It Happened at Niagara Falls

Melanie Robertson-King

King Park Press

Published by King Park Press

It Happened at Niagara Falls is a work of fiction. Names,
characters, places and incidents are the product of the
author's imagination or are used fictitiously. Any
resemblance to actual events, locales or persons, living or
dead, is purely coincidental.

ISBN: 978-1-990371-10-3

DEDICATION

For anyone still looking for their happy ending.

ACKNOWLEDGMENTS

Thanks to everyone who put up with my daft questions during the research of this novel. Without your help, the book would not have come to fruition.

Huge thanks to my eagle-eyed proofreader, the phenom with the red pen, Leona Berrea.

If I've missed anyone by name, I apologize.

Special thanks to my husband, Don, who continues to support and encourage me, and provides a shoulder to cry on when things don't go well. He redesigned my website making it mobile-friendly and taken charge on the domestic front giving me time to write.

One

Howard Johnson Hotel, Victoria Avenue, Niagara Falls, Ontario

May 19, 2018

Michael Scott woke with a sense of anticipation, throwing off the covers and stretching. He scrubbed his hands down his face, walked to the window, and pulled the curtain aside. The sun shone, promising an exceptional day of touring. He planned to explore Niagara Falls after eating breakfast at the Denny's restaurant beside the hotel.

His seminar the day before was a triumph, well-received by the Canadian audience. This was a significant milestone for him; it was his first time presenting in Canada. He often lectured in England, sharing his experiences from various archaeological digs throughout the UK. With his youngest sister Melissa's wedding approaching, he decided to combine this trip with some well-deserved downtime before travelling to

Percé, where the event was being held.

After an arduous journey, Michael's GO train left Toronto for Niagara Falls, which took him until one in the morning. The relief of arriving at the hotel on Victoria Avenue, despite it was going on two, was pronounced. Now, it was around noon, and his stomach growled, reminding him he had eaten nothing since supper the previous day. He looked forward to a satisfying meal.

First; he needed to shower. The hotel room, with its cozy bed overlooking the bustling Victoria Avenue, was a welcome sight after his trip. Tea and coffee facilities were in his room, but he'd wait until he got to the diner for breakfast before he had his first cup. Denny's restaurants used to serve breakfast all day. He hoped this one still did.

When Michael arrived, the restaurant buzzed with activity. After about thirty minutes, the hostess ushered him to a table next to the windows, offering an outlook of the cityscape. She left the menu for him to peruse the tantalizing array of options, but he had a straightforward decision. He ordered the Lumberjack with eggs, hash browns, sausage, ham, bacon and toast, a hearty meal that promised to satisfy his hunger. While waiting for his breakfast, he sipped on his first coffee of the day, the aroma and warmth comforting him.

When had he been here last? It had to have been when he was a kid, a time of innocence and wonder. He, his parents, and his siblings piled into the family's station wagon and off they went, embarking on a journey filled with laughter and anticipation. It was before Melissa was born. If he could depend on his memory, he and his twin, Amy, would have been about six, their world still revolving around games and toys. Roger would have been a year older, and Christopher would have been about five years older, their youthful energy filling the air. When his breakfast arrived, the enormous plate of food surprised Michael. Still, he was starving, and it took no time to clean his plate.

When the server brought his bill, he asked, "It's been many years since I was here. Can you tell me how to get to the waterfalls?"

"When you go out the front door, turn left and continue down the street until you reach Clifton Hill. Take it; it will bring you to the Parkway almost across from the American Falls."

"Thanks."

When he exited the restaurant, the sky had clouded over, but the sun still peeked out from behind them, casting a golden hue over the city. It would be an excellent day to walk to the falls and take in the view, a view that in all likelihood had changed since his last visit. The city had transformed, proof of the passage of time and the march of progress. More hotels, souvenir shops, restaurants and bars, and people, a bustling city that had grown with the times. But it was the first long weekend of the summer, a time of celebration and joy, so that was to be expected.

Michael sauntered down a path that meandered through the park. It was less crowded in here than out on the sidewalks, so he strolled along, enjoying the scenery. The flowerbeds were a riot of spring colours, their sweet scent filling the air. The ponds had fish swimming in them, their scales glinting in the sunlight. The steady rush of the water cascading over the falls roared, echoing through the park.

"Zeus! Stop! Come back!" a female voice called.

A pug, with a mind of its own, dashed across the grass, its leash trailing behind it. In a moment of serendipity, Michael sprang into action and stepped on the dog's lead, halting the animal in its tracks.

A young woman with long blonde hair, dressed in a white T-shirt, beige, thigh-length cardigan, jeans and running shoes, approached him and the dog. She struggled to walk on the uneven ground despite using a cane. "I can't thank you enough for catching him."

Michael bent down, lifted the dog, and placed him in her arms. Her green eyes sparkled as she spoke. "I don't know how to thank you for rescuing this bad boy."

"Be my plus one at my sister's wedding next month," he

said.

"You want me? We're complete strangers." She tucked her hair behind her ear.

Michael saw the uncertainty in her eyes, and guilt for putting her in this position washed over him. But there was something about her, something that made him want to get to know her better.

"I'm Michael Scott."

"Jennifer Fox."

The two shook hands.

"Do you want to find a bench and sit down?" he asked.

"Sure."

"I'll take care of the escape artist, and you can use your free hand to take my arm."

When they made the exchange, Michael held his arm out for her to put her hand through. She turned to him and smiled. Sadness filled her eyes, along with a story he wanted to learn. Like something tragic in her past had happened. Never mind that for now. If he was correct in his interpretation, she'd tell him in her time, and if she didn't ... oh, well. Why did he ask her to be his guest at Melissa's wedding? Because his sister expected him to bring someone? Because this girl was gorgeous? Because he didn't want his family to know he still wasn't in a meaningful relationship? He couldn't put his finger on it, but something about her intrigued him.

Low-hanging, black clouds formed beyond Horseshoe Falls. A storm approached. It began with random drops and became steadier. When it came down, they hadn't reached the first available place to sit. "Here, take Zeus, is it?" He handed her the leash, shrugged off his jacket, and held it over them to shelter them from the rain. "So, Jennifer Fox, what do you do for a living?" he asked, trying to keep the conversation going despite the rain.

"I'm a bartender. I used to work at the Fallsview Casino, but moved on. I'm at the Outback Steakhouse now."

Michael recalled walking by that restaurant. It was almost straight across the street from his hotel room.

"And you, Michael Scott, what is it you do?" she asked,

her curiosity piqued.

Michael, always one to share his passions, explained his work, his eyes lighting up as he spoke. "I'm an archaeologist with a minor in mummy studies and another in Egyptology. An archaeological team in Egypt has approved me to go on a dig with them, pending the government approval of my applications, visa, and other red tape."

"Wow."

"Remember hearing about Richard III being discovered under a car park in Leicester? Well, I was there for that one. What a thrill, even though I'm not the one who found him."

"Are you from England? I detect an accent."

"Born and raised in Ottawa, but studied at the University of Manchester and come home to visit my family every other year."

Two

Queen Victoria Park, Niagara River Parkway, Niagara Falls, Ontario

May 19, 2018

This man, huddled under a makeshift rain shelter in the heart of a green space in an otherwise concrete jungle, didn't look like an archaeologist. But then, what did one look like? All she had as a reference was Harrison Ford in the Indiana Jones movies. Not much to go on. He had a scholarly appearance about him with his light brown hair. It was short on the sides, over his collar at the back, peppered with grey in places. His beard made her think of a teacher from back in high school.

That man was eccentric, to be sure. Did this man also have quirks? Other than asking her on a date before they exchanged names.

The clouds started to break up. The rain had let up, but the question remained, for how long. The skies remained ominous, hinting at the possibility of another downpour at any moment.

"It's almost stopped raining. You can put your jacket back on now," Jennifer said.

"Well, we won't be sitting outside for a while. How about we sit inside, and I buy you a coffee?" Michael asked, a smile playing on his lips.

"Most places don't allow dogs."

"Okay, I'll still buy you a coffee. The crowds have thinned out, thanks to the rain. We can take advantage and drink our coffee on the other side of the road where we can walk on even footing."

"Sounds fine to me."

"Where can we buy coffee to go?"

"Up here. In the gift shop. A bar and grill is above it, but it will be packed."

They made their way to the spot Jennifer pointed out, their steps careful and deliberate, as if navigating a minefield.

"You take the escape artist again. How do you like your coffee?"

"Cream and sugar. One of each."

"I'll be back in a flash."

Jennifer put Zeus on the ground and leaned against a fence that separated the entrance from a patio area while she waited. The place was busy, but once summer came, when wasn't the city busy? And down here, it was always a zoo. The sound of rushing water rumbled, mingling with the chatter of people and the occasional bark of a dog. Freshly brewed coffee wafted from the nearby cafe, mixing with the damp earthiness of the rain-soaked ground.

Michael gave Jennifer his arm. "I'll carry the coffee. Think you can manage the dog and your cane?" he asked with concern in his voice.

She bristled at the last word. She hated that thing, but it was her fault she had to use it. "I'll be fine."

They strolled to the street and reached the median before they had to wait for cars from the other direction to pass. "Guess we're invisible," Michael said.

As if divine intervention shone down on them, the next car stopped, as did the one in the curb lane.

Michael guided Jennifer and her pug to the railing and handed her a coffee. "Good thing we take our coffee the same way. Saves getting them mixed up."

She smiled at him and took a sip.

"Do you walk down here often?" Michael asked.

"Once a week, I bring my car and park it in the big lot down by the power station," she said, pointing to the location. "The rest of the time, I stick closer to home when I take Zeus out." Did she say too much? Would it lead him to ask where she lived? She'd already told him she worked as a bartender and where. Sure, he was easy to talk to, easy to look at, too. But was he ready for the horror story that she was? Not likely. She couldn't risk it.

Jennifer sipped her coffee. It had to have been a fresh pot. The bitterness associated with one that had sat for a while wasn't there. She glanced at Michael, who stared off towards the Horseshoe Falls. "Penny for them," she said.

"Thinking about the last time I came here. I was a kid with my parents, two brothers, and my twin sister. The youngest, the one getting married, hadn't been born yet. I remember we stayed in a motel out on Lundy's Lane. I don't know if it's still in business."

"That would have been a special trip."

"We drove down from the motel and parked in the same lot you're in now. We visited Marineland, too. I remember that day well; it was cold. Even though we were fairly high in the stands, we still got wet from the whales splashing."

"I've never been."

Michael turned to her. "You've never been? And you live here."

"I know. Crazy, eh?"

Jennifer inhaled a shuddering breath and hoped he didn't detect it. Hers wasn't an everyday family life post-accident. Many days since then, she wanted to turn the clock back to the day before her life unravelled.

"If you don't mind me asking, why the cane?"

She didn't want to bring this up at their first meeting. "Accident."

"Recently?"

"No."

Please just drop it, she begged. She wanted to forget, but not that she'd ever be able. The scars reminded her every day. She sighed and a tear fell onto her cheek, and she dashed it away before Michael saw it.

"Hey, I didn't mean to make you cry."

Too late. He saw.

"We don't have to talk about it. We can find something else to talk about."

"No. We've started. Might as well finish. Mind you, after I've told you, you'll likely turn your back and run."

"Nothing is that bad, is it?"

"I was fifteen. A bunch of us were at my friend Emma's house. Her parents were out of town. I was supposed to be the only one at her place that weekend. The news got out, and a gang of kids turned up. Some of them, we didn't know. Anyway, we were drinking. It got loud, and the neighbours called the police. When the others heard the sirens, they took off, leaving the two of us there. The cop dragged us off to the station." She paused and sipped her coffee. "Our parents were called to come and pick us up. The police charged Emma and me with underage drinking. That did not go down well with my folks. Anyway, on the way home, a driver ran a red light, broadsided us killing my parents and my younger brother. I spent a couple of months in the hospital, most of which I spent in a coma, and had multiple operations on my leg and hip. I have more hardware in my leg than most home improvement stores' entire inventory."

Michael sat in silence. He'd asked the question. He didn't like the answer, but it was from the past. Jennifer had no doubt learned the hard way, turned her life around, and made herself a better person. Now he understood the sadness in her eyes.

"I'm sorry." Clichéd or what. Isn't that what everyone says, whether they mean it? He genuinely meant it. Change the subject. Perhaps talk about his family instead. "My father is dead, too. Not in a car accident. Cancer. Mesothelioma from working at the mill in Hull; exposed to asbestos all those years.

That was in 2015. The year before that, my brother Roger's wife committed suicide. The toughest thing about that was Adam found her. That's my nephew, Roger's son. And in 2016, the Alberta wildfires, my oldest brother, Chris, his house burnt to the ground. He works in the oil sands. You're not the only one whose family is a train wreck."

Jennifer smiled but didn't say a thing. Her eyes glistened with unshed tears.

"And I still want you to come with me to Mel's wedding."

"Oh, all right. You twisted my arm, but don't expect me to wear a dress. Or heels."

"Deal." Michael rubbed his palm on his thigh. It went easier than he figured it would. "Now, we need to work out the logistics of getting there. The wedding is on June 6. So I think to make our connections, we'd have to leave here two or three days before to ensure we arrive in plenty of time."

"Do you want me to look into it?" Jennifer asked.

"Why don't we both? Then, we can compare results. We won't book anything until we agree on the travel arrangements."

"I have to book the time off work. It's not much lead time, so it might be difficult." She glanced at her smartwatch as she spoke. "I've got to go. Take this one home and get ready for work." Jennifer stood.

"I'll walk you to your car. Come on, Zeus. You're with me."

Michael walked Jennifer to the parking lot. As they reached the bright yellow Smart car, it started to rain again. He helped her in and put the pug in the passenger seat.

"You'll get soaked walking back to your hotel. I'll give you a ride," Jennifer said.

He could walk and enjoyed it. But the skies were darker now than when it had rained earlier. He hesitated, considering the offer. "As long as giving me a lift won't make you late for work." He squeezed his six-foot-tall body into the car.

"I won't be. You said your hotel was near my work, so that's where I'll drop you."

Once Michael worked his way inside and fastened his seatbelt, he discovered the car was far more roomy than he expected. Just getting in and out posed a problem for his height, like a giraffe trying to fit into a rabbit hole.

It took less than ten minutes to reach their destination once Jennifer exited the lot. If it wasn't pedestrians sauntering through like cattle, it was other drivers circling for parking spots or leaving them. She turned left onto Fraser Hill and drove by a stone building, which she told him housed the power station, and then left onto the parkway. After another wait in traffic, she turned left onto Murray and up the hill. Michael tried to memorize the street signs to use this route as an alternate way to go from his hotel to the falls. Another right on Fallsview. The farther they travelled in this direction, the narrower the street became. What started out as multi-lanes in each direction narrowed to one each way, with what might be parking or bus stops on each side. Finally, she turned right onto Ferry Street, which turned into Victoria Avenue.

"There's no parking here, so I've got to drop you off and leave. You never know when the police will make a random pass-through," Jennifer said when she stopped the vehicle in front of the Outback.

"Thanks, Jennifer. I appreciate not getting drowned. I might come here for supper tonight. I'd like to get to know you better." Michael moved the pug off his lap and extricated himself from the tiny car.

As she navigated her way into traffic again, the canary yellow car disappeared, swallowed by the larger vehicles surrounding it.

Three

Jennifer's House, Orchard Avenue, Niagara Falls, Ontario

May 19, 2018

From the time Jennifer dropped Michael off in front of the Outback, she pondered over his invitation. Yes, she had agreed, but was he serious? Who would want to be seen anywhere with her? She walks with a cane and sometimes does not do that well. Despite all the hardware in her left leg and the nerve damage to her arm on the same side, she persevered. Sometimes, her hand was so numb she couldn't pick anything up, or if she did, she dropped it. That was why Zeus got away from her. Earlier today was a perfect example. Her hand had lost sensitivity, and she only thought she had a good grip on the dog's leash.

The numbness caused problems for her at work, too. More than once, she'd dropped things at the casino. They had suggested she take up another line of work. And now, she was performing the same job, but at a different venue. Most of her co-workers discovered the signs of her hand going numb and stepped in to prevent a filled glass from being dropped on the floor. A few weren't so kind. None of them knew of the accident. Until she told Michael today, no one other than her grandmother, fellow students at her high school, and Emma, who got busted with her, knew. The consequences were severe. Emma's parents sold the house and moved to another part of the city before her father accepted a transfer that took the family out of the province.

She pulled the car into the driveway, turned the engine off, and grabbed Zeus's leash. With the fenced-in backyard, she opened the gate and let him run around off-leash while she entered the house and got ready for work.

Her shift started at four o'clock, so she had time to shower before work. Once Jennifer had stripped down to her bra and panties, she stood in front of the full-length mirror on her bedroom door and appraised her reflection. Her left knee pointed inward; her ankle fused, so it no longer flexed. A scar ran down her thigh from her hip to just above her knee. Those were the physical scars.

The mental ones were as bad, if not worse. Jennifer avoided driving anywhere near the intersection where the accident had occurred — terrified it would happen again. Her grandmother persuaded her to get her driver's license. The woman also encouraged her to take driver's education in high school or at least lessons from a reputable school.

Despite Jennifer's fears, she learned to drive.

All this ruminating over an invitation and self-pity over her physical appearance sent grief coursing through her. Something she hadn't experienced in a long time.

She forced herself into the bathroom and showered, then donned her navy blue velour housecoat. Dressed in her robe, Jennifer padded to the backdoor and brought Zeus into the house before she continued her preparations for work.

Once she put on her work clothes — a black Outback-branded T-shirt, jeans of the same colour, and non-skid shoes — she applied makeup and blew her hair dry. The last thing she did before leaving the house was grab a hoodie off the hook by the side door.

Four

Outback Steakhouse, Victoria Avenue, Niagara Falls, Ontario

May 19, 2018

Jennifer maneuvered her car into one of the scarce parking bays. As she spotted the familiar vehicles of her co-workers, a sense of camaraderie washed over her. Their shifts often overlapped, but she worked with the reliable ones tonight. The ones who saw the signs of trouble were always ready to lend a hand.

"Hi!" she called as she stepped in the back door. She pulled her timecard from the rack and punched in.

"Hey, Jen," Andy said. "Gonna be a busy night, it being the long weekend."

"I know." She grabbed an apron from the peg and tied it around her waist.

"Wonder if the fireworks will go ahead with it raining?"

"I hope not. Zeus hates them even though we're a long way from where they set them off. He'll be cowering under my bed when I come home."

She worked her way around the end of the bar to serve the lone waiting customer.

"What can I get you?" Jennifer asked.

Engrossed in the television's flickering light, he turned, and Jennifer's breath caught in her throat. Was this guy for real? Her heart skipped a beat, and she gripped the counter for support, her mind racing with questions.

"I didn't mean to frighten you. I said I might come over for supper since my hotel is close."

"Sorry. I must have forgotten you mentioned it. Brain like a sieve. Guess I wasn't expecting to see you sitting here. I thought you'd be more comfortable at a table."

"Now, if I sat over there, I wouldn't be near the prettiest girl in the place."

No one had ever said anything so kind about her looks, and his comment flattered her. It made her tongue stick to the roof of her mouth, rendering her speechless.

She swallowed hard and asked again. "What can I get you?"

"Stella. Pint, please," Michael said.

"Large or small?"

"Better make it a large. And a blooming onion. I've heard good things about them but have never had the chance to try one," he said.

Jennifer turned and punched his order into the computer, then pulled his pint. "You said you wanted a large," she said when she sat the drink before him.

His eyes grew as big as saucers, and Jennifer's lips tugged into a smile.

"Wow. Now that's what I call a pint," Michael exclaimed.

Jennifer giggled at his reaction.

Soon, another employee placed his blooming onion before him.

Michael savoured the beer and the onion. The dip that accompanied the appetizer was spicy, but not so much that it displeased him.

From his seat, Michael asked, "What time are you off tonight?"

"Ten."

"Did I read somewhere that they have fireworks every night?"

"Yes. The display starts at ten during the summer, and eight in the winter. I'm not a huge fan. I shouldn't say that. I don't mind them, but Zeus is terrified of them."

"Well, I was going to ask you if you wanted to go with me, but by the sounds of things, you need to go home to your dog."

"How long are you in town?" Jennifer asked.

"I'm flexible. As long as I'm in Percé, in time for my baby sister's wedding. You haven't forgotten your invitation, have you?"

"N-no."

Nervous. Jennifer probably thought Michael was an axe murderer or stalker or some other pervert with the way he asked her to go with him.

"Look, I said I'd go."

Oops. A little too strong. That was his tendency. Go in, all guns blazing. But he didn't want to scare Jennifer off.

"I'm sorry if I came on too strong when I asked you to come with me. Sometimes, my mouth works before my brain catches up."

Jennifer smiled and chuckled, her tension easing. Crisis averted. Should he tell her he'd checked into the train? Why not? In for a penny and all that.

"I checked out the train. We can go from Toronto to Montreal, then catch the train to either Gaspé or the one to Halifax. If it's the latter, we'll go as far as Campbellton, New Brunswick, and take the bus from there to Percé."

"You've been busy."

"This helps." Michael pulled a book out of his jacket pocket. *Canada By Train* by Chris Hanus and John Shaske. "I bought it at Union Station. According to the book published in 2016, a train goes from Montreal to Gaspé. It's possibly outdated now. The Halifax train is an overnight one, but since we're not going the full distance, I don't think we'd need sleeper accommodations."

Sleeper accommodations? No way; she was independent,

and resolute in her decision not to compromise on sharing a bed.

"No. We won't need a bed. The seats recline, don't they?"

"Yes. And Zeus can travel in his carrier if it fits under the seat in front of us. He's not that big, so it shouldn't be a problem. We'll take him out before we board in Toronto and when we arrive in Montreal, and once more before we catch the next train."

He had it worked out — right down to the last detail — except he had mentioned nothing about how much this trip was going to cost. And once they reached Percé, where would they stay? Five siblings, their partners, and his mother. He had only mentioned his father's death, so his mother was still among the living. Friends of the bride, too. A twinge of uneasiness being with so many strangers gripped her. Was she up to the trip? These thoughts filled her with anxiety and excitement.

When her parents and brother died, their estate passed to her grandmother and then to her after her gran's death. It was a large sum of money — more than she ever thought. Being a minor, it passed to her grandmother, who held it in trust until she came of age. She thought nothing of it then, but was glad her grandmother kept it longer. She wasn't ready or responsible enough at that age to manage money.

So, the trip cost wasn't a concern unless it meant dipping into her investments. Jennifer had done her financial planning, a task she never thought would interest her. With her local bank's guidance, she had set up a plan that offered flexibility if she needed cash. The house on Orchard Street was mortgage free, and the last payment on her car was due next month.

"I've got another customer. I'll be back." Jennifer moved off to serve the people who came in and sat at the bar's opposite end.

Michael pulled out his mobile phone when Jennifer returned from serving the other customers. "Why don't I text my sister and see if she can shed any light on the trains since she lives down that way?"

She nodded as his thumbs flew over the screen. Before he

hit send, he turned his phone to show her his typed message.

Hey kid. Do U know if a train still runs from Montreal to Gaspé?

"Now we wait for her to reply."

"Will she know it's you?"

"She should when it comes up with an overseas phone number and with the question I asked her. I know she hightailed it to Percé last summer when she and her fiancé parted ways."

"But isn't she the one who's getting married?"

"Met someone new. And the ex got himself killed in an accident. Took on a train at a level crossing and lost."

A startled squeak escaped from Jennifer's mouth.

"She was supposed to marry the ex on New Year's Day this year."

"Your sister didn't waste any time finding a new man."

"True enough. Apparently, Mel caught the ex in bed with his boss's wife. Mom said that when she phoned me to tell me the wedding was off. And she didn't find the new man. He found her."

"Sounds like your family has strange ways of meeting people."

Michael chuckled. "That we do," he said.

Jennifer excused herself again to serve other customers.

Melissa replied to his text message while Jennifer served customers elsewhere.

It would have been nice if it still ran. I could have gone by train from Moncton to Matapédia and changed trains for Gaspé, which stopped outside Percé. Where are you?

"So, we'll have to take the Halifax train. It's not as convenient as the other one, but it's the best option," Michael said when Jennifer returned from looking after the other customers.

In Niagara Falls. Spoke in Toronto at an archaeological conference. Thought I'd do some sightseeing before coming to your wedding.

Michael took another mouthful of Stella and sat the

gigantic mug down. If he ordered another, it would be a small one. He picked away at the blooming onion, pulling off segments one at a time like plucking the petals from a daisy.

Five

Niagara Falls Bus Terminal, Erie Avenue, Niagara Falls, Ontario

June 3, 2018

This morning, Michael and Jennifer had to be at the bus terminal to catch their bus to Union Station in Toronto. The worst thing was that they had to be down there by six thirty. None of the other buses to the city coordinated with the train they had to take to get them into Montreal early enough to catch the Ocean to Campbellton. From there, it was a short (by comparison) bus ride to Percé and the venue for his youngest sister's wedding.

He hated making Jennifer get up that early. They arranged to meet at the station. Michael was packed and checked out by six o'clock, which gave him plenty of time to walk to his destination. It was chilly at that time of day, and he was glad he had put on a jumper under his multi-pocketed vest. A slight comfort in the face of the early morning chill.

Since he had arrived in the city in time for the previous month's long weekend, Michael hadn't walked this far down Victoria Avenue. He'd only gone as far as Clifton Hill, a popular tourist spot. From there, Louis Tussaud's Wax Works, towered ahead of him, but he still hadn't visited it. Just beyond that and on the other side stood the upside-down house, a quirky landmark.

A peaceful time to be out with the streets sparsely populated. Only a few early morning dog walkers crossed his path. Michael took a moment to enjoy the quiet before stopping at a Tim Hortons to buy a coffee. They'd get breakfast once they arrived in Toronto.

He took a taxi to his hotel when he first arrived in the city. The same route on foot was so different. There were the sights, the fragrance of the seasonal flowers, restaurants gearing up for the day, and exhaust fumes from the buses and personal vehicles.

He almost took a wrong turn at the roundabout with Thorold Stone Road but righted himself before he'd gone too far in that direction.

At the end of Erie Street, the bus station was on his left, and the train station was straight ahead. Now, he had to find a place to wait for Jennifer. He didn't have long. A cab pulled up, and she sat in the back. "Hey, you made it!" he said with a smile.

Michael walked to the car, helped Jennifer get out, and picked up Zeus, her pug, in his carrier. They had a few minutes to let him out on his leash before confining him again.

"As your plus one at your sister's wedding, I'm questioning my decision," Jennifer quipped, stepping out of the taxi. Michael had always been adventurous; after all, he was an archaeologist and had travelled worldwide; Jennifer was more reserved.

"I'm sorry I had to get you out so early in the morning. With the transit schedules not helping us, it was the only way."

Their bus to Toronto's Union Station pulled into the lot. Jennifer gathered Zeus up and returned him to his carrier. Michael grabbed her suitcase and his, since she needed a hand for her cane.

About ten minutes after they boarded, they were on the

road. The traffic was minimal at this time, and the air was crisp and cool. If it were Monday, the morning rush hour would have started. Soon, they reached St. Catharines and were crossing the Garden City Skyway. Because of the walls on the bridge, most of the city remained out of sight, but Lake Ontario sparkling in the sunshine took her breath away.

When they passed the old rusted ship near Jordan Station, Jennifer pointed to it and said, "They claim it's a replica. Sure looks like the real deal to me."

"I agree," Michael said. "The landscape is mind-blowing, with wineries and vineyards everywhere."

"Crazy, eh? Most of the land now growing grapes used to be fruit trees. Orchards of pears, apples, peaches, and cherries."

"Shame."

Jennifer fixed her gaze on the passing scenery. As she ventured beyond St. Catharines for the first time, a sense of adventure and curiosity filled her — a new world waiting to be explored.

Soon after the bus passed through Grimsby, the rural setting disappeared, replaced by a sprawling urban landscape. The transition was stark, starting with Stoney Creek and then Hamilton. Once they crossed over the Burlington Skyway, it was the city of the same name, Oakville, then Mississauga. They stopped at Winston Churchill Boulevard before arriving at the train station in downtown Toronto, a world away from the quiet countryside they had left behind them.

Michael, a seasoned traveller, turned to Jennifer. "Why don't we get something to eat and take in some sights near the station. We have about three hours before the train leaves for Montreal."

"I am hungry."

Michael pulled his phone out and brought up the maps app. "There's a Tim Hortons on York Street about a block away. Or, there's a pastry place right here in the station. The smell of their fresh baked goods is making me hungry."

"As long as I can get something to eat. I think my blood sugar is tanking," Jennifer said.

"You're not diabetic, are you?"

"No. But I've had breakfast before now. As in, length of time since I got up this morning."

"Pastry it is, then."

Michael put Zeus's carrier on his wheeled suitcase and trundled them to the eatery. He grabbed Jennifer's in his other hand.

He led her to a table, their footsteps inaudible in the bustling station. He walked to the counter, the aroma of coffee and pastries wafting through the air, and ordered two breakfast sandwiches and two coffees.

When he returned with their food and drink, Jennifer was as white as a sheet.

"Here, get this into you. I don't want you fainting," Michael said, placing the tray on the table. "I got you a veggie sandwich. I hope that's okay."

"Yes." Jennifer took a bite. "This is amazing!"

Michael tried his. He wiped his mouth with the paper napkin. "You're right. I'll have to remember this place when I'm in the station."

The two finished their meal in silence.

When they were done, he asked, "Better now? You're not as pale as earlier."

"Much," said Jennifer with relief and gratitude.

"Why don't we check our bags and Zeus's carrier? That way, we won't have to drag them all over with us."

"If we can. We might need to keep his carrier because he must be in it when we board."

Michael made the inquiries, ensuring they could check everything and retrieve it when they returned to catch their train.

"So where would you like to go? There are parks close to here."

He conferred with the map app again. "There's Roundhouse Park almost across from the CN Tower or do you want to go up it? They claim on a clear day, you can see Niagara Falls."

"The park is fine as long as there are benches and grass."

As they strolled through Toronto's concrete jungle, Zeus kept his nose to the ground. The unfamiliar odours must have been overwhelming for the small dog, but he didn't stop too long at any single place.

When they reached Roundhouse Park, emotion overcame Jennifer. She dashed a tear away from her eye and hoped Michael didn't see her in this state.

"Hey, what's wrong?"

So much for him not seeing. "Kevin would have loved this place. He was a train nut."

Michael wrapped his arms around her and held her close. In his embrace, she felt safe. Still saddened by the idea, her brother didn't live to see this park and the trains.

They had just arrived and were returning to the station. Jennifer had taken some pictures of the trains with her phone. If she got around more easily, she might consider visiting again when she had more time.

They had walked Zeus, fed him and gave him water. He'd done his business, so he'd be fine until they reached Montreal.

When they returned to Union Station, Jennifer found a place to sit down and waited while Michael retrieved their luggage and the carrier for Zeus. If it didn't cause a problem, she'd like to leave him out of it until they had to board.

Michael assisted Jennifer in loading Zeus into his carrier. They descended the ramp towards the track, where their train awaited. A short escalator ride later, they found themselves at the track level. Michael managed the two-wheeled suitcases, relieving Jennifer of any immediate worries. He was also prepared to take care of Zeus, ensuring their journey was as smooth as possible.

If Melissa had any inkling of the hurdles, he had to overcome to reach Percé for her wedding, she would be astounded. Perhaps he would share the details with her after the ceremony when they could both laugh about it.

The train set off about five minutes after the two settled into their seats. The rhythmic chugging and gentle swaying of the carriage soon lulled them into a peaceful state. As they traversed the Distillery District, the once familiar aroma of aged whiskey was now a distant memory. The last operational distillery had shuttered its doors years ago, transforming the area into a hub of commerce and dining. A massive stone building bearing the sign Gooderman & Worts Ltd. stood as evidence to the district's previous life. Michael strained to read the smaller text beneath it as the train sped up.

A few signs of countryside popped up in patches, along with the occasional grazing cow, but until they got beyond Oshawa, urban settings filled the vista.

Between Cobourg and Belleville, a sight caught Michael's eye. "Look, Jennifer, turkeys. A whole flock of them." He pointed out the window.

"Turkeys. Like the kind you eat at Thanksgiving and Christmas."

"Not quite. These are wild. I've never seen so many in one place before. And they're something we don't have in England."

Okay, she'd give him that. To her, they were just a flock of enormous birds — nuisances like Canada Geese. But out in the countryside, a world of wonder opened up: animals, domestic and wild, herds of cows, horses, dogs, and birds of all sizes. As they passed, a grand bird with a white belly sat on a tree branch. Its feathers glistened in the sunlight and stirred a sense of awe in her.

"What kind of bird is that?" Jennifer asked.

"Red-tailed hawk," said Michael.

Red-winged blackbirds perched on cattails. In a small clearing, Jennifer spotted a doe and her fawn. The sight took her back to her childhood and the book *Bambi*. In it, Bambi's mother died. Would the same fate befall this little one's mother? The thought filled her with sadness and hope, a bittersweet nostalgia for the innocence of youth.

It didn't take any time after the stop in Belleville to arrive in Kingston. After that, it was a long stretch to get to Cornwall. Once they crossed into Quebec, the countryside became flatter.

The mountains on the south side of the river — she wasn't sure of their name — poked up from the horizon. It was a clear sign of transforming from the peaceful countryside to the bustling urban areas.

Bridges, rivers, and more urban sprawl again became the norm as they approached the second to last stop, Dorval. The announcement came over the speakers to de-train here for the airport. The cityscape, a sprawling tapestry of glass and steel, unfolded before her, opposite of the serene countryside they had passed through so far.

As they approached the Montreal station, train yards, freight cars, and engines surrounded them. The tang of diesel made the air thick, and the rumble of engines filled her ears. In the distance, the sign on the Five Roses Flour building, a memory of her mother's baking, caught her attention — the brand her mother always bought. More nostalgia. The last thing she needed.

The best thing about the station here was that she didn't have to navigate steps to get off the train. There was a ramp from the car to the platform, but she still had an escalator to deal with to reach the concourse.

Michael stepped aside and let Jennifer go ahead of him. He was accustomed to the unique sensory overload of train travel, the bustling stations with their distinct blend of coffee and diesel fumes. They were almost always the same, yet each journey held its own charm.

The layover in Montreal, a necessary pause before boarding the Ocean train, was shorter than earlier in the day. Jennifer's pallor had improved, no longer on the verge of fainting. They had grabbed a snack on the train, and he had a beer to unwind.

The complex was a culinary haven, offering an abundance of dining options. From high-end restaurants with liquor licenses, serving gourmet dishes, to fast-food outlets, dishing out quick and tasty burgers and fries, there was something to pique everyone's interest.

Once they'd taken care of Zeus, and put him back in his

carrier, Michael led the way to a place where they would have supper.

He chose one with tables outside the establishment, right on the concourse. That way, they shouldn't object to Jennifer having a dog with her, and Zeus could enjoy the fresh air and the bustling station.

They each had a burger. Jennifer drank iced tea, and he had Stella. It wasn't on tap, but it was still refreshing.

When it came time to board the Ocean, they rode the escalator back down to track level.

Six

VIA Rail Station, Roseberry Street, Campbellton, New Brunswick

June 4, 2018

The train arrived in Campbellton, New Brunswick, just before eight o'clock in the morning. The overnight trip had been uneventful, the rhythmic chugging of the train lulling him into a deep sleep. He hoped Jennifer slept, too, her soft breathing a comforting sound in the darkness. Once the sun dipped below the horizon, there was nothing to see but the occasional flicker of lights from passing towns.

Now, they had to gather their belongings and catch the bus that would transport them to the village of Percé. In an ideal scenario, they had a mere twelve minutes to disembark, collect their things, and reach the bus. The bus terminal and train station occupied the same building according to Google maps, but Zeus needed a comfort break. His little bladder was surely about to burst.

"Time is at a premium, thanks to the train being late getting in," Michael said, attempting to hurry Jennifer along. The train delay had thrown off their planned schedule, and now they had to race to catch the bus.

"Okay."

"I'll take Zeus and his carrier. With any luck, the bus will give us a couple of extra minutes to let this guy have a wander and do his business."

Michael stepped aside and let Jennifer out into the aisle. He handed her suitcase to her, pulled his luggage down from the overhead compartment, and they made their way to the carriage's exit.

When they were off the train, Michael scanned the area for the bus terminal. The platform was a bustling hub, with people rushing to catch their connections and others strolling towards their next destination. There was no signage for the bus terminal amidst the sea of people and luggage.

"Excuse me," he said to one of the VIA employees, a young woman with a friendly smile. "My friend and I need to get a bus to Percé. Can you tell me where the bus depot is, please?"

"Out the front doors, turn to your right, and it's about a two-minute walk to the Irving Oil gas station. The bus goes in and out of there."

"Thank you so much."

Undeterred by the time constraint, Michael followed the girl's directions and led the way, Jennifer by his side. A two-minute walk if he was alone, perhaps. But with Jennifer, who could not walk fast, it was a different story. Yet, they reached the bus stop in time. Michael let the pug out of its crate and clipped his leash to his harness, ready for the next leg of their journey.

"Come on there, my boy, let's see if you need a comfort break."

Zeus, stretched, put his nose to the ground and sniffed. Relief washed over Michael who had left the carrier and the bags with Jennifer, taking the pug to the grass boulevard next to the road. It took a while, but the animal did his business. The bus pulled in just as the two returned to where Jennifer had waited. They had made it, overcoming the challenges and keeping Zeus comfortable during the journey.

"Sorry, sweetie, but you have to go back in the crate,"

Jennifer said as she bundled the dog into the carrier.

"Anything to go in the baggage compartments?" the driver asked.

"No, thanks. We've just got these," Jennifer said. She handed Zeus's crate to Michael and then boarded.

Once she reached the top step, Michael returned the crate to her. She started down the aisle until she found two seats together. "Are there seat numbers on our tickets, Michael, or is it wherever you want to sit?"

"Right there will be fine," the driver said.

Michael stowed their bags overhead and put Zeus's carrier on the floor.

Jennifer settled into the window seat on the right-hand side of the bus, her heart brimming with anticipation. Despite the restless night on the train, she caught some sleep. Perhaps she would doze off again on this leg of the journey to Percé.

"What did you think of the train ride from Montreal to here?" Michael asked.

"Long."

"It was that. Did you get any sleep?"

"A bit, but not well."

"As I walked Zeus around, I glimpsed the bridge we're about to cross. It's a sight to behold, super impressive," Michael said.

The bus door sealed shut with a reassuring thud, and the engine roared to life. In moments, they were in motion, the wheels turning, propelling them forward on their journey.

When Jennifer mentioned her restless night, Michael's heart sank with guilt, mirroring the waves they traversed. Perhaps they should have opted for two cabins on the overnight train, prioritizing comfort over economy. He resolved to explore the possibility of upgrading their tickets for the return trip. After all, he could sleep anywhere, but Jennifer's rest was not as easily won.

The steel cantilever-through-truss bridge left a lasting impression on Michael. Painted a soft green, it stood against the tests of time and traffic. In a blink, they had crossed the water and entered Quebec. The traffic lights hung in a horizontal orientation rather than vertical. This unique feature was not exclusive to Quebec, as Michael had noticed a similar set in Campbellton. The two provinces may have shared this design because of their proximity.

Not that he drove back in England, but the traffic lights were a complete contrast to those in Canada. There, the sequence was red, orange, and green. Here, it was a red, green, orange. Whenever he had a moment to relax and take in the surroundings, he chuckled at this quirky difference.

Once they travelled east again, a rail line ran next to the road. At first, Michael couldn't tell if the tracks were still there, but the crossing signs and signals still stood at one crossroad. Farther along the road, the rails were visible. Did any trains use them these days? When Melissa ran off to Percé the previous year, she had to take the bus from Campbellton, just like they did now.

The highway ran too far inland to see the water. And even if it wasn't, trees blocked the view. They looked like pine or spruce. The speed they travelled made it difficult to tell. This section of the road was desolate. A few houses, spread far apart from one another, with manicured lawns, broke up the monotony of trees, trees and more trees. At least now, there was birch mixed in with the evergreens. Their distinctive white bark gave them away. Some were dead, others leaned on angles that defied gravity but were living.

The trees on the right side of the bus cleared, and a sliver of water shimmered in the distance.

"Look, Jennifer. There's the bay," he said, pointing towards the horizon.

"Hmm? You say something?"

She had been sleeping, and he woke her. Guilt overcame him once again.

Jennifer put her hand up to shield her eyes as they drove over a section of road where the sun's brilliant rays shone straight in the bus windows. Their warmth painted the interior with a golden hue. There must be more to see along the route.

She inhaled the Christmas tree smell of the pines as they passed by trees, which took her back to her childhood. The occasional house stood with no others near it. Rock cuts where crews blasted to keep the road reasonably flat. Guard rails in places where the road was higher than the surrounding land.

A few more houses came into view, their quaint charm adding to the journey. A gas station, out of place in this serene landscape, appeared on the left. Michael pointed it out, drawing Jennifer's attention to it.

The railway tracks, a throwback to the area's industrial past, ran parallel to the shoreline, separating them from the Bay of Chaleur. Beyond the trees, the bay glistened like a field of diamonds under the sun's caress. The trees thinned out, revealing the water in all its glory. The muted green-blue hues of the land, a characteristic of this region, enhanced the picturesque scene.

Jennifer tried to capture the beauty with her phone, but the bus's speed made it a challenge. A few cottages stood on the shore. What a beautiful view to wake up to every morning.

The road started curving away from the water, and the scenery out the windows returned to trees. An enormous mountain stood in the distance straight ahead. A few seconds later, the water was next to the road again with the tracks between them.

The mountain in front of them earlier now stood on their left, its imposing presence reminding them of the journey's grandeur. At least now, the sun was high enough that Jennifer no longer needed to shield her eyes from the glare. With the change in light levels, the next time a sliver of water became visible, it took on a different colour. Now, it looked more orange, hinting of the sunset to come.

Michael's unasked question about the rail line still being in use, received an answer. Five hopper cars, frozen in time, stood on the tracks. A weathered green sign on the side of the road proclaimed that Nouvelle, translated to English, was new, was fourteen kilometres ahead and New Richmond was fifty-nine.

On the right, what appeared to be a small campground,

with a handful of permanent caravans, came into view. They traversed another bridge. The creek, or so it seemed, had adopted the green hue of the evergreens beside it. A tall pole stood on the opposite bank crowned with an osprey's nest. He strained for a better look, hoping to spot the birds, but they were nowhere to be seen.

They passed a deer crossing sign, a common sight in these parts. However, when they crossed the border between New Brunswick and Quebec and embarked on the road to Percé, the signs warned of moose. Neither had graced them with their presence, even if only a fleeting glimpse. Some transports they met had moose bumpers installed on the fronts of the tractors, a precautionary measure in this wild terrain.

A military helicopter flew by them, going in the opposite direction. Michael knew of only one base in this area, CFB Gagetown in New Brunswick. Would a chopper from there be that far from its base? But then, how far away were they? Perhaps not far at all.

The bus approached another green sign along the side of the road. They had reached Nouvelle. It was so small that if a person blinked; they missed it. There was not a single house on either side of the road. A bit of civilization came along on the north side of the highway. About half a dozen homes were there, and one stood on the south.

The other thing that struck him as odd was no farms stood along the road. At that moment, a farmhouse and barn with a fair chunk of land appeared. But no livestock. Up ahead, there were more houses, maybe a couple of small stores, and the tracks crossed at a level crossing. A lumber mill stood next to the tracks on the south side. This must be Nouvelle. More houses, a post office, and a gas station. More rail cars waited here. It appeared as if wood shavings or sawdust filled the containers.

There was a river named after the village. Or was the village named after the Nouvelle River? Kind of like which came first, the chicken or the egg?

Another village spread out along the north side of the road. Given the proximity of the water to the road, it was once a fishing village. The farther east they travelled, the more quaint and colourful the houses that dotted the shore became.

It had been two arduous days of travelling. Jennifer had dozed off and on throughout the bus ride. The hum of the tires on the asphalt had made her sleepy. She checked her watch, just after eleven o'clock. They should soon be in Percé. As the bus rounded a corner, the rock with its arch appeared.

"Look, Michael," she said and pointed.

"I see it. That's the place where Gareth had to rescue Melissa. It must be high tide because the arch is invisible from here."

Shrouded in mystery, the gigantic rock remained hidden from view for a few minutes. A sprawling campground stretched alongside the road on the waterside, teeming with colossal motorhomes, trailers, and other campers. When it revealed itself in its entirety, Jennifer gasped at its sheer magnificence.

"I can't get over the size of it. It's enormous," Jennifer said, trying to comprehend the sheer size of the rock's immense stature.

"When we arrive at Danielle's guesthouse, you'll realize its enormity." Michael assured her and indicated a tiny speck atop the cliff. "That minuscule dot of white is Danielle's house."

Jennifer couldn't make it out. Once they got closer, it would be easier. It was amazing how buildings a fraction of the size obliterated something that massive from view.

The village of Percé burst at the seams with life. Cars, trucks, and pedestrians lined the streets and filled the parking lots. People strolled across the street, oblivious to the world around them, lost in the village's charm. The bus slowed and pulled off to the side of the road.

"Percé. Anyone for Percé?" the driver asked.

Jennifer stood, her body stiff from sitting for so long. She stretched her arms and legs, the tension in her limbs dissipating. The excitement of reaching Percé replaced the weariness in her muscles.

Getting off the bus and stretching after the long trip felt good. Michael opened Zeus's carrier and clipped the leash onto his harness. The dog walked in circles, sniffing the ground before he did his business.

"So, where is this place where your sister is getting married?"

"Up the hill. See that white house with the red roof?" He pointed towards the property.

"That's a long way from the bus stop. Can't we check in at one of the motels here and rest for a while?"

"We can do that. I'll text Mel's friend who runs the guesthouse. She might pick us up later?"

"That sounds wonderful."

Michael had never considered how exhausting the trip would be for Jennifer. She looked shattered.

"Let's check the tourist information office. Ask them where the closest pet-friendly place is, and we'll go there."

She nodded.

When the traffic cleared, they walked across the street from where the bus had dropped them.

"There are a few stairs. You okay to do them?" Michael asked.

"Yes, I'm not that crippled," she snapped.

The heat rose up his neck. "They have an accessible parking spot, so they must have a ramp. You're tired. I don't want you to trip and get hurt. Besides, with these suitcases, the ramp will be easier for me, too."

The two worked their way around the side of the building and up the ramp. Michael held Zeus's leash in one hand and his suitcase with the pet carrier on top of it in the other. Jennifer pulled her bag behind her. Thankfully, they all had wheels.

"Hello," Michael said to the girl behind the counter. "My friend and I are looking for a hotel or motel room for a few nights. We'd like one close to here, and it has to be pet-friendly for this little guy."

Her straight, jet-black hair fell over her face when she leaned over the counter to see the dog.

"Pet-friendly. The closest one is the Hôtel Motel Fleur de Lys at 247 QC-132. It's about a ten-minute walk west of here."

"Thanks. Ready, Jen?"

"I guess I don't have any choice."

Michael held the door to allow Jennifer to exit the building. "Since the tourist information has an even street number, the hotel will be on the other side of the road, so we might as well cross here."

The longer they walked, the more Jennifer's leg throbbed. After they checked into the hotel, a comfortable bed, pain medication, and sleep topped her priorities. She didn't care if they only had one room as long as it had two beds.

When they arrived at the Fleur de Lys, Michael opened the door and allowed Jennifer to precede him into the compact but neat lobby. A chair sat in the corner, but she'd never get back up if she sat down now. Besides that, how many bums had sat on it over the years? It looked clean, but worn. Jennifer turned to the rack of predominately French brochures. Some also had English on them in smaller print, and a few were English only.

A tourist town, for sure, much like Niagara Falls but on a smaller scale. Most hotels and motels along the highway closed up at the end of the season. She couldn't see much to do in the winter in the village of Percé. So far, they had no problems with the language thing. Did Michael speak French? She hoped he did because she didn't.

"Désolé, monsieur, une seule chambre est disponible."

"Excuse me? I'm sorry, I don't speak French."

"So sorry. Only one room is available, but it has two beds."

"Is that all right with you, Jennifer?" Michael asked.

She nodded.

"Is it on the lower level?"

"Oui, monsieur."

Michael completed the check-in and accepted the key. He turned to Jennifer, "Shall we?" he asked.

Again, he held the door while she exited.

"This way."

Jennifer followed him. Their room was at the end of the porch on this level. She waited while he unlocked the door and pushed it open. She had said one room and two beds would work for her. She'd get dressed in the bathroom, or he could. They'd fine-tune those arrangements once they got settled. She lifted her bag onto the luggage rack and then unzipped it. The trouser suit she'd packed to wear to the wedding needed to be hung up so the wrinkles would fall out with help from steam. Jennifer grabbed a hanger and put it on the hook on the bathroom door.

She should have put her medication in her purse. That way, she'd have it when she needed it. In hindsight, oh well. Her extra-large cosmetic bag worked just as well for pill bottles as for makeup.

Jennifer took the bag into the bathroom, shook a couple of pain pills out of the bottle and swallowed them. She washed them down with water from the tap and collapsed on the nearest bed.

Michael placed Zeus's carrier in the corner of the room and left the door open. It gave Zeus the option of sleeping there, although after being in it throughout their travels, he doubted the dog would want to spend any more time in it.

He took his suit out of his case. It wasn't too wrinkled, so it should be all right. The shirt was still in the store's packaging. If he had to, he knew how to use an iron and press the garments.

Soft snoring filled the room; Jennifer, flaked out on the bed, sound asleep. He took the extra blanket from the closet shelf and covered her.

"Looks like it's just you and me, Zeus," he whispered to the dog.

He didn't know what time everyone planned on arriving at Fortin's Guesthouse. He'd text Mel but would turn his phone down so the ringtone didn't disturb Jennifer. As an extra precaution, he walked onto the porch and typed a message.

In Percé. What are the plans for today? Everyone meeting up somewhere?

While waiting for a response, he grabbed the room key and Zeus's leash. As soon as he did, the pug scrabbled over to him. They would go for a short walk and let Jennifer sleep. When he walked out the door, he pulled it closed softly.

A red Dodge truck with Alberta plates parked between their room and the water. Chris's truck?

A boardwalk along the shore started at the end of the parking area. The two walked towards it. Michael and his charge hadn't reached it when his phone pinged.

Where are you staying?

He typed the message slowly because of the spelling.

Fleur de Lys. Needed pet-friendly for Jennifer's dog.

Michael didn't want to venture too far from the motel if Jennifer woke up and thought he'd abandoned her.

Gareth is staying there for the same reason. Roger and Adam, too. Not sure about Chris. Amy isn't coming. Can't afford it.

At least some of the family had booked into the same place. If they were already in Percé, he could meet up with them before the wedding, and spend all day tomorrow together, too. Too bad that his twin wasn't coming.

Everyone getting together at Danielle's this afternoon. We're on our way. Roger's bringing Mom.

A pre-wedding gathering. That would be great fun. The crowd might overwhelm Jennifer, although she seemed to cope at the bar filled with punters. Over his years spent in England, he'd picked up and used their terminology.

Tired from travelling. Both of us. Jen's napping at the moment. I doubt she'll want to hike to the guesthouse. Can someone come here and uplift us and put us down later?

He hated to impose, but he knew Jennifer was in extreme pain from walking the distance from the tourist information office to their hotel. It would only be one way because some of the family members stayed in the same place, and they'd have to come here later, anyway. They'd ride back with one of them. It would also explain why only one room remained. The Scott clan and the soon-to-be member took over the entire establishment.

Danny's brother is there. You remember Paul Sutton. He's there, too. I'll text her and ask if one of them will.

Jennifer woke with a start. It took her a few minutes to get her bearings. She calmed once she realized she was in the hotel room in Percé. When she flaked out on the bed, she didn't have a blanket over her. Now, she did. Michael must have covered her.

Speaking of Michael, where did he go? Zeus, too? Both had disappeared. The pet carrier sat in the corner where Michael had put it. His clothes for the wedding hung in the closet. But where were they?

The nap and the pain medication helped. She threw the blanket off and stood. So far, so good. Jennifer hobbled to the window. Michael and Zeus were down by the water. Since they got off the bus, she hadn't been good company. Chronic pain had plagued her since she came out of the coma after the accident. In the beginning, the medical team thought her pain would go away in time. How much time did it need? It hadn't lessened. In her mind, it was worse. Spending all that time on the trains and buses aggravated it. But it was always there. A constant reminder of that night.

Jennifer scanned the desk for the room key, but it wasn't there. Michael must have taken it with him. She grabbed her cane and walked to the shore where they stood.

Seven

Hôtel Motel Fleur de Lys, Highway 132, Percé, Quebec

June 4, 2018

"Hey, sleepyhead, how are you feeling now?" Michael asked when she approached.

"Much better. The nap helped. So did the Tylenol and Motrin."

"So you're up to going to Danielle's?"

Jennifer pulled her hair behind her and twisted it. "Are we walking there?"

"No. I've been texting with Mel. The plan is for us all to get together at Danielle's today. Someone from there will come and pick us up when we're ready. I have to text Mel, and she'll contact Danielle. And returning later won't be a problem because Mel's fiancé, my brother, Roger, and his son are staying here, too. They needed pet-friendly accommodations, also. We can hitch a ride back with one of them." He scratched his beard while he waited for her response.

"I'm not so sure. Are your friends and family going to like me? What if it turns out to be a huge mistake? We've only known each other since the May two-four weekend." She cast her eyes downward.

Michael placed his fingers under her chin and raised her head to meet his eyes. "They will love you. You don't have to mention the accident. They won't hold it against you because you must use a cane. I've known Danielle and her brother, Gilles, since we were kids. And there's Gilles' friend, Paul. They're all younger than me."

A tear escaped and dripped down her cheek. Michael wiped it away with his thumb.

"And you won't be the only one there who's past is tragic. My oldest brother, Christopher, had taken his girlfriend, who was about to be his fiancée, to the Rideau Centre in Ottawa. There to collect her engagement ring and propose to her on the spot. Some thug gunned her down in a random shooting in the mall before they got to the jewellery store. I think I told you, he lost his house in Fort McMurray during the wildfires."

"I know, but if it was a competition, he'd win hands down," said Jennifer. "Okay, I'm up for it."

"Good. Do you want to change before I text for a ride?"

"Shower, too? Do we have time?"

She was trying to make a good impression. Michael had given her the opportunity, and she didn't have to prove anything to him.

"Take all the time you need."

Michael took her hand, and they returned to their room.

Jennifer grabbed a change of clothes and a hair towel from her suitcase and headed for the bathroom to shower. The way Michael talked about his family made them more human. Not the gods she'd envisioned since he'd first brought up the idea of attending his sister's wedding with him. They were an average, everyday family who had terrible luck happen — some worse than others.

She adjusted the water to the highest temperature tolerable and climbed into the tub under the spray. There hadn't been many opportunities to get clean while travelling. Just what you could do in the bus or train station bathrooms.

Once she finished, she wound her hair up in the towel she'd brought, dried herself, and dressed. She'd put her makeup on in the room if Michael also wanted to shower.

"I didn't use all the hot water; if you want to shower, too." She had her cosmetic bag in her hand and sat at the desk. "I'll do this out here, so the bathroom is yours."

Armed with his shaving kit and a change of clothes, Michael withdrew to the bathroom. The lock clicked after the door closed. Did she lock the door? Did he not trust her? Did he not want her to bust in while he showered? Or, growing up with that many siblings, it had become a habit.

She continued applying her makeup. About five minutes later, Michael emerged from the small bathroom.

"I think Chris is staying here, too. There's a truck in the lot with Alberta plates."

"And?"

"I was thinking, if you'd rather share a room with another woman, I'd swap places with her. I share Chris's room. You and she share this one."

That would work. Jennifer would still keep her scars hidden. But, at least she'd be sharing a room with a member of the same sex.

"Maybe," she said.

"Shall I put the wheels in motion?" he asked.

"Yes. It will take some time to relay messages and for someone from there to come for us."

Michael picked up his phone and tapped out a text message to his sister.

We're ready if you can get word up to Danielle.

That part's done. Now, the waiting game. Melissa might not text back until she knew who was coming for them.

Jennifer had chosen a white top with navy stripes and jeans. A matching hoodie hung on the chair. He'd opted for navy cargo pants, a T-shirt, and a jean shirt. It was early June, so the weather still got cool at night, and being near the coast, it was downright cold.

Paul is coming for you. He drives a BMW.

If Paul owned one of those, he'd done all right for himself. Michael decided Jennifer would sit in the front, and he would take the back. Even if the car was a four-door, getting into the back seat could be awkward, no matter from which side of the vehicle you entered.

We have a dog. Will that be a problem?

It might be trouble leaving Zeus behind at the hotel. Yes, the place was pet-friendly, but he didn't think it extended to leaving the animal behind when you left for the day. The pug was sleeping on the mat by the door. For a small dog, it snored for England. Louder than Jennifer earlier when she fell asleep.

No prob. Paul doesn't mind.

"Let's wait outside," Michael said.

Jennifer responded by slipping into her hoodie. She picked up her cane and started for the door.

Michael lifted the dog's leash, and the pug opened its eyes and stood.

They had just settled on the porch when a vibrant red BMW glided into the hotel's lot. The driver, Paul Sutton, emerged from the car.

"Good to see you, Mike," Paul said as he strode around the front of the car. "Who are your friends?"

Michael, smiling, began the introductions.

"Nice to meet you, Jennifer," Paul said, extending his arm to shake her hand. "We all ready to go?"

"Yes," said Jennifer.

Michael inspected the car for ease of getting in or out, his eyes scanning the vehicle. "You take the front, Jennifer. Zeus and I will ride in the back." He opened the passenger door with a gentlemanly flourish and held it until she was inside and situated before he closed it and climbed into the back.

Paul couldn't have had the car long because it still had that new car smell, a mix of leather and fresh air. Either that, or he had it detailed often, the scent of cleaning products lingering in the air. The leather seats were smooth and soft, inviting to the touch. Michael hadn't driven in years but had his license. He got it before he moved to Manchester to attend university, but it was far easier and cheaper to use public transit. When he travelled back to Canada, a train took him to the airport terminal.

"So what do you do these days, Paul?" he asked.

"Lawyer. Based in Halifax. And you?"

"Archaeologist specializing in mummy studies and Egyptology."

"That must be," Paul paused, "interesting."

"It's had its rewards."

"Michael was on the dig where they discovered the remains of Richard the something under a parking lot somewhere in England," Jennifer said.

"Third, and in Leicester." Michael filled in the blanks.

Jennifer had done well remembering the location details and the first name. Besides her severe leg injuries, she suffered a fractured skull in the accident and some memory loss. Too bad, the night of the accident wasn't one of the things she'd forgotten. It was never anything significant, only little things. A name. The full details of what Michael had told her. Turning out a light. She'd left the oven on overnight once.

"Well, here we are," Paul said as he stopped the car in the parking area next to the guesthouse. He came around the BMW and opened the door for Jennifer.

Half a dozen vehicles sat in the parking area already. Were all these people related to Michael?

Michael set Zeus on the ground and took Jennifer's free hand. He leaned over and whispered, "You'll be fine."

"Here they are," Paul said as he walked through the door first but held it open for them.

A girl with long blonde, curly hair rushed to meet them. "Michael. I don't believe it. It's been forever."

"Danielle? Danielle Fortin?"

She nodded and smiled.

"I haven't seen you since you were a kid. You're all grown up now." Michael leaned in and hugged her. "This is my friend, Jennifer Fox. And down here, this little monkey is Zeus."

Danielle hugged Jennifer, who was unsure what to do. She had no family or any close friends who would be this friendly anymore. After a moment's hesitation, she returned the embrace.

"Come in. Sit. What can I get you to drink?" Danielle asked.

"Just water for me, thanks," said Jennifer.

The room opened into an enormous open-plan kitchen, living room, and dining room. An island separated the latter from the former. Beyond stood a stainless steel fridge-freezer.

Michael steered her towards the main room.

Jennifer felt like she was on display. All these people seemed friendly enough. At work, she always dealt with people — co-workers and customers. She was never as out of place as in this large room full of Michael's family and friends.

Roger, a tall man with a friendly smile, stood up as Michael and Jennifer approached. "Mikey, good to see you, kid." The two hugged and thumped one another on the back. "This is my friend, Serenity."

"Is that Adam? My, oh my, look how much you've grown since I last laid eyes on you." Michael exclaimed as he introduced Jennifer to his nephew and brother's friend.

"How come you walk with a cane?" Adam asked.

And Michael said no one would notice. Liar.

"I broke my leg when I was a teenager, and it never healed right," she said. She told the truth and hoped the young boy didn't pursue the matter any further.

A stout woman with short, grey hair walked towards them. "Mom, good to see you." Michael bent down, hugged his mother, then straightened and introduced Jennifer.

"Lovely to meet you, Mrs. Scott," Jennifer said, extending her hand and expecting a handshake. To her surprise, Michael's mother pulled her into a warm, enveloping embrace, a gesture that made Jennifer feel welcomed and accepted.

Gareth's parents introduced themselves before Michael held her hand and led her to the island. Danielle handed her a tall glass of water with a chunk of lemon and lots of ice. Another couple stood over by the window with their backs to them.

Stacks of paper plates, napkins, and platters of veggies and dips filled the surface of the kitchen island. Not store-bought, either, but fresh vegetables prepared here.

The girl on the other side of the room turned around. She held another platter of food. She looked familiar, but Jennifer couldn't place where she would have met someone from down here back home. Then, she realized; this had to be Michael's twin sister.

"Michael," the girl exclaimed, handing the platter off to the man beside her. She rushed over to hug her brother. He embraced her just as warmly.

"Jennifer, meet my twin sister, Amy. Amy, Jennifer Fox."

This time, a handshake was acceptable.

Eight

Fortin's Guesthouse, Rue Mont Joli, Percé, Quebec

June 4, 2018

The man who had been with Amy brought the food over to the counter. It was Danielle's brother, Gilles. He was closer in age to Michael but still younger. Unlike his sister, whom Michael didn't recognize at first, he had changed little.

Amy started chatting with Jennifer, which was a good sign. Everyone had accepted her. Only Adam mentioned the cane. He was just a kid, so he didn't know any better.

"Okay, everyone. We can't wait to eat any longer," Danielle said. "There's plenty here. Come and get it."

Cheese, pickles, cold cuts, buns, butter, and vegetables sat on the platters on ice inside larger containers to keep everything from spoiling. Mason jars filled with plastic cutlery and a stack of napkins sat at the end.

"What would you like, Jennifer?" Michael asked. "I'll fix you a plate."

"No, you're okay, I can do it."

The screen door slammed, and he turned to see who came in. Christopher, a girl, and a dog as big as a horse stood in the opening. That made three dogs in the house now. The black

Labrador lay on the floor in the front room where Roger, Adam, Gareth's parents, and Roger's friend … Serenity, sat. It took a few minutes, but her name finally came to him. Zeus, who had found his way under the table. And now this one.

"Sorry, we'd been for a walk on the beach and lost track of time. Mel not here yet?" Christopher asked.

"Not yet," Danielle said.

He unclipped the leash from the Great Dane. "Wolfgang, sit." The dog dropped to his haunches.

Christopher and his girlfriend walked to where Jennifer and Michael stood and made the introductions.

"So you're going to marry this guy?" Michael asked when Lori held her hand out to show off the engagement ring.

"He proposed on the first anniversary of our meeting."

"I suppose your meeting is as out in left field as the other family members?" Jennifer asked. "Michael told me that Gareth found Melissa. Not sure how Roger and Serenity met. I met Michael when Zeus got away from me, and he caught him."

Soon, Roger stood in the group with them. "I met Serenity thanks to Tori jumping on her and knocking her down."

Lori took over. "Chris was stuck at the work camp. I'd been watching the wildfires news coverage and saw his Great Dane, although I didn't know it was his straight away. He bolted whenever someone got close enough to get him into a vehicle to evacuate him. I drove up from Calgary to try. Worst that would happen is I wouldn't be able to get him either. Well, I got him and found out who his owner was. Once the authorities evacuated the work camp, I agreed to meet Christopher at Lake Louise near the chateau on May 18, two days after the evacuation. He couldn't return to Fort McMurray right away, so we spent a lot of time together. He surprised me with a trip to Lake Louise, where we met originally, one year to the day after we met and asked me to marry him."

"That's what I call a story," Michael said.

"So, will there be wedding bells for you two soon?" Christopher asked.

"We've only known each other since the May two-four

weekend," Jennifer blurted out.

"While it's just the four of us, sort of, for the moment. I wondered if the girls would be more comfortable sharing a room, and I'll bunk in with you, Chris. I assume your room has two beds," Michael said. "I mentioned it to Jennifer before Paul picked us up."

"It's up to you, Lori," Chris said.

"It's only for a couple of nights. It's not like I won't see you. Sure, if Jennifer's more comfortable with me sharing the room, we'll make the swap when we go back to the motel tonight."

There was no time to think about Jennifer's reaction because Melissa and Gareth had come in the door. And two more dogs. They had barely entered the house, and Gareth's parents rushed to meet them.

The gentleman who had been speaking with Melissa's brother and his family earlier strode towards them. "Gareth, my boy. We thought you changed your mind and ran off, but if this lovely young lady is the one you were running off with, well done."

Mel's curiosity as to the man's identity was satisfied.

"Evie, come and meet Gareth's fiancée," he called across the crowded room to his wife.

When she arrived at her husband's side, Gareth made the introductions. "Mom, Dad, this lovely girl is Melissa. Mel, these are my parents, Kenneth and Evelyn."

"Ken and Evie, please," said Mrs. Young.

"Pleased to meet you," she said and extended her hand. "I see you met my brother, Roger." Melissa turned to Gareth. "Well, shall I introduce you to the rest of the crowd?"

He sucked in a deep breath. Melissa switched Percy's lead to his right hand and took his left — his discomfort unmistakable. Under her breath, Mel begged him to hold it together and not break down.

The couple worked their way around the room. Melissa introduced her siblings but depended on them to present their plus ones. "Michael, I'm so glad you got here from England," she gushed and hugged him.

"Pleased Mom contacted me when she did, or I would have been across at New Year's. By the way, sorry to hear about Iain."

"Thanks. Gareth, this is my brother, Michael. I'm afraid I don't know your name," she said to the girl on her brother's arm.

"I'm Jennifer. Jennifer Fox."

After chatting with them, they moved on to Christopher and his guest and, in time, made it to the island where Amy stood with Paul and Gilles.

"I thought you weren't coming, Amy," Melissa said.

"Had to have some surprises for you. And to be honest, I didn't know if I could swing it. Who's this handsome boy?" she asked, looking at the golden retriever.

"He's my emotional support dog," he said.

"Gareth served in Afghanistan," Melissa explained but said nothing more than that.

"You and your mom will share the room you stayed in last summer. All right with you?" Danielle asked.

"Sure."

"I gave Gilles and Paul the room with twin beds, put Serenity in one double, and Amy in the other."

"That sounds perfect."

Emotional support dog. Gareth must have PTSD. She had something in common with him. She'd suffered from flashbacks and nightmares since the accident. It had gotten somewhat better. Especially after she got Zeus. She didn't need a big dog. She couldn't handle a large dog. Sometimes, her pug was too much. Like the day she met Michael.

"Excuse me," Jennifer said to Melissa. "Everyone here has a meet-cute that involves their pet. Mine was when my pug, Zeus, got away from me, and Michael stopped him. I've heard the other stories. All I know about yours is that Gareth found you, not the other way around. If you want to tell me."

"I'd come here to stay for a while after my fiancé and I broke up. Buddy, my dachshund, and I had walked out to Percé

Rock at low tide. It's something you should do. A storm blew up, and the tide came in sooner than I expected. Buddy got away from me, and I didn't catch him until he reached the rock's arch. Gareth was on the quay and persuaded the pilot of a whale-watching tour boat to come out and save me."

Since she had no family, belonging to one had never meant much until today. The five siblings, each with their own stories, were friendly and warm. She had that until her grandmother died, but after that, only her. No younger brother anymore to be a pain — and he was one. Her parents had been only children, so no cousins, aunts, or uncles existed. That was why she and Emma were so close, well, until her parents sold their house and moved on.

She slipped out the door and sat on the verandah. The tears threatened to flow, and she didn't want to cry in front of everyone. They'd think she was an emotional mess and not someone who should be with their brother.

"So that's where you've gone, Jennifer. I wondered. One minute I saw you talking to Mel, the next you'd disappeared." Michael sat in the wicker chair beside her. "Are you crying?"

Jennifer didn't raise her head.

Michael patted his pockets, his fingers fumbling in search of a tissue. He found one, crumpled but unused. "Here, take this." He held it out to her, his hand trembling.

She accepted it and dabbed at her eyes but didn't look at him.

"We are overwhelming when you put us all in one room. I'm sorry it got to you," he admitted. This time, she turned towards him, her eyes red and glassy with unshed tears.

"I'm being silly and feeling sorry for myself." Jennifer stood and walked to the railing. Michael joined her.

"It's seeing you all together. The banter, the affection you have for one another. It's something I'll never have. My only brother is dead, thanks to me. My parents, also. All I had after that was my grandmother, and she's gone now, too."

"You're always welcome to become part of this crazy family."

She shrank back from him.

"I know. It's early days. We need to spend more time together and get to know each other. I'm willing to try it."

"I'm scared. I'm scared because everything and everyone I cared for until now is gone. It's possible I'm not supposed to be happy. This is my punishment for what happened when I was fifteen."

"It may appear like that, but you've suffered enough. It's time for Jennifer Fox to be happy again. Dry your eyes, and we'll go back in and join the others."

Jennifer, her heart heavy with the burden of her past, took a shuddering breath, attempting to steady herself before stepping back into the guesthouse. A change of scenery, a respite from the memories that clung to her, seemed like a distant hope.

Michael, a tower of strength in her life, guided her back inside when she was ready to face everyone again. As a child, she never fathomed that someone with his background and life experience would find her intriguing. A bartender in a restaurant/bar, she believed the intellectual types kept to their own. Yet, Jennifer found solace because Michael was different. Perhaps, with time, their connection would pave the way for her long-awaited happy ending. After all, sometimes, miracles happened. They hadn't happened to her ... yet.

Nine

Fortin's Guesthouse, Rue Mont Joli, Percé, Quebec

June 4, 2018

It was well after nine o'clock and for Adam past his bedtime. His father, Roger, noticed his son's tiredness as he sat at the table, elbow on the surface, propping his chin up with his hand.

"Looks like it's time to get this one to bed. Anyone want a ride to the Fleur de Lys?" he asked. He walked to Adam and touched his shoulder to rouse him. "Come on, sport. Time to get you to your bed."

"Aw, Dad, do I have to?" Adam whined, reluctant to leave despite his sleepiness.

"Say your goodbyes, and we'll head out."

Roger's girlfriend, Serenity, met him about halfway across the room. She placed her hands on his hips. "I'll see you tomorrow," she said, kissing him on the cheek.

Adam worked his way around the room, his tiny figure weaving through the crowd. Some of his goodbyes took longer than others. The people he'd met today for the first time received shorter ones, and his aunts and uncles got longer ones.

When he arrived at his father's side, his voice was filled with tiredness.

"Can Jennifer and I hitch a ride with you? We're both tired after a few days of travelling on trains and buses," Michael asked, his voice tinged with anticipation for the comfort of a car ride.

"Absolutely."

"Room for one more?" Lori asked. "If I hitch a ride back with you guys, I can move my things into your room. I just need to ensure I have my key."

"Yup. But how will Chris get back?"

"He takes Wolfgang out for a long walk every night. So for them, walking will be normal."

Michael scooped up Zeus and helped Jennifer to the door where Roger, Adam, and their dog, Tori, waited.

"Bye, everyone," he called loud enough to be heard over the din.

Roger held the door open and waited for his passengers to exit before closing it behind him. He pressed the button on the key fob, and the tail lights flashed.

"Right over here, folks," he said.

"Wait for me," Lori said, jogging to catch up with them.

Roger raised the lift gate, and Tori jumped into the back.

"Do you want to put your little guy in there, too? There's plenty of room."

"No, I'll keep him with me if it's all the same to you," said Jennifer.

"Not a problem."

Roger opened the rear passenger door for Adam. After helping Jennifer into the front, Michael eased in the back beside his nephew. Lori got into the backseat on Adam's other side.

At the age of ten, Adam was already weary, yet he clung to the party. He was no longer a baby; he was growing up, navigating a world of mysteries. How did Jennifer break her leg? She never shared the reason, leaving him with a lingering curiosity. The impression she left made it obvious that it was not his business. He didn't need to know anymore. He didn't need to know what she told him.

Adam, in his own perception, was more mature than his age suggested. He had, after all, posted his father's profile on dating sites last year. The memory of that act still haunted him, a constant reminder of his premature stab at adulthood.

He held a special fondness for Serenity. She was a kind lady, kinder than anyone who would have responded to his dad's dating profile. The sadness she carried had started to fade. Deep within, Adam nurtured a secret hope — a hope that Serenity and his father would unite in marriage, bringing stability and love into his life. Yet, he dared not voice this dream, fearing that its mere utterance would shatter their budding relationship.

Serenity lived just a stone's throw away, close enough that she and his father spent many of their evenings together. His Auntie Mel also lived in Quebec City, working at the same place as Serenity.

His soon-to-be uncle was in the military. Melissa said he had served in Afghanistan when she introduced him to his Auntie Amy.

The next thing Adam knew, Roger pulled up outside the hotel where they were staying.

Jennifer had chosen the bed closest to the small bathroom again. Before settling in, she retrieved a pair of flannel pyjamas from her suitcase, a comforting reminder of home, and slipped into the bathroom.

Changed into her night clothes, she brushed her teeth and pulled down the covers.

About five minutes later, a knock sounded on their door. Michael opened it.

Once Lori arrived with her things, Michael gathered his together and made the move to the room next door.

Lori entered the room, her arrival announced by the hum of the wheels on the large suitcase she dragged behind her.

"I'm done in the bathroom, so it's yours now, Lori."

With little effort, Lori hefted her bag onto the other bed

and retrieved a pair of cotton sleep shorts and a T-shirt. With a swift motion, she zipped her bag and tucked it away in the corner.

Michael kissed Jennifer on the cheek, got the key to the other room from Lori and left.

With any luck, tonight would be a dream-free one for Jennifer. Nightmare-free was more like it. And she'd had some doozies over the years since the accident. Usually, they occurred when she was overtired. Jennifer napped in the afternoon after they arrived in the village, so that shouldn't be an issue tonight.

As the days led up to Melissa's wedding, Jennifer found herself with a whole day to spare. The previous day, she had glimpsed the boardwalk when Michael had arranged their transportation from the hotel to the guesthouse. The question lingered in her mind — could she conquer the entire length of it?

Her gaze fell upon the corner where Zeus's carrier sat, and there he was, snoring on the rug. Comfort washed over her, and she took a shuddering breath, snuggling deeper under the blankets.

Ten

Hôtel Motel Fleur de Lys, Highway 132, Percé, Quebec

June 5, 2018

The digital alarm clock's red numerals glowing seven-fifteen roused Michael. He slid out of bed, mindful not to disturb his brother, Christopher, who had returned with his Great Dane, Wolfgang, after a late-night walk. The two brothers, despite their differences, shared a deep bond. The exhaustion hit Michael the minute he settled under the covers.

Michael, moving with the precision of a cat, navigated the room. He tiptoed around the end of his bed and along the foot of both beds, his every step carefully planned. Michael misjudged the corner of Chris's bed and stubbed his toe on the frame, disrupting his stealth. He bit down on his knuckle, stifling a yelp of pain, his concern for his brothers' sleep overriding his own discomfort.

Wolfgang raised his head, his ears perked up in recognition. He stood and sniffed Michael, his large, wet nose brushing against Michael's hand. The dog's warm breath and the slight dampness of his nose brought a smile to his face.

"It's okay, boy, go back to sleep," Michael whispered.

He made it the rest of the way without incident and closed the door behind him. Thankfully, the light switch was inside the bathroom. Michael blinked after he did; the fluorescent glare bouncing off the white walls. With the heavy curtains drawn on the window, the rest of their small, cozy accommodation was enveloped in darkness, compared to the blinding glow in here.

Danielle had mentioned breakfast back at the guesthouse the previous night. Michael's mind couldn't help but worry about Danielle's financial situation. The thought of her struggling and having to provide all this food alone weighed on him. However, if her business was as successful as it seemed, she might manage. Perhaps she would have to consider raising her rates for future guests after the Scott clan left, a decision that Michael knew would not come easy for her. And perhaps, Mel and Gareth were footing the bill as part of their wedding?

It was about seven in the morning when Jennifer woke. Zeus snored on the rug outside his crate. She hadn't encouraged him to get into bed with her since the hotel might not like it although they ran a pet-friendly establishment.

A bare leg poked out from under the covers of the other bed. It took a minute before Jennifer remembered that Michael and Lori had switched rooms.

Jennifer crawled out of bed and climbed into the shower. The hot spray soothed her leg and mind. She turned so the water poured down her scarred limb. She wasn't a party pooper. The village didn't seem to have anything to do. There were some stores, but most of the main street was full of hotels, motels, and restaurants. Michael didn't have any trouble with the tourist information yesterday, but when they checked into the hotel, the man at the desk spoke French first. If they ate at a restaurant, would the servers only speak the official language? Would the menus only be in it, too? She would ask Danielle about it later. What was there to do in Percé?

Before leaving the bathroom, Jennifer slipped into her jeans and an Outback-branded T-shirt. It was an old one that she didn't need at work any more since the logo on the merchandise had changed appearance.

Lori sat cross-legged on her bed, checking her phone.

"Bathroom is yours if you want it," she said when she came out.

A knock sounded on the door — not the bathroom door but the entrance to their room. Jennifer opened the door a crack and stuck her head through the opening.

"Adam and I are heading up to Danielle's if you two want to hitch a ride with us," Roger said.

"Michael's bunking in Chris's room. He and Lori swapped last night when we got back. Give me ten minutes? I shouldn't be longer than that."

"Okay."

"I'll check with the guys and see how they want to play this."

Michael knocked on Jennifer's door.

"You want me to take Zeus for a walk while you finish getting dressed?"

"Sure." Jennifer clipped the dog's leash to his harness and held it through the opening.

"Roger was here and wanted to know if we wanted a lift to Danielle's. I wasn't sure what to tell him. Lori is in the shower now. She might like to drive up with Christopher?"

Michael led Zeus to the far end of the parking lot but only halfway to the boardwalk. From here, he thought the tide was out, but as educated as he was, it wasn't in maritime or lunar studies. Where Michael travelled on digs, the locations were far enough inland that the tides did not affect them. The arch in Percé Rock, the infamous location of Melissa's and Gareth's meeting, was visible.

An emotional support dog meant the man had PTSD. How severe, Michael didn't know, and he wasn't about to ask. His baby sister was a big girl now and could look after herself. She didn't need his help. Their mother appeared to like Gareth. That and Melissa loved him were good enough for him.

Mrs. Scott had always been an excellent judge of

character. When he was younger, if she disapproved of the people he hung around with, she told him in no uncertain terms. Most of the time, Michael listened. When he didn't, he got an earful from her later. A couple of his former friends turned out to be rotten apples — right to the core. One ended up in jail for attempted murder after a bar fight in which he'd stabbed a guy with a broken bottle. The other ended up dead. Drug overdose.

Michael bagged up Zeus's mess, and the two walked back to the room. He dropped the baggie in the trash barrel for that purpose.

Jennifer stood by the window, her eyes fixed on Michael as he handled Zeus with little effort. The pug had warmed up to him, thanks to his natural charm and ease with animals. Jennifer found herself drawn to him, although she hadn't sought a romantic connection that fateful day they crossed paths.

He proved kind and caring during their trip from Niagara Falls to Percé. It proved a long and arduous combination of train and bus travel and station layovers. He never once complained. She supposed it was better than being bent over in a hole, poring over the ground to find the tiniest artifact. She wouldn't last two minutes in that profession. First, there was her lack of mobility and flexibility. Second, she didn't enjoy squelching in the mud.

Then it hit her. Lori, who came in with the enormous Great Dane. She limped. The two had something in common. And they weren't family members. Maybe they could spend time together before the wedding.

When Jennifer emerged from the hotel room, she wore an Outback-branded T-shirt and jeans. Was it one of her work shirts? She took Zeus's leash.

"Okay, I've got to get ready now," he said. "Chris was in the bathroom, so I took advantage and came for Zeus."

Michael entered the room he shared with his brother, grabbed what he needed and headed into the room vacated by him. He stood in front of the mirror. He should shave. At least trim his beard line, but that would be better tomorrow. No, just a quick shower, change of clothes and brush his teeth. Besides, Roger stayed back to give them a ride. He didn't want to keep his brother waiting, even though he had returned to his room.

When he finished, he and Jennifer walked to Roger's room and knocked on the door.

Michael thought his and Jennifer's travels were brutal; how about driving from Alberta to here? And with that great horse of a dog. That didn't bear thinking about.

Eleven

June 5, 2018

Around mid-morning, everyone, including close friends and family, had gathered at Danielle's guesthouse for a hearty breakfast the day before the wedding. The table groaned under the weight of a delightful spread — crispy bacon, fluffy scrambled eggs, Eggs Benedict, fried mushrooms, home fries, ham, and sausages. And to keep the conversations flowing, an endless urn of coffee sat on the counter. It seemed endless because everyone there had gone back for seconds and thirds, and there was no sign of it running dry. As they enjoyed their meal, they couldn't help but discuss the spectacular flower arrangements.

"What are your plans for today?" Gareth asked, his eyes gleaming.

"I don't know. We hadn't thought about it," Jennifer said. "Melissa mentioned we should walk out to Percé Rock at low tide. After what happened to her last summer, I'm not sure I'm up to that."

"Fair enough. I took Mel on the bike to a beach north of here last summer and to a secluded waterfall. Both are great places."

Michael walked over and joined the conversation. "Trouble is, we don't have a car," he said.

"That poses a problem. It would be quite the hike to get there."

"We might go on a whale-watching tour. I hear they're fun. I've been checking them online. The afternoon tour starts at two o'clock from the quay. We can book the tickets online or at the tour office. It's a great opportunity to see these magnificent creatures up close."

"I haven't done that. Once breakfast is over, Percy and I need to make ourselves scarce. I'm surprised Mel consented to me eating breakfast here this morning."

"I'm surprised how composed she is," said Jennifer. "If I was in her place, I'd be a babbling idiot by now."

"What do you want to do today?" Michael asked Jennifer.

"Whale-watching? At least I can sit if I want."

"Okay."

"Anyone else want to go out whale-watching today?" Michael asked.

That wasn't one of his brightest suggestions. Jennifer gave him a stink eye, her disappointment obvious.

"I'm sorry. I thought some of the others would want to come, too."

Regret flooded Michael's heart. He should have expected Jennifer's wish for some quality time with only the two of them. Could they bring Zeus on the boat? No, it would be best to leave him here at the guesthouse if Jennifer agreed to let someone else care for him for a few hours.

"Would you be kind enough to let Zeus stay here while Jennifer and I go on a whale-watching tour today, Danielle?" Michael asked, anticipating a negative response.

"I'd love to. The dog gets along well with Melissa's pooch, Buddy, and all the other dogs."

While he had been talking to Danielle, Jennifer had disappeared. Michael found her on the porch. She had her back to the door and likely taking in the view of Percé Rock.

"All settled. Danielle says Zeus can stay here. You and I are off to see whales. None of the others were interested in going, so it will be just us." Michael put his arm around Jennifer's shoulders and pulled her close.

It was petty of Jennifer to be upset because Michael asked the others if they wanted to go whale-watching. Since beginning this trip, she had been on an emotional rollercoaster. Highs, lows, and in-betweens. Right now, she was on a low. These feelings frightened her. She'd never had them like this. When she was with Michael, she felt safe and cared for, an emotion she longed for since her parents died. That was different. That was family. This was with a man. As a teenager, she never had a boyfriend. After the accident, none of the boys she attended school with showed an interest in her. Most of them steered well clear, afraid Jennifer would bump them off, too.

With a deep breath, Jennifer leaned her head on Michael's shoulder, a subtle act of seeking comfort. "If we're going whale-watching, I insist on paying for *my* ticket," she declared.

Michael's response was not one of agreement or disagreement but a challenge. "We'll see what happens when we get there," he said. His tone added a layer of tension to their interaction.

Twelve

Quai Percé, Percé, Quebec

June 5, 2018

Michael held the ticket office door open for Jennifer. She was already at the counter, having purchased tickets for both of them before he had the chance. It should have been his treat, he mused. After all, he was the one who had convinced her to embark on this wild adventure. But with the expenses of trains, buses, rooms, and meals, she might have thought he'd already spent enough. Rather than argue, he accepted she had treated him.

"The next tour is in about one and a half hours. Do you have warm clothing? It's cold out on the water," the clerk said. The ticket office was warm — a stark contrast to the chilly breeze that seeped in through the open door.

Jennifer wore a light sweater, and he was in short sleeves. The realization hit him like a cold gust of wind. Did he have time to go back to their rooms and get them each a jacket? If Michael went by himself, then yes. If he took the boardwalk, in even less time.

"Have you got your room key?"

"Yes, why?" Jennifer asked.

"I'll get us something warmer to put on when we're on the boat," Michael offered, his concern for Jennifer's comfort clear.

Did the thought of Michael rummaging through her suitcase, which contained her intimate apparel, make Jennifer uncomfortable? Had she packed anything heavy? Her jacket from the day they left Niagara Falls should have been hanging in the closet, but other than that, Jennifer had no warm sweaters or sweatshirts. She handed him her key and told him where to find her coat.

"Why don't you wait outside on the boardwalk for me. There are benches where you can sit and watch the birds and the water and get some good views of Percé Rock. I'll be as quick as I can." Michael said.

Jennifer nodded, a silent affirmation of her decision to buy the tickets. There was no turning back now. Most importantly, she didn't want to be cold when they were on the water. She followed Michael out the door and walked to a nearby bench.

The sun was bright, casting a warm glow over the shore. When the wind changed, a gentle mist of brackish spray kissed her skin. Where the water landed on her was cool, a refreshing contrast to the day's warmth. She dug into her bag and pulled out her sunglasses, a comfort amid this tranquil scene. She should have worn them on the bus when they came yesterday. But, no, she didn't.

The water shimmered like a million diamonds, each reflecting the sun's brilliance. It was a dazzling sight without her shades, almost too much to bear. At least when she put them on, it helped tone the brilliance down to a tolerable level, allowing her to appreciate the beauty of the sea.

Michael returned in about half an hour. He had his hands full with Jennifer's jacket, a sweatshirt each, in case the coat wasn't enough for her, and his multi-pocketed vest, anticipating the upcoming adventure.

"Here you go. I also have an extra jumper in case you need more than your coat," Michael said.

"Whale-watching is new to me. Do you think we'll see any?" Jennifer asked.

"Hard to say. I hope we'll see at least one since we'll be out on the water for two and a half hours."

"What kinds will we see?"

"Dunno. Blue and minke, maybe Belugas."

"They had Belugas at Marineland. I don't know if they still do. They're white, aren't they? Do they have a funny-shaped forehead?"

"That's them."

"I've never seen them except in the Marineland ads on TV."

The boat, a sturdy vessel with comfortable seats and a sheltered area, arrived and berthed at the quay. Michael and Jennifer opted to board then rather than wait and enjoy the warm sunshine longer so they'd secure an excellent location to watch.

He chose the aft of the boat, where they'd be able to feel the gentle breeze and have a clear view of the horizon. There were seats and a sheltered area in case of bad weather or heavy seas, ensuring their comfort throughout the journey.

Before the scheduled departure, more and more people straggled down the quay and stepped onto the vessel. The weather was favourable at the moment. He hoped it continued.

Employees untied the ropes at the scheduled departure time, and the boat cast off.

"Good afternoon, ladies and gentlemen. I hope you're excited about today's whale-watching tour. We're not out to chase the whales, but watch for them breaching the surface. What you should be watching for first is the blow. That's a column of moist air expelled through the animal's blowhole when they surface to breathe. You can see it from quite a distance on a day like today. Once someone spots that, we'll go in that direction. Everyone ready? Remember, no sudden movements or loud noises that might startle the whales. Let's respect their space and enjoy this unique experience together."

A chorus of ayes came from the passengers. Michael held Jennifer close to him. He didn't want her to fall overboard.

As if on cue, Jennifer's eyes widened with excitement as she spotted the first blow. "There, I see it," she yelled, pointing off the starboard side. The thrill of the moment was infectious.

The captain turned in the direction she pointed. Soon, the aquatic mammal breached the surface. Only its back came out of the water, but even that excited Michael. He let out a gasp of awe with the thrill of the sighting.

By now, they were well past Percé Rock.

Jennifer's heart raced with exhilaration as she witnessed not just one but multiple majestic whales. The entire boat buzzed with excitement, cameras poised for the anticipated breach. In her awe, Jennifer captured the breathtaking creatures on her phone, and snuck in a couple of selfies with Michael. The sheer thrill of the moment was clear.

The skies to the east grew ominously dark, a storm brewing. Jennifer, who had never experienced the Maid of the Mist back home, found herself in a similar, if not more perilous, situation in the Gulf of St. Lawrence. The waves loomed, threatening to swallow their boat whole. The rain began, at first with a few scattered drops, then pouring down, intensifying her sense of dread. Yet, amidst the fear, there was a glimmer of hope, a belief in their survival that refused to be extinguished.

People scattered to get out of the foul weather. She and Michael remained on the aft but under the shelter formed by the upper deck. The swells heightened, terrifying Jennifer. Then someone else who had stayed outside started singing the theme song of *Gilligan's Island*, most notably the part about the weather and the ship being tossed. She had seen reruns of the television show and knew things didn't turn out well for those onboard the Minnow.

Gripping Michael's hand, she prayed for their safe return to land. In a comforting gesture, he wrapped his other arm around her and the vertical pillar they stood beside. Though not wholly dispelled, his action eased her fears somewhat at that point. However, the genuine sense of relief would only wash over her once they docked, and the solid ground was beneath her feet. The joy of being back on land was overwhelming, a sensation of safety and comfort that was unmatched.

Once the weather turned, the whales made no more appearances. It was disappointing, but the ship being buffeted by wind and waves was frightening.

Soon, they approached the back side of Percé Rock. A vast crater had formed near the top. Weather like this caused the rock to erode. Was that how the arch formed at the far end? And what about the stack just beyond the promontory? Was it attached at one time as well?

After they rounded the rock, it wasn't long until the the pilot and awaiting crew tied the vessel up to the quay.

Jennifer couldn't wait to get off. And when she did, the sensation of being still onboard and in the rough seas for the first few moments remained.

While the weather had not cleared completely, it had let up considerably, and the sun broke through the cloud cover, creating a rainbow.

Thirteen

Fortin's Guesthouse, Rue Mont Joli, Percé, Quebec

June 6, 2018

Roger had driven Michael, Jennifer, and the rest of the gang to the guesthouse around one-thirty. Rather than burden Danielle with another meal, the group, including Gareth, ventured out for breakfast in the village. After all, it was bad luck for the groom to see the bride before the wedding.

White paper lanterns hung from the gazebo, casting a soft glow. Delicate gauze curtains, tied to the posts, billowed at the top and pooled at the bottom. Neatly arranged rows of white wooden folding chairs, separated by a wide aisle faced the pavilion. A table, adorned with a fitted covering, stood as the altar, where the bride and groom would soon sign the register.

Family members began to arrive before two that afternoon for the three o'clock ceremony. The location of the gazebo and rows of seats were outside the kitchen window. Christopher and Michael escorted people to their chairs. Danielle had secured an officiant from the village who stood before the makeshift altar.

Soft music floated in the air, a gentle backdrop to the family's conversations. Jennifer sat with Lori, and her presence was comforting. Christopher and Michael sat with their mother. Amy, Serenity, and Danielle began their walk down the path to the altar. Roger and Melissa followed. As they reached the last row of seats, Gareth, a vision in his full-dress uniform, stood. Paul and Gilles by his side, and Percy and Buddy, the couple's dogs, wore black tuxedo bandanas with matching bow ties.

Zeus sat by Jennifer's feet. She'd picked up a black bow tie to attach to his collar before she left Niagara Falls and had affixed it before they came earlier. Wolfgang had settled by Lori. He, too, sported a black bow tie on his collar. "After all, you can't attend a wedding without a tie," Lori whispered. "I love your trouser suit, by the way."

"Thank you." Jennifer had chosen this because the wide-legged pants appeared skirt-like. The longer tailored jacket came just below her buttocks. When she first found the ensemble and tried it on, the ivory colour washed out any colour she had because of her blonde hair. The store clerk found another one in her size but in royal blue. She wore blue in various shades often, which suited her much better.

Lori wore a floor-length, poppy red, halter dress. The colour worked well with her hair colouring and skin tone. But unlike her, Lori wore sandals with about a one-inch heel. Jennifer wore a pair of ivory flats.

The ceremony was brief but poignant. As Jennifer observed the joy and unity of the Scott family, she wondered about her future. Would she ever find herself in a similar situation? Would a family as warm and close-knit as this welcome her into it? The thought lingered in her mind, even as the event demanded that she set any personal conflicts aside.

Jennifer had met Gareth's parents when she and Michael arrived. Another couple sat on the groom's side, about the same age. An aunt and uncle, perhaps?

After the newlyweds signed the register, congratulatory handshakes, hugs and kisses made the rounds as the bride and groom walked down the aisle between the guests' chairs.

"Congratulations, Gareth," said the man from the other couple seated across the aisle when he and his wife stood.

"Madame Courcy. Monsieur Lévesque. What a

surprise," he exclaimed, pumping the man's hand. "How?"

"Your lovely bride invited us."

"Oh, Mel." He enveloped her in a hug. "You don't know how happy this makes me."

A loud shrieking whistle sounded, and a silence fell over the crowd.

"Photo time," Christopher announced.

Pictures with Gareth's parents and Mrs. Scott. More with Lévesques, his late friend Normand's parents. Still more with the Scott clan. The dogs were front and centre in every photograph. The shoot finished with just the newlyweds and Buddy and Percy.

His baby sister was now married. He knew little about Gareth, but if he was the man who made Melissa happy, then Michael was, too.

Michael pulled his cell phone out of his pants pocket and turned it on. He had shut it off before the ceremony so it didn't interrupt the proceedings. He checked his emails and text messages, but there was still no word on whether he'd passed muster to go on the dig in Egypt. It was an archaeologist's dream to go there and work alongside the best in the field. His minors in mummy studies and Egyptology at the University of Manchester got him considered by the head of the team. Now, it was waiting for the Egyptian government's approval, visas, and umpteen other hoops to jump through.

Jennifer walked over to him. "Still no word?"

"No. And it's beginning to get frustrating. Not to mention discouraging."

"I'm sure you'll hear soon. The team wants the best, and you're it." She rubbed his upper arm.

"You and Lori appear to have hit it off," Michael said, changing the subject.

"Yes, we have. Guess it helps that both of us have a physical disability."

Michael frowned. He never considered Jennifer disabled. Many people used a cane, so it wasn't a big deal to him.

"Lori fell down the stairs at her house as a kid. Broke her

ankle and never had it looked at."

"Why wouldn't she have gone to the hospital?"

"I don't know. That's all Lori told me."

Michael turned to Jennifer and tucked an errant lock of hair behind her ear. "Have I told you how beautiful you look?"

Jennifer never considered herself beautiful, so Michael's statement caught her off guard. Some days she didn't think of herself as pretty. She turned away and looked out over the Gulf of St. Lawrence. In her mind, she didn't deserve to have this kind of attention lavished on her. Jennifer killed her parents and brother. Okay, she didn't shoot them or stab them or bludgeon them to death. Didn't hit them forty whacks with an axe. The cops hauled her off to the police station for underage drinking, and her parents had to come and get her. Her brother was young enough that they couldn't leave him at the house alone, so they had to wake him up and bring him along.

Jennifer hated the intersection of Stanley and Highway 420 with a passion. That was where it all happened. If her father had only used Portage, where there was an overpass, the accident would never have happened. Her family would still be alive. But he was so furious with her he wasn't thinking straight. She never saw her father as angry as he was that night. So, she killed her family.

Once the photo session ended, Melissa had time to speak with her brother and Jennifer. "Sorry I haven't been able to socialize with you guys too much, but I've been preoccupied."

"You're fine, Mel. No one expected you to drop everything for them. You had your wedding to get through. Far more important matters to deal with," Michael said.

"I know, but I still feel bad."

"I love your wedding gown. Where did you ever find one this fancy?" Jennifer asked.

"It started out as a winter wedding dress. I bought it in Saint John, where I lived at the time. I couldn't return it for a refund. Then I transferred from the store I worked at there to the main one in Quebec City. Their alterations department did a fantastic job of converting it from one with a jacket to this," Melissa said.

Michael removed his hand from Jennifer's and put his arm around her shoulders instead.

"So what's the deal with you two?" Melissa asked.

"No deal," Michael said.

"When I asked your brother how I could repay him for rescuing my dog, he said to be his plus one at your wedding. It seemed a simple enough request."

"And let me tell you what a royal pain in the butt getting here was. It might have been easier to fly to Quebec City, rent a car and drive the rest of the way. Planes, trains and automobiles, but in our case, it was buses, trains, and automobiles."

"Hey, you're forgetting that I went through the same thing when I came here last summer."

"Come and eat, you three," Danielle called out the kitchen window.

"Where are you and Gareth going for your honeymoon?" Jennifer asked as they started to make their way into the house.

"He won't tell me. Says it's a surprise."

As Jennifer pondered the possibility of a future with Michael, her mind wandered to potential honeymoon destinations. Yet, she knew better than to let her imagination run wild. The odds of them tying the knot seemed slim despite Michael's impeccable character and how he treated her with respect and kindness.

He held the door for his sister and her and they entered ahead of him.

The feast unfolded in all its splendour. A majestic three-tiered wedding cake reigned over the kitchen island, while a cornucopia of mouthwatering dishes graced every inch of space. The dining table, laden with an abundance of food, was a shimmering sea of stacked plates and gleaming cutlery.

Seeking solace from the bustling kitchen, Jennifer found refuge in the other room. The kitchen, since the ceremony, had transformed into a hub of activity, unable to contain the multitude of guests. The contrast was stark, with the living room offering a quiet retreat amidst the celebration. Even the dogs, sometimes mischievous, seemed to sense the solemnity of the occasion, showing a rare restraint with the amount of food.

Fourteen

June 7, 2018

Despite the distance they had to cover to get to Percé, they were fortunate to have two full and two partial days. The time had come for the challenging journey back to Niagara Falls. Jennifer, mindful of her work commitments on the twelfth, had planned a few extra days off, unsure of the reliability of the return trip's connections. If they returned earlier, she'd have time to rest and rejuvenate.

With a meticulous eye, Jennifer packed her suitcase, ensuring no single item remained behind. Her decision to not wear any jewellery was a wise one, eliminating the risk of an earring or ring being overlooked.

Having packed his case, Michael was waiting outside with her beloved dog, Zeus, possibly accompanied by Michael's brothers, Chris, Roger, and Lori, Chris's fiancée. The shared anticipation of the journey back home created a sense of camaraderie and warmth.

Once satisfied that everything she had packed everything she had brought, Jennifer zipped up her case. She placed it on the floor next to Zeus's carrier and stepped outside to join Michael.

Melissa and Gareth, embarked on their honeymoon soon after the meal; they had already cut the cake the day before. Mrs. Scott, Serenity, and Amy stayed at Danielle's. Roger planned to return home, accompanied by his mother and partner. He had agreed to drive Amy to Quebec City to continue her journey to Sudbury by train.

Michael put his arm around Jennifer's shoulders when she arrived at his side.

"So, bro', when will there be wedding bells for you?" Christopher asked.

"I could ask you the same thing."

"And what about you, Rog? Wedded bliss coming any time soon with you and Serenity?" Michael asked.

His brother said nothing, just smiled.

If Michael was going to marry Jennifer, he'd like to know her better, not jump into things after only a few weeks. Chris and Lori met in 2016, so they had spent the better part of two years together. Roger and Serenity, a minimum of six months. If anyone was going to marry, it should be one of them.

"All packed?" Michael asked Jennifer.

"Yes."

As Michael turned to retrieve the bags from their room, the sound of Paul's BMW pulling in reached his ears. The car was driven by Danielle, his fiancée, having become engaged at Melissa's wedding.

"We couldn't let you go without saying goodbye," Mrs. Scott said, climbing out of the front passenger seat.

Amy and Serenity stepped out of the car, their presence adding to the warmth of the gathering on the verandah outside their room. Everyone hugged and kissed one another, including Jennifer. He and his friends and family had accepted her as a member of his family.

"When do you go back, Rog?" Michael asked.

"We leave tomorrow. Take Amy to mine, and she'll return to Sudbury from there."

"If you didn't mind sitting in the back with Wolfgang, we'd offer you a lift. We have to go right by Sudbury on the way back to Fort Mac," Chris said.

"Thanks, but no thanks," Amy said. "I like Wolfgang, but it's a long time in a small backseat. No, I'll stick with my original plan." They met her decision, though independent, with understanding and acceptance.

She petted the dog's head to prove she liked Chris's Great Dane.

"You're still welcome if you change your mind," Lori said. "At least then I won't be outnumbered."

Everyone laughed.

It didn't take any time, from when they said their goodbyes to the family to when Michael, Jennifer, and Zeus were on the bus headed back to Campbellton. He kept checking his phone for news, but there was still nothing.

As the bucolic scenery passed the window, thoughts of Jennifer and their potential future together consumed his mind. The prospect of marriage loomed, casting a shadow of uncertainty over their relationship. If they married, where would they live? It would be a straightforward decision for him to stay in Canada, given his citizenship. However, it would mean a complex process of applying for and getting a visa for Jennifer if they moved to England. He experienced this when he had to secure a student visa before heading to university. Before graduation, he had to apply for a different one to remain in Manchester. The path seemed more straightforward for him to come home, but what about Jennifer?

Would Jennifer be content to stay in Niagara Falls, or would she prefer to start anew in another part of Ontario? And more importantly, would she want to marry him if he were to propose? These questions swirled in his mind, each one adding to the uncertainty of their future. The possibilities were endless, and the unknown was both thrilling and terrifying.

Michael's fervour for this dig was not a mere interest but a burning passion. It wasn't about the desert sand but the exhilaration of discovery, the rush that came with unearthing something significant. Even a minor find was a cause for celebration in scientific circles, and he still basked in the Richard III discovery. This unwavering passion had convinced the leader of the dig team to include him. He had been part of many other digs in the UK, some with significant finds, but none compared to the car park in Leicester.

Fifteen

Montréal Central Station, Montréal, Quebec

June 9, 2018

With his palms sweaty from nervousness, Michael logged into the train station's Wi-Fi to recheck his email. Still no word. He had submitted his proposal months ago. Why was it taking them so long to respond? He stood and paced back and forth in front of the seats where Jennifer sat with Zeus in his carrier on the floor next to her.

"They get dozens of applications daily. It will take time to sift through them all and decide you're the best person for the job," she said as she reached out and touched his arm. "Come sit down. You getting worked up will not make them respond any quicker."

"You're right. Still, I can't help thinking they've passed me over." Michael rested his chin in his hands, his elbows on his thighs. It would sting if they rejected his proposal, but not knowing was far worse. He refreshed his email for the umpteenth time. Still nothing.

"Is there something in your past that would make them turn you down?" Jennifer's voice was concerned as she twisted in her seat and caught his eye.

"I don't think so."

"Not even when you were a student working in the field?"

Michael pondered her last question. Did he do something wrong back then? His class travelled to Cambridgeshire when he was a second-year student. Flag Fen. He'd forgotten all about that. They weren't involved in any of the actual work. It was a field trip for them to observe.

"Not back in Uni, but 2009 at the Staffordshire Hoard. I handed an object to someone I thought was the team leader on the site, but I found out the recipient wasn't. I was concentrating on the ground before me and reached out with the object in my hand. Once I realized my mistake, I yelled for someone to stop the guy. A lot of explanation and grovelling, but the misallocation of the artifact was only moments long. Another member recovered it and handed it off to the proper person. I handed it off to a guy who wasn't even involved in the dig. Surely, they wouldn't hold something like that against me?"

"I don't know what to tell you. I'm sure it would all be forgotten if it was resolved as quickly as you said. It's not as if you tried to pocket the artifact."

Michael leapt to his feet, seething with indignation. "I'm not a thief," he declared, his words echoing in the station.

"I know, but do you think the authorities in Egypt think you are."

Well, that turned out well. Not. Jennifer hadn't just accused him of being a thief. She had torn into him, her words like daggers, slicing through his defences. She had tried to be sympathetic to the situation he had been in at the Staffordshire Hoard, but her words had been laced with doubt. Of course, he'd be paying attention to the ground where he'd discovered the artifact. There might be more, and he'd worry about damaging them. That was the Michael she knew, but now, she seemed to question even that.

The authorities in Egypt were a whole other story. Over the centuries, looting of sites occurred and artifacts stolen. Of course, they would be leery. It made sense. These were not merely objects; they were their cultural heritage, a thread connecting them to their ancestors. They needed to regulate the participants in digs in their country to protect this fragile link to their past.

"I'm sorry," Jennifer said. She reached out and tried to take his hand, a silent plea for forgiveness. He shook her off, his hurt too deep to be assuaged by a simple touch.

He needed more than a few moments to cool off. With luck he'd be in a better mood when they boarded the train bound for Toronto. She pulled her phone out of her hoodie pocket and loaded up a solitaire game, giving him the space he needed.

The boarding announcement sounded. Michael stood and extended the handle on his suitcase. His and Jennifer's boarding passes were open on his phone.

"Do you want me to take Zeus or your suitcase down the escalator?" he asked.

"Suitcase."

Once the business class passengers had their boarding passes scanned, they took the escalator down to the track level. He liked this station because the platform was step on, step off, mind the gap like in England.

On the train, Michael switched Wi-Fi networks to the one he'd use en route to Toronto. It wasn't until the train pulled out that the email he'd waited for arrived. He was too nervous to open it in case it was a rejection.

"The email is here," he said.

"Well, open it," Jennifer urged, nudging him with her shoulder.

"I'm sorry I blew up at you earlier. I know you were trying to help."

"You're forgiven. Now, are you going to open the email? If you don't, I will." She reached for his phone.

Michael pulled the hand in which he held his mobile back towards him. "Ah, no. I'll do it." He tapped on the email icon and read.

"Well? Are you going to keep me in suspense?"

"They've accepted me! I can't believe it. The site leader wants me to come and work with the Egyptian-German team that is currently there. All my paperwork is in order. I'm free to join them as soon as I can."

In his excitement, Michael put his hands on the sides of Jennifer's head and kissed her square on the lips. "I can't believe it," he said again after the kiss.

"I'm happy for you. I know how much you wanted this."

That kiss was a complete surprise. Jennifer didn't mind it. He was the first person who hadn't bailed on her once he discovered her disability and her past. He took her as she was. The accident was tragic. It changed her forever. At least she hadn't suffered facial cuts in the accident. Why did that pop into her mind? Was it because of what just happened? Was she that vain?

"Champagne. We need champagne to celebrate," Michael said.

His enthusiasm pulled her out of her reverie. She was thrilled for him and this grand adventure that awaited him. If there were ever any clouds of doubt that lingered over the fiasco in Staffordshire, this would lay them to rest. The Egyptian authorities wouldn't allow archaeologists with less than stellar credentials into their country to work alongside them. One question remained. When would he leave?

"I have to fly to Manchester. Things I need to do there. Then, another flight to Cairo. I have to tell them what flight I'm coming in on, and they'll send someone to meet me at the airport."

"When are you leaving?"

"As soon as I can get everything arranged. I checked out of the hotel, so I don't need to go all the way with you. I'll see you onto the GO Train in Toronto, and then I'll take the UP Express to Pearson."

Sooner than expected, Michael was leaving. A pang of disappointment caught Jennifer off guard. She had somehow expected him to return to Niagara Falls with her. It made no sense for him to pay for a hotel room he wasn't using. They had spent so much time together before their trip to Percé, during their train and bus rides, and the wedding. She had grown accustomed to his presence. She would miss him.

"But you want to celebrate with champagne. We can't do that if you don't return with me."

At that moment, a VIA employee came down the aisle.

"Excuse me, but is there any champagne on this train? We want to celebrate," Michael said.

"Not here, but business class might have some. I'll find out."

Michael pulled his credit card out of his wallet and sat it on the tray table.

When the crew member returned, she carried a bottle of bubbly and two glasses. "It's Prosecco. Will that do?"

"That's fine," Michael said.

"Celebrating something special?" She asked as she unwrapped the foil from the bottle.

"Yes," they said in unison.

"Tell her, Michael," Jennifer said.

"The Egyptian-German archaeology team has accepted me to join them at Saqqara."

"Oh … I thought you had asked the young lady to marry you."

"We've only known each other since the May two-four weekend," Jennifer said, accepting a poured glass of Prosecco.

"Well, best of luck. I hope your trip is successful." She handed Michael another glass. "Enjoy."

"She thought we'd got engaged." Jennifer giggled before taking a sip of her sparkling wine.

"It's not a bad idea."

"It would be a long-distance engagement," she replied with playfulness in her voice. "Don't you think it's better to get to know me better before committing?"

"I know you hog the bathroom. Your makeup, shampoo and stuff fill the countertop. You and Zeus both snore."

"You don't know if I can cook," she countered. "Yeesh, when you get something in your head, you go off with guns blazing."

"That, too," he replied, a mischievous glint in his eyes. They clinked their glasses, their playful banter filling the air. Michael's smile threatened to melt Jennifer's heart.

Sixteen

Between Montréal, Quebec and Toronto, Ontario

June 9, 2018

Did he suggest that he and Jennifer get engaged? The idea seemed preposterous. They knew so little about each other, yet here they were, contemplating a lifelong commitment. It was a spur-of-the-moment decision that she accompanied him to Melissa's wedding. He got carried away, but this was a whole new level of impulsiveness.

At a minimum, he wanted to keep in touch with her while he was abroad. He had a plan. He'd tell her about the work, the discoveries, the challenges, as far as possible breaking no confidentiality clauses that might be in place on this site. Selfies with the vast expanse of the Sahara behind him and not too much of the area they were excavating were the safest thing to do. It was a way to share his journey with her, if only a glimpse.

He sipped his Prosecco and turned towards Jennifer; her gaze fixed on the passing scenery from her window seat. What was she thinking? The thought of leaving her at Union Station was unbearable, but this opportunity was too good to pass up. It would catapult him into the elite who's who in archaeology.

Michael had dreamt of this day since his first day at university in Manchester, even before that. Perhaps since the first Indiana Jones movie came out. That's what influenced him to go into that field of study; now, it was all within reach, and the thrill was intoxicating.

The past three weeks had flown by, filled with the best moments Jennifer had experienced since the tragic loss of her family. But now, in a few scant hours, she would be thrust back into the icy embrace of loneliness. No more warm smiles to greet her, no more feeling like she was the centre of someone's world. It would be back to the status quo. Just her and Zeus. Perhaps this was the destiny she was meant to endure. A life of solitude.

She had a decent rapport with her co-workers, but their interactions were confined to the restaurant. The same was true for the customers, most of whom were transient tourists. No, her life would be her and her pug, Zeus, until the day he crossed over the rainbow bridge. Their bond was the only thing she had to cling to, the only thing that gave her life any purpose.

Tears pricked her eyes, threatening to spill over. She fought to keep them at bay, not daring to turn around. If she did, there would be no way of stemming the flow. Her loneliness pressed down on her, threatening to crush her spirit.

The thorough task of preparing for the dig engrossed Michael. Every item he needed, except for the clothes he had brought to Toronto, was waiting for him in his Manchester flat, organized and ready to be packed.

Michael recognized needing the trip to England. The decision to close up his flat was a strategic one. As a Canadian citizen, living in Canada wouldn't pose a problem. This prudent move would allow him to find a new place in England upon his return, considering the possibility of being away for months.

He'd have to take some tools with him, but they would be small hand ones. The more oversized items required would be onsite. They might even have some digging machinery, like a small excavator.

Security was of the utmost importance, and was not to be taken lightly. While staying in a hotel might be an option, much would depend on what they had already unearthed. Looting, though less frequent than before, was still a concern. Guards would be on duty around the clock, and a boundary around the excavated area was definite. The width of the perimeter was yet to be determined. However, one thing was sure: they would only admit authorized personnel within its confines, underscoring the significance of the site and its findings.

Michael's excitement was palpable, his spine-tingled with anticipation. It was as if all the joy of Christmas had converged into this moment. The last time he had experience this level of exhilaration was when he received the news of his acceptance at the prestigious University of Manchester.

Seventeen

Michael's Flat, South Hall Street, Manchester, England

June 10, 2018

Jet-lagged from his flight following the long bus/train combination from Melissa's wedding, Michael collapsed on the sofa. At that moment, all he wanted to do was sleep. A few hours later, somewhat rested, he woke.

When he rented the furnished flat, it was only a month-to-month lease, so it was easy to get out of. He'd have to pay for June, but once he handed the keys back to the landlord, it was no longer his problem. Before he left for his speaking engagement in Toronto, he had emptied the fridge of anything that would spoil. Some canned goods remained in the pantry, but he'd leave them there for the next tenant and advise the landlord. The flat was in much better condition than when he first moved in, so he didn't foresee any objection.

As he packed his belongings, bidding farewell to the place he had called home since his graduation from University and the start of his associate professorship hit him. It was more than a house; it was his sanctuary.

The duration of his stay in Egypt, ranging from a month to

a year, was uncertain. However, the rush of being part of such a significant project sent excitement through him, making his heart race with anticipation.

Living a minimalist lifestyle for as long as he had, there wasn't much that needed to be packed up. Some clothes and textbooks still had pertinent information, and he had a few hand tools he used on digs in the UK.

With his departure from Manchester set for June 16, he had a long journey ahead. His five o'clock flight, with a layover in Istanbul, put him in Cairo in the early hours of the following day.

Eighteen

June 17, 2018

After Michael cleared Customs, a surge of anticipation filled him. His heart pounded as he strode through the facility to the arrivals hall. Men and a few women held signs bearing names. He scanned the crowd until he found the one with his name on it.

"You are Michael Scott?" the sign bearer asked.

"Yes."

The man lowered the sign and shook Michael's hand. "I'm going to take you to the excavation. I am Ahmed Abdel Rahman," he said, shaking his hand again. "Please follow me." The man picked up one of Michael's bags and turned towards the exit. "So, Mr. Michael, what brings you to the Saqqara dig site?" Ahmed asked, trying to make small talk.

"Are you involved in the work at the site?" Michael inquired, his curiosity piqued. "Have there been any intriguing discoveries yet?"

"I am the chauffeur. If they're not staying in the onsite accommodations, I shuttle people to and from the airport to the location or their hotel."

"I see." Tents, camp beds, and a mess tent for meals were not the most luxurious. He was here and ready to embrace the adventure, even if it meant putting up with the lack of modern comforts.

He pulled out his phone. He had turned it on in the car after they left, and it had synced to the new time. Michael searched his contacts list for Jennifer's name. When he did, he sent her a text message.

Arrived in Cairo safely, now headed to the site. Catch up with you later.

He debated adding *x o* to the end of the message but in the end decided against it. Unsure what time it was back in Ontario, he turned his phone off and shoved it away, not expecting a reply soon.

Roughly an hour and a half later, Ahmed pulled into the sprawling complex, with several Jeeps parked side by side at one end. Beyond that, a vast area of excavated earth marked out in a grid pattern, waiting to reveal its secrets, was being searched. He parked next to the last Jeep, ready to send his passenger on his new adventure.

"Come, I will take you to Ramadan Badry Hussein, the leader of this team. You can leave your bags. Someone will put them in the tent for you."

Michael, filled with excitement and anticipation, followed Ahmed. As they approached, one guard on the site stepped aside, acknowledging Ahmed's authority and the new member to the team.

"Ramadan Badry Hussein, this is the new member of your team, Michael Scott," Ahmed said, emphasizing Michael's role.

"You're the one from England. What were your studies?" the man asked, placing one hand on Michael's right upper arm while shaking hands with his right.

"I come from Canada and studied at the University of Manchester in England where I majored in archaeology with minors in mummy studies and Egyptology." Michael returned the handshake.

"I don't think I have to tell you how important this dig is. If you find anything, you drop your tools, raise your hands, and yell, 'Found something.' No matter how trivial you think the piece might be. You do not touch the artifact again until you are told."

"Got it." It made perfect sense. The Egyptians didn't want any finds damaged or stolen.

Ramadan handed him a small hand trowel. "Come."

Michael followed the man to the excavation site, a vast expanse marked in a grid pattern with stakes and string. The sand, packed firmer than he expected, crunched under his boots as he descended the makeshift steps to the bottom of the pit, the air thick with anticipation.

"This is your grid. Go slowly and carefully."

Under Ramadan's watchful eye, Michael got to his knees and began scraping the sand away. It was painstaking work, and only removing the smallest layer at a time, highlighting the precision and care involved.

Someone yelled from the pit's far end, "Found something."

Michael stopped and waited, his heart beating like a drum in his chest. Something significant? He watched as Ramadan, the team leader, climbed out of the pit and made his way to the find. What was it? Was it a piece of history waiting to be unveiled?

It turned out the find was nothing more than a brass button. Someone on a previous dig must have lost it or buried it for a future archaeologist to find.

The cook served a delicious meal. Michael recognized the Shawarma, having eaten it in England. He had to be told what some of the other dishes were. One was Koshari. It consisted of rice, lentils, and pasta and topped with a spicy tomato sauce, caramelized onions, and chickpeas. Michael picked up his fork in his left hand and ate. Everyone at the table stopped and stared at him. He was left-handed. He had never had people he was with react that way before. They nodded and smiled when he switched the fork to his right hand. The food was delicious. There were also salads and fresh fruit. By the time he finished eating, Michael was stuffed. He made a mental note to always eat with his right hand while here, including finger food or fruit.

He checked his phone for messages. Jennifer had replied, and his heart soared, and he hadn't opened it yet.

Glad you got there okay. Miss you. x

She ended her text with an *x*. He would do the same.

Miss you 2. Will try to get pics tomorrow. x

Jennifer had said theirs would be a long-distance engagement. She was right about the distance aspect. He scrolled through the photos on his phone. There were selfies from the day they met at Niagara Falls, Zeus front and centre, along with them. There were more from Melissa's wedding. They weren't selfies, but someone had used his phone to take pictures of them together in their wedding finery.

He wasn't a monk. He had dated but never anything serious. He watched Christopher's downward spiral after his girlfriend's shooting. And the mess with the way his relationship with a fellow student ended. Those events made him gun-shy with his feelings until it came to Jennifer. Something made him want to seize the moment. But what did he do? He came to Egypt instead.

Nineteen

Saqqara, Badrshein, Giza Governorate, Egypt

June 18, 2018

As promised, after Michael had eaten breakfast, he took pictures of non-sensitive areas and a couple of selfies for Jennifer. He sent them off and tucked his phone in his pocket. Despite the heat, he wore a long-sleeved shirt and long pants to protect himself from the sun and any potential hazards in the desert. Michael also had a hat which covered the back of his neck and kept his face shaded. The sun was brutal out here in the desert, and the last thing he wanted was a sunburn.

He resumed working on the grid he'd toiled in the day before, showing his unwavering dedication to his task, and carried on where he left off. Nothing deterred him, not even a few clumps of sand that, when the trowel hit them, they disintegrated.

The cook served up a midday meal much the same as the previous night, but included Ta'ameya. This time, he also tried the other dishes on offer, including Mahshi. The fresh fruit at the end of the meal was a welcome treat. As was the supply of drinking water. Dehydration was possible in this heat. He drank as much as he could.

Twenty

Jennifer's House, Orchard Avenue, Niagara Falls, Ontario

June 18, 2018

    Jennifer checked her phone when she woke up. There was a brief message with half a dozen pictures attached. The desert was endless. The sky was bluer than she'd ever seen. Michael hadn't been there a full twenty-four hours, yet his face showed the effects of the sun; his nose showed signs of sunburn.

    She clutched her phone to her chest, attempting to keep the moment alive. Before Michael put her on the commuter train at Union Station, he told her he'd be in Egypt for at least six weeks. Maybe longer. Jennifer marked the squares on her calendar in red to signify the days they had been apart. The days stretched to what seemed like weeks without him around.

    "Come on, Zeus, let's go walkies."

    The pug raced to the back door. Jennifer put him into his harness, and they walked into the backyard. She turned right towards Dixon Street when she got to the sidewalk in front of her property. A walk around the block. They'd go out later before she left for work. Another left turn onto Dixon followed by another at Ralph. Zeus stopped and sniffed at every tree, signpost, and fire hydrant along the route. Sometimes, he replied to the messages he had picked up left by other dogs.

Twenty-One

Saqqara, Badrshein, Giza Governorate, Egypt

July 1, 2018

The archaeological site, a sprawling expanse of sand and history, stretched from Michael's quadrant to the Step Pyramid of Djoser, a majestic structure undergoing restoration. This pyramid, believed to be the earliest large-scale cut-stone construction, was a treasure trove of ancient secrets.

Amidst the vast expanse of desert, a sudden cry pierced the air, *I found something, I found something!* The words echoed, reaching Michael and the others who toiled nearby. What had stirred such excitement in this barren land?

Did his team members rush to see what all the fuss was about? They would on their own dig site, but this was another area, not one being searched for artifacts. The unexpectedness of the find only added to the intrigue.

The hubbub died down, and Michael returned to work, his mind buzzing with anticipation. Whatever it was, the news would travel fast. The jungle drums, albeit in an arid climate, would beat out the news. By supper time, they'd know, and the entire team would share in the excitement.

By comparison, the day here at Saqqara was dull. There

were no finds, no excitement, just painstaking work, sweating, and stiff joints.

Ramadan joined them at supper. The man was in charge of both sites, which was a tremendous responsibility. He had raced off not long after the find was shouted out to anyone within listening distance.

"I'm sure you are all aware of the excitement earlier. The finding was significant. They uncovered a statuette of Osiris in a small gap between the blocks of the Step Pyramid of Djoser, eastern façade."

"What are we expecting to find here? There must be something of interest, or we wouldn't be here," Karl, one of the German contingent, asked.

"We'll know it when we find it," Ramadan said.

Twenty-Two

Saqqara, Badrshein, Giza Governorate, Egypt

July 14, 2018

It had been two weeks since the discovery of the Osiris statuette, a significant artifact in Egyptian mythology. Michael wished for something of similar interest being unearthed on this site. Today, the team had hit the motherlode.

They discovered five stone coffins in an underground vault. Beyond that, they unearthed a mummification workshop, another rare find. It was complete with tools such as embalming knives, hooks, and linen bandages, providing valuable insights into the ancient Egyptian mummification process. The workshop contained buried chambers that dated back to the twenty-sixth and twenty-seventh dynasties. A gilded mummy mask adorned with semi-precious stones lay over the face of one mummy.

That same day, the Minister of Antiquities, Khaled al-Anani, a key figure in preserving and promoting Egypt's cultural heritage, announced the discovery at a press conference. He highlighted the government's support and involvement in the archaeological research.

Following the significant discovery, Egyptian officials heightened security at the site. The coffins and mummies, not to mention the workshop tools, were invaluable. The government, recognizing how priceless these artifacts were, took immediate action to secure them. Until they were in the hands of the authorities, the guards allowed no one in or out of the site, preserving these historical treasures.

At least the dining tent, porta-potties, and sleeping accommodations were within the site's boundaries so the archaeologists could eat, sleep, and relieve themselves.

Michael spared a few moments and sent a text to Jennifer.

Big find here today. Still buzzing from unearthing such significant artifacts. x

When they ate, the topic of conversation was the discovery. What it meant? What more would they find? How long would it take to discover anything else?

By early evening, the government trucks had arrived. Under the watchful eyes of the guards on-site, workers loaded the artifacts, and the doors latched and sealed. Michael and a few of the crew members watched the process.

There was never any mention of family or loved ones at home waiting for them. Ahmed, the driver, returned home every night after he ferried people between Cairo International and the job sites. Everyone else stayed there.

Later that night, after the authorities secured the artifacts, the dig team piled into the vehicles on-site and celebrated in Cairo. They started at Viola Rooftop, ate a delicious meal, and spent some time in the nightclub. Afterwards, they headed up the street to Bears, one of the many bars in the neighbourhood.

A few of the German team members came back to the site early, so Michael hitched a ride with them. Celebrating was great, but it would have been so much better with Jennifer.

Went out with the team tonight to celebrate. Wasn't much fun without you. x

Michael decided that wasn't enough. Once settled, he telephoned Jennifer.

"Despite the excitement of the dig, I miss Niagara Falls. I

miss being with you, and I even miss Zeus. I've committed to six weeks here at Saqqara and am about halfway through. I've booked my return flight to Manchester for August 5. I plan to spend a few days there to catch up on some things, and then I'll hop on a plane to Toronto. I can't wait to be with you, Jennifer. I miss you so much."

"I miss you, too," Jennifer said. "I shouldn't keep you on the phone too long. This call is likely costing you a fortune. It's great to hear your voice and your passion for your work. Speaking of work, I have to get ready. We'll talk again soon. Bye."

Jennifer disconnected the call, leaving Michael bereft.

Before his return, Michael was determined to find a unique memento to bring back for Jennifer. But for now, he would settle for text messages, eager to share every detail of his adventure with her.

After he sent it, he realized she hadn't replied to the one he sent earlier in the day telling her about the discovery. He hadn't told her much, just that they had uncovered something big. Was she upset with him? Michael sat his phone down and opened his laptop. The site didn't have Internet access, but he documented each day in a Word file.

His phone vibrated on the table.

Glad you're making progress. x

That was the response from his message telling her of the find. Michael typed up his notes from the day. Perhaps someday, he'd turn them into a book. It would contain everything you wanted to know about archaeology but were afraid to ask, although the title sounded pretty lame.

Day off after tomorrow. I'm planning to do the tourist thing. I'll be visiting Giza, see the Pyramids, and the Sphinx. I wish you were here with me to share these experiences. I'll take lots of pics to send you. x

Twenty-Three

Jennifer's House, Orchard Avenue, Niagara Falls, Ontario

July 14, 2018

Despite her physical infirmity, Jennifer envied Michael's adventures in Egypt. Tossing her phone onto the couch, she pondered over her own travel limitations. International travel appeared out of reach, but she had managed the journey to Percé. The thought of surprising Michael in Cairo sparked a glimmer of possibility. With her physical constraints, would she manage a trip of that magnitude by herself?

Imagining her journey, Jennifer saw herself on the GO train to Toronto with her suitcase in tow. She had done it once before. Then, the UP Express to Pearson, a flight to Cairo. But the reality of her situation hit her. The metal detectors in the airport would surely go off with the amount of hardware in her left leg. And there was Zeus. She couldn't take him with her. He would have to stay at the kennel or with a co-worker. No passport, and not enough time to get one. It was mid-July, and Michael was flying back to England on the first Sunday of August.

As Jennifer contemplated her options, a plan started to

form. She would apply for her passport, and perhaps they'd go on a trip together later in the year. After all, they might invite Michael back to work with another archaeological team.

Her shift started at four, so she had time to take Zeus for a walk before work and enough time to shower in between.

With Michael away, Jennifer hadn't gone to the park by the falls with Zeus. That was a two-person operation. There was no guarantee he wouldn't do the same thing again. If he did, it might mean the end of him. Some people only looked out for themselves. Several people that Zeus raced past paid no attention and did not stop him, until Michael. He heard her panicked cry and spotted her pug racing towards the road, a potentially fatal move. He stopped him just in time, averting a tragedy.

The only walks Zeus got now were around the block. She changed it by turning in a different direction from her house and sometimes did the bigger block by going as far as Level Avenue. When Jennifer walked there, the Minolta Tower was visible. Some time ago, developers converted it into a hotel, but she never had a desire to go up. She felt detached from the touristy side of her city. Same with the Skylon Tower. Tourist traps they both were, as were most attractions in the city.

Twenty-Four

Khan el-Khalili, El-Gamaleya, El Gamaliya, Cairo Governorate, Cairo, Egypt

July 16, 2018

This was Michael's first day off since arriving. Others were available, but his desire to find something motivated him to stay onsite. There might be more yet to be unearthed, but it would be some time before the excavation grew to a size large enough.

One of the Egyptian team members recommended Khan el-Khalili to Michael. Instead of his original plan of visiting the Giza plain, he travelled there instead. Ahmed drove him into the bazaar and said he would return later to pick him up. Ahmed shared stories about the bazaar and its history as he drove, making Michael even more excited about his visit.

Michael strolled through the vibrant streets, his senses overwhelmed by the sights and sounds. The aromatic smells of exotic spices tickled his nose, and the colourful textiles in the craft shops caught his eye. The tourists' chatter and the locals' haggling filled the air. There was so much to see: souvenir shops, craft shops housing textiles, papyrus paintings, clothing, linens, and pottery. Spices and food were out because rules might prohibit him taking them home.

The window of a jewellery shop beckoned him. Gold and silver earrings, necklaces, pendants and rings sparkled in the artificial light. He walked into the store, his mind filled with thoughts of Jennifer. "I'm looking for something to take back to Canada for a lady friend. She's a special person in my life, and I want to give her something unique and meaningful."

"May I suggest a cartouche pendant?" The woman behind the counter pulled a tray out from beneath the counter. "Like these. In ancient Egyptian script, you can engrave it in hieroglyphic symbols representing the wearer's name."

Michael pondered the idea.

"You can also have semi-precious stones or enamel added to it."

"Can you do her birthstone and her name?" Michael asked, his mind already envisioning the perfect piece. This was not a gift but a representation of their connection.

"Yes. What is the month?"

Had Jennifer told him about her birthday? He pulled out his phone and sent her a text.

What month were you born? Don't ask. x

"I'm embarrassed to say I don't know. I've sent Jennifer a message. Hopefully, I'll hear from her soon," Michael said. His heart pounded with anticipation, unable to wait to share this special gift with her.

"What size? Small and delicate or a larger statement one like this?"

"I think I like the bigger one," he said, imagining how it would look on Jennifer. He considered her style and how she might wear it, wanting to choose something that would suit her. This was a decision he wanted to get right.

"Gold or silver?"

"Silver. I think the gold would get lost since she has blonde hair." Michael's phone vibrated.

October. Why?

"Her birthday is in October," he said. "She just replied to my message."

"We have opal or pink tourmaline. They are both October

birthstones."

"Two? I don't think the opal would show up. So, I guess it's the other."

"And her name?"

"Jennifer."

"You come back in a week, and it will be ready. That will give our silversmith time to do it properly."

"Do I pay you now?"

"A deposit only. The balance will be due when you pick it up."

Michael pulled a banknote out of his wallet. "Will this work for a deposit?"

"Yes, fifty Egyptian pounds. A generous deposit. Thank you, sir."

Michael had used an ATM on the night of the celebration to have cash on hand in case he needed it. Right now, he was glad he did. He left the jewellery store a lucky man, a weight lifted off his shoulders. Jennifer would love this piece. He'd decide if he needed a chain when he picked it up.

Michael walked to the spot where Ahmed had dropped him off earlier. The man waited in his car for him.

Twenty-Five

Jennifer's House, Orchard Avenue, Niagara Falls, Ontario

July 16, 2018

Why did Michael inquire out of the blue about the month of Jennifer's birth? The question hung in the air, devoid of any context. Jennifer, perplexed, re-read the text message. It was cryptic, with an explicit instruction not to seek answers.

Jennifer marked today with a red X on her calendar, a symbol of her longing for Michael's return. His date of arrival, hidden in the next month, remained a mystery. She had taken Zeus for a walk, leaving him in the backyard as she prepared for work. Michael's absence was a void she tried to fill with routine.

Once dressed in her work attire, Jennifer put on her makeup. Her routine was simple, limited to eyeliner, mascara, and lip gloss. She gathered her belongings, brought Zeus back inside, and locked the door behind her, ready to face the day.

When she arrived, the restaurant and bar were busy. On sunny and warm days, like today, the place was dead until closer to mealtime. This was the middle of the afternoon.

Jennifer took her position and began serving the customers. The bartender, whose shift was ending, brought her up to speed on who was drinking what and whether they had paid yet. "Have a good night," the other employee called as he walked through the employee's only door.

A man at the far end of the bar raised his glass to get her attention.

"What can I get you, sir?"

"How about you?"

"Sorry, no can do. I'm spoken for." The drunken lout didn't need to know if she was. "I think you've had too much to drink, and it's time to settle up and leave. And call a cab. You're in no fit state to drive."

He pulled a hundred-dollar bill from his wallet and threw it on the counter. "Keep the change." He staggered towards the door.

Working in the restaurant section, Sadie came to her after the man left. "You okay?"

"I've had worse. At least this guy wasn't grabbing at me and trying to paw me," Jennifer said. "I can deal with the mouth. I say I'm engaged to a guy who's six feet eight inches tall and weighs 275 pounds, and that he chews up guys like him and spits them out. This guy took the hint before I had to use that line."

"Good one," Sadie said. "I'll have to remember that when the drunks hit on me. Better let you go. It looks like the natives are getting restless."

"Okay, gentlemen, let's tone it down a couple of notches and have a bit of order in here." Jennifer had to yell to be heard over the din. It was turning into a bartender's worst nightmare.

The duty manager came into the bar area from his office. "Everything okay in here, Jennifer?"

"Nothing I can't handle, Gregg."

"If you need me, say so."

She might be only five feet four inches and 115 pounds, but she had frogmarched many a drunk out of a bar in her career. It hadn't been necessary since she started her job at the Outback, but at the casino before that, many times.

Thankfully, the men settled down. Jennifer hadn't bothered looking at the TV to see what was playing. Sports of some kind, and with the volume turned all the way down, you wouldn't know unless you looked at the screen.

After that group left, another came in and took the recently vacated stools. This latest bunch was both men and women. Their actions said they all knew one another. Jennifer took their orders and entered them into the computer in the correct pairings. The last thing she wanted was to charge the wrong person. She pulled pints and delivered them, and poured glasses of red and white wine. During their stay, one of them told her they were going to the fireworks later.

Those damn things. Poor Zeus. The noise from them terrified him. If only they would use silent ones. They existed. But the loud bangs, and rifle repeats were too much. The evenings were peaceful during the few months in the winter and spring when there were none.

110

Twenty-Six

Khan el-Khalili, El-Gamaleya, El Gamaliya, Cairo Governorate, Cairo, Egypt

July 23, 2018

Michael entered the jewellery store in Khan el-Khalili. The shopkeeper recognized him right away, reached under the counter, and pulled out a box. "Here, open it. I think you'll be pleased."

The cartouche was a masterpiece. The intricate craftsmanship took Michael's breath away. In its centre was a lifelike depiction of an Egyptian priestess, her serene face etched in silver. A tear-shaped pink tourmaline, the stone of love and compassion, adorned the top. Beneath was Jennifer's name, a personal touch that made the gift more special. Engraved on either side and the top were hieroglyphics, a secret message only they would understand. Dotted around the edge were pink stones, the same shade as the gemstone, adding elegance to the piece.

"Your lady friend must be someone special."

Michael, lost for words, gazed at the cartouche, his heart swelled with love and uncertainty and he wondered about Jennifer's reaction. Did she wear necklaces? They had shared unforgettable moments in Niagara Falls and on their trip to Percé, but her jewellery preferences remained a mystery. Rings were not part of her attire, but beyond that, he was unsure. Yet, he was determined to make this gift special, proof of his love and appreciation for her.

Before leaving the shop, Michael secured a silver chain for the cartouche and a delicate opal necklace. Ahmed had advised him to negotiate the prices, but the pieces were worth every penny. Michael charged the balance to his credit card. With care, the shopkeeper packed the gift boxes into a bag, and he stowed them away in one of his inside vest pockets. Satisfaction washed over him.

He met Ahmed at the same place as on his previous trip to Khan el-Khalili. Inside the car, he showed his driver the gifts.

"Beautiful. Your friend will love them."

"I hope so."

Twenty-Seven

Saqqara, Badrshein, Giza Governorate, Egypt

July 23, 2018

When he returned to the camp, Michael stowed the bag in his suitcase. His faith in the men at the dig site was unwavering, yet he locked the luggage with a combination lock. This was his way of ensuring that his purchases remained untouched by any potential sticky fingers.

He caught up with Ramadan, who briefed him on where they were in the project. The team had unearthed nothing since their find a little over a week ago. They walked around the perimeter of the excavation. Ramadan pointed out the quadrants they would concentrate on beginning the following day.

The team made their way to the mess tent. The men ate many of the same things as before, but there was also Ful Medames tonight. This was a staple on their breakfast menu, but it went well with the other dishes and ensured no one left the table hungry. Salads and fresh fruits finished the meal.

After eating, Michael retrieved his laptop and wrote the day in his journal.

I wasn't sure what to expect when I collected the

cartouche today. When I first ordered it, I wasn't sure what I wanted other than Jennifer's name and birthstone. Who would have known that October had two birthstones? Opal and pink tourmaline. I hadn't thought the opal would show up well on the silver background, so I opted for the other. I was gobsmacked when I picked it up how beautiful it was. The silversmith did an excellent job. It left me speechless. Then, I decided before I left I would get Jennifer an opal necklace, too. It's delicate, and the stone shows up well. I hope she likes them.

Reflecting on the day's work, I realized I had missed nothing on the dig site. While there were no new discoveries, Ramadan showed me the area we would focus on starting tomorrow. This sense of progress and anticipation left me content and satisfied with the day's efforts.

When he finished writing, he saved the document and shut down his computer. Without the internet, there was no point in staying on it once he'd finished. At one point, he had a couple of games on it, but he grew bored with them and uninstalled them.

The sun was setting as Michael ambled to the camp's sleeping quarters. The western skies were a breathtaking blend of apricots at the horizon, transitioning into a vibrant red at higher altitudes and deep purple. Captivated by the spectacle, he pulled out his phone and captured the moment. In the short time he stood outside, the sky transformed again, resembling a fierce fire. He stood there, mesmerized, as darkness descended and the stars emerged.

Once he had settled on his bunk, Michael previewed the pictures. The images turned out just as the sky looked. Sometimes, the pictures turned out brighter, but not this time. He selected a few and attached them to a message, anticipating Jennifer's response.

Gorgeous sunset tonight, so I thought I'd share some pictures with you. x

With the seven-hour time difference, it would be mid-afternoon and Jennifer might be working. If that was the case, she wouldn't be able to look at his message until she was on her break. How did he fall for her so hard, so fast? It had never happened to him before. His last relationship had ended on a sour note, and he swore then not to get involved with another woman — EVER. Yet, here he was, unable to resist the pull of his emotions for Jennifer.

When she accepted his invitation to be his guest at Melissa's wedding, it was as if all his Christmases came at once. His family members liked her. Most importantly, he loved her. The next question was whether she felt the same way about him.

His phone pinged.

Pictures are beautiful. Miss you. x

Her message was brief, but he sensed the warmth and longing in her words. It made him miss her even more.

At that moment, he didn't recall who started ending their text messages with an *x* signifying a kiss. It wasn't important. The fact they still did it was what mattered. It was their secret code, saying 'I love you' without saying it in words.

Another text came in from Jennifer on the heels of her response to the picture message.

Counting the days. x

That was a good sign. Jennifer was happy that the authorities accepted him on this dig because it was important to him. Still, she was disappointed when she found out how long he would be away.

Me too. x

Would it be possible to get to Niagara Falls sooner than he'd mentioned? August 5 was a Sunday, and the day he returned to Manchester. If he wrapped things up quickly, he could leave for Canada on the seventh. He'd ended his business by closing the flat before coming to Egypt. Now, it was the University. Turn in his notice. Michael decided to keep that tidbit of information to himself — surprise her. Her face lighting up when Michael arrived earlier than expected excited him. He didn't want to disappoint her if it didn't work out, but he would take the risk.

Twenty-Eight

Howard Johnson Hotel, Victoria Avenue, Niagara Falls, Ontario

August 8, 2018

It didn't quite work out to plan, but Michael returned earlier than his original estimate. He had been careful not to drop any hints in his messages to Jennifer. When he arrived, he checked into the same hotel where he had stayed in May, having booked the room on his return to Manchester. With it being peak tourist season, Michael didn't want to leave anything to chance. As it was, he got the last room. It was on the end of the building, but the Outback's entrance was visible from his window. Not that it was of much value. The employee entrance was at the back.

After he checked in, Michael put the two gift boxes in the leg pockets of his cargo pants and zipped them closed. No, still taking too much of a chance. Any pickpocket worth his salt would get in there without his knowledge. He'd secure them in the room's safe for now. It was too hot to wear his vest with pockets inside and out. He'd wait until he knew where she would be. Maybe catch her at work, dash across the street, retrieve the jewellery, and return to the Outback in minutes.

Late afternoon, and he'd been on a long flight followed by two trains to get from Toronto Pearson International Airport to Niagara Falls. The last thing he wanted was to stay in the hotel room. He tucked the room's keycard in his cargo pants pocket, grasped his phone and headed for the elevator. A trip down to the falls might help him keep awake. Jet lag sucked. It didn't matter if he flew from England to Canada or vice versa; it knocked him for six every time. Jennifer might have been in the park with Zeus if he were lucky.

Michael took a different route this time. Instead of the usual left turn from the hotel to Clifton Hill, he veered right, cutting through the lot at the Courtyard by Marriott to Clark Avenue. From there, he navigated more lots by the Skylon Tower. The landmark had always fascinated him with its towering presence. He then crossed a bridge and emerged onto Murray Street. This alternative path, discovered on Google Maps, promised a quicker journey with fewer people. He was eager to explore this route, as it offered a unique perspective of the city.

Once at the Niagara River Parkway, he headed to the right towards the car park where Jennifer's compact was the day they met. He strained to see the canary yellow Smart car, its vibrant colour standing out amidst the sea of darker vehicles. It might be there, but with so many larger vehicles parked in that area, he'd never see it. The little car blended into the background like a chameleon in a forest.

He retraced his steps, heading back in the direction he'd come from. At the base of the inclined railway, he turned towards the Welcome Centre. An overhead walkway attached the building to the one on the opposite side of the street. This structure, a blend of attractions, restaurants, and souvenir shops, stood as confirmation of the changes over the years. As he walked, he reflected on the transformations he had seen since his first trip to the city as a boy on holiday with his family. New buildings had sprung up, the old ones torn down, reminding him of the passage of time, of the constant evolution of the world around him.

The falls were a sight to behold, as breathtaking as when he'd been here as a child and more recently when he met Jennifer. The old scow still clung to its perch above, a sight that never failed to inspire awe. Someone had anchored it there to prevent it from breaking free and tumbling over the precipice. That thing was as iconic as the waterfalls. The sunlight danced on the droplets of moisture in the air, creating a vivid rainbow, a natural wonder that always left him speechless. In the distance, the tower of the Sky Screamer ride at Marineland poked above the trees, a reminder of the modern world beyond the falls.

Michael approached the railing, drawn to the base of the falls. He observed the people in their yellow rain capes, their excitement noticeable despite the soaking cement. A wave of nostalgic memories from his family's visit flooded back of the proper raincoats, hats, and boots they wore, all in black. The bright yellow capes of today's visitors were a stark contrast, thanks to the changing times. He remembered the ritual of entering a room to don the gear before venturing to the tunnels behind the falls and the viewing platform.

The wind changed and blew a spray of water over him. It was time to leave. Five o'clock. Time to think of grabbing a bite to eat.

Michael, filled with anticipation, took the familiar route back to his hotel on Victoria Avenue. Instead of his usual routine of crossing the street to his room, he found himself drawn to the Outback on the same side. A young blonde woman, her hair piled on top of her head in a messy bun, worked behind the bar. Even with her back turned, he knew it was Jennifer.

A vacant stool beckoned from this side of the counter. Michael made his way to it, settling in as he waited for her to turn around. And turn around she did, her eyes widening in surprise, her mouth forming a perfect *O*. The shock of seeing him showed in her every feature.

"Michael," she exclaimed, "When did you get back?"

"A couple of hours ago."

She raced around the end of the bar and threw her arms around him.

"I've missed you so much!"

"I've missed you as well," he said, hugging her back.

"Tell me all about Egypt," she said.

"I will, but first, I've got to nip over the road. I'll be back as quick as I can. Wait here."

Without hesitation, Michael dashed out of the restaurant, his eagerness to return palpable. He navigated the busy street with practiced ease, his mind filled with thoughts about the coming conversation.

That was odd. What urgent matter compelled Michael to leave at that precise moment? Jennifer pondered, her curiosity piqued. She shrugged, returning to her post. The pint of Stella she had poured for the man seated at the far end waited, so she made her way towards him.

"Thanks, love. Boyfriend, is he?"

Jennifer was used to customers making small talk and engaged with them as often as her workload allowed. Sometimes, it was too busy, but at the moment, the time was there.

"We're friends," she said. "Good friends." At least, she hoped they were. She wanted to know more about his trip and their findings. He had told her bits in messages, but they were short. While there, he might not have been able to discuss it. Regulations and whatnot. She wasn't an archaeologist, so she didn't know.

"So what does your friend do?"

"He's an archaeologist and is just back from spending six weeks in Egypt on a dig."

"He cracks stones, and you get folks stoned," the man said, chuckling.

Jennifer shivered, anticipating Michael's return. He settled on the vacant stool beside the man, engaging in a lively conversation with Jennifer.

"Close your eyes," he instructed.

She did. What was Michael up to?

"You can open them now."

When Jennifer opened her eyes, a gift box about the size of her cell phone sat on the counter.

"What's this?"

"Open it and find out," Michael said.

She picked up the package with trembling hands, her fingers shaking with anticipation. Jennifer removed the lid, revealing a layer of foam. As she lifted it off, her breath caught in her throat. It was breathtaking. A statement pendant of some sort with an Egyptian priestess in the centre. Her name was at the bottom, and a pink gemstone over part of the woman's headgear. Other stones, also pink, dotted the outside. Jennifer was speechless, her eyes welling up with tears of joy.

"Turn around, and I'll put it on you."

Michael took the pendant from her hands, undid the clasp on the chain and fastened it around her neck.

As Jennifer turned to face him, her eyes welled up with tears, her emotions too overwhelming to contain.

"Come here, you daft thing," Michael said.

Jennifer came around the bar again and walked straight into Michael's open arms.

"One of the Egyptian team members told me about the Khan el-Khalili bazaar in Cairo. On one of my days off, I discovered this jewellery store that makes bespoke pieces. I only knew I wanted to bring something back for you. The shopkeeper suggested this. It's a cartouche. I didn't know it would turn out this beautiful. The big stone is a pink tourmaline, one of the October birthstones. I know that only because the woman in the store told me. I chose that stone for this piece and told her to surprise me. The silversmith's craftsmanship is amazing. I was gobsmacked when I saw it. I had no idea it would turn out so well."

"It's beautiful ... no, it's gorgeous. I love it! I don't want to take it off — ever."

"Not even if it's for this?" Michael pulled another box out of his pocket.

"What?" This was way too much. The pendant she had

around her neck must have cost him a fortune. He didn't need to be spending all his money on her. As it was, the text messages, along with the pictures he sent to her, would be expensive.

Michael held out the second box.

At least her hands had stopped trembling. Jennifer opened it and uncovered a delicate opal necklace. The stone was the same shape as the one in her pendant but with the broader end at the bottom, set in a delicate filigree and a finer chain.

"Can I wear them both?" she asked.

Michael took the piece from the box and fastened it around her neck.

Jennifer hugged him, her heart overflowing with gratitude. Never had anyone showered her with such love and attention as Michael. She raised her hand to the opal. It hung just above the pendant, a token of their deepening bond.

A regular customer finished his first pint and ordered another. His chosen stool, always the same, evidence of his routine. The days he looked forward to the most were the ones when Jennifer was on duty. Her friendly and courteous nature was a delight to witness, and her ability to switch to a no-nonsense mode when needed intrigued him.

In the past, his wife had possessed a similar charm. He had spent his working years at Nabisco until his retirement. Jennifer seemed familiar. Could she be the daughter of a former colleague? Was that the connection? Besides the company he enjoyed in the afternoons, was he here to be a protective figure in her life? Just before his retirement, when he had begun to care for his ailing wife, a tragic accident had taken the life of one of his colleagues from the plant. The man died along with his wife and son.

As he savoured his pint, he found himself engrossed in a spirited conversation with Michael about Egypt. The two men exchanged tales and perspectives, their mutual fascination forging a strong connection.

"So what's it like over there? All desert, isn't it?"

"There is lots of desert, but it's also lush and green in

Cairo." Michael pulled out his phone, brought up the photos app, and scrolled to the pictures he'd taken. He handed the phone to the gentleman.

"It's quite the place. Hard to believe that in all that sand, there is so much to see. I would think there would be some mighty sandstorms."

"Luckily, there weren't any when I was there. You're right, though; there have been some beauts."

Twenty-Nine

Outback Steakhouse, Victoria Avenue, Niagara Falls, Ontario

August 8, 2018

Michael ate a filling meal, completely different from those he had eaten in Egypt. The steak, cooked to perfection, and the baked potato, tender and fluffy. He also indulged in the house salad with honey mustard dressing.

He anticipated his reunion with Jennifer and stayed at the restaurant until closing. As the evening progressed and it got busier, he had less time to talk with her. Still, he was within feet of her, and until she was off work, he would settle for that. They'd been apart for over six weeks.

When Jennifer finished her shift, they stepped outside. The first bang of the fireworks display sounded, filling the sky with glittering sparks. They strolled down to the Niagara Sky Wheel and the Dinosaur mini-golf. They were far enough from the falls that there weren't many people, yet close enough to watch the pyrotechnic exhibition.

"I should be getting back home. Zeus hates fireworks," Jennifer said, taking Michael's hand in hers. "But I'd rather be with you."

That was a good sign. He could arrange for the two of them to spend time together and comfort the petrified pug.

"I can always go back to yours for a while," he suggested, understanding her dilemma. "Be together and be there for wee Zeus."

Jennifer looked up at him and smiled. She turned and started back towards the restaurant's employee parking area. She still held Michael's hand, and despite her not moving fast, he had to take a couple of long strides to catch her.

Jennifer eased into the little car. She had to lift her left leg in thanks to all the pins and screws she carried with her. At one time, the orthopaedic surgeon mentioned once everything had healed, he would remove her *accessories*. That wasn't how she thought of them. To her, they were a hindrance. A pain. The cold bothered her more. In the dead of winter, her leg ached. Still, she never had another surgery to rid herself of them. No, they were hers to bear since she killed her parents and brother because of her stupidity and weakness.

Five minutes after pulling out of the Outback lot, she pulled into the driveway of the house she inherited after her grandmother's death.

"Here we are," she said. "Be it ever so humble."

"It's a cute place." Michael unclipped his seatbelt and exited the car.

The next thing she knew, he stood at the driver's door, opening it for her and helping her get out.

"I supposed you'd like the grand tour."

"If you're offering."

The first thing Michael noticed when Jennifer let them in through the side door was the stairlift from the main level of the house to the basement. Did Jennifer have to use it? He didn't want to bring it up in case it set her off, so he decided against it.

"My grandmother had it installed. She had arthritis and the stairs were difficult for her. After she died, I never bothered having it removed. There's nothing down there but a washer and dryer, water heater, and the furnace. It's not finished. I don't plan on doing that."

They walked up the first set of stairs, about five in total.

"Front door, off to the right beside it, is a small bathroom. This way, the living room, family room, kitchen and dining room are at the back," she said as they walked through the main level.

Michael nodded. He liked the looks of the house. Big open rooms, like his flat. As spacious as it was, it would fit in the central part of Jennifer's house.

"My father added the kitchen and dining room. He didn't do the work, but he hired the contractor. Can you imagine those two rooms crammed into these spaces?" She stretched out her arms as she spoke. "Do you want a coffee? I can put a pot on if you do."

"Not at this time of night. I'm still feeling the effects of the flight."

"Something else then?"

"Nah, you're fine."

Jennifer led Michael to the front of the house via the long living room. Another stairlift was fitted to the staircase leading upstairs.

"Upstairs are three bedrooms, two enormous closets, and another bathroom. Go on in and sit down. I'm going to go upstairs and bring Zeus down. I know he'll be happy to see you."

His other question was answered without him having to ask. This was Jennifer's childhood home. It still didn't answer the stairlift question that niggled at him.

"You want to see the upstairs, too? I'd like to move the washer and dryer to that level someday since I generate most of the laundry there."

"Nah, you're all right." Michael sat on the sectional. It had a chaise at one end and a blanket folded on it. He surmised Jennifer slept down here on days when she was in a great deal of pain. The whir of the stairlift caused him to look up. About halfway down the last set of stairs, Zeus launched himself off

Jennifer's lap and raced towards Michael. He didn't have time to ask if the dog was allowed on the furniture. The pug was on the sofa beside him.

"Zeus, are you being a pain?" Jennifer asked.

"He's fine." Michael continued making a fuss over the dog and rubbing Zeus's belly.

Exhausted from work and excited by Michael's presence, Jennifer shared a personal story. "My grandmother lived in an apartment when my parents passed away. She moved there after my grandfather's death. Then, after the accident, she came to live with me. She was in a seniors' building, and they didn't allow underaged residents."

Michael didn't care about all that, but it was something she'd told no one. She'd told him bits of it before when she told him about her parents and brother being killed on the way back from the police station.

She was happy that someone besides her dog was in the house with her.

"You're sure I can't get you anything?"

"Yes." Michael reached up and put his arm around her.

Jennifer's hand reached for the pendant and the opal necklace, a tangible reminder of the reality she was living. It wasn't a dream. Not anymore. Until today, no one had ever brought her a gift from their holiday. His wasn't a holiday — it was work, but a first. Curled up next to him on the sofa, she felt safe and protected. There was no reason to feel otherwise without him here. Her house was in a safe neighbourhood. The place was secure. When the sliding patio door was closed, a tension bar kept someone from opening it. And with the fenced backyard, they had to get into it before entering the house.

The motion sensor light over the door flicked on, casting an eerie glow over the backyard. Jennifer's heart skipped a beat, and her breath caught in her throat. All these thoughts about being safe vanished, replaced by a primal fear that gripped her. Someone or something prowled in her backyard — the safety she experienced with Michael shattered in an instant.

"I'll go," Michael said, his voice steady and reassuring. Jennifer felt relief wash over her, and she was grateful for his presence and willingness to protect her.

"I'm coming, too." Jennifer stood, her legs shaky, and followed him to the back of the house. She needed to be close to him, feel his strength and presence, and reassure herself that everything would be okay. The light was still on when they reached the doorway.

"There's the cause of your light coming on. Right there on the deck. A trash panda."

Jennifer peered around Michael, her eyes widening in surprise. A big, fat raccoon stared back at her, its eyes gleaming with mischief. Despite the moment's tension, a small smile tugged at the corners of her lips. It was a comical sight, this unexpected visitor in their tense situation.

"I've never seen them in this area. What's it after, I wonder?"

"Scraps of food from people's bins. Where is yours?"

"In the garage."

"Good place. Must be casing the street for something to eat and was just passing through your yard on his way to the next."

The masked bandit stared at them, scampered across the yard and up the fence and disappeared into the property next door.

"I should be going. I don't want to keep you up all night," said Michael. "I've got to get myself back on Canadian time."

He turned and gathered Jennifer into his arms. Her eyes were glassy with tears when he stepped back.

"Hey, don't cry. I'll see you tomorrow." He brushed her cheeks with his thumbs. "Promise."

Jennifer nodded.

Again, Michael wrapped her in his arms and brushed his lips against hers before the kiss intensified.

This time, it was Jennifer who pulled away. Did he do something wrong?

"No one is guaranteed tomorrow," she said. "I know that

better than anyone. So don't make promises you can't keep."

Thirty

Jennifer's House, Orchard Avenue, Niagara Falls, Ontario

August 9, 2018

It was well past midnight when Michael walked back to his hotel. Jennifer's words about the uncertainty of life resonated within him. The thought of a bus accident, a sudden end to his life, seemed insignificant compared to the confusion he felt about her reaction to his kiss. It was a kiss meant to express his love, not scare her. Why did it frighten her? That was not his intention.

He puzzled some more as he continued his walk. What could he do to make it up to Jennifer tomorrow, convince her of the depth of his love, a love that was so strong it was almost painful?

Jennifer, her heart heavy with unresolved emotions, locked the side door with a sigh after seeing Michael off. She let Zeus out one last time and waited by the patio door for him to return. After he came inside, she put the bar across and flipped the lock.

Why had she reacted the way she did? If she ever saw him again, she'd have to apologize. Was it because her whole family, whom she loved with all her heart, was taken away from her? The pain of that loss was still fresh; was she scared Michael would be, too?

She brought her hand to her chest and touched the cartouche pendant. Michael must love her. Why else would he spend so much money on gifts for her? As much as she appreciated the gesture, she couldn't help but feel unworthy. The fear of ruining him, of causing his downfall, was a constant, suffocating weight on her heart. The decision to end her relationship with him was a battle she was losing. If she spent too much more time with him, she'd ruin him. No, she'd have to tell him she was ending it. The thought of it was unbearable, evidence of her deep-rooted fear.

Jennifer reached behind her neck and undid the clasp for the opal necklace, fastening the chain again so it wouldn't knot before returning it to the box. She repeated the process with the cartouche. The next time she saw him, she'd tell him she couldn't see him anymore.

Her loyal companion, Zeus, sat on the floor next to her, his warm presence a balm to her turbulent thoughts. Jennifer almost tripped over him when she tried to cross the room to her bed. A small moment of levity in her otherwise heavy heart reminded her of the love and comfort the pug had brought to her life.

Since it was after midnight, she was grateful for the respite from work until the weekend. She climbed into bed, her heart filled with sorrow, and cried herself to sleep.

Michael lay on his back in his hotel room, hands behind his head, staring at the ceiling. What went wrong? He replayed the day over in his mind. Every time, it came back to the kiss. It was a moment of vulnerability, a gesture meant to show his affection and his growing feelings towards her. But had he misread the situation? Had he backed her into a corner by doing that? Did she feel uncomfortable? It wasn't his intention. He sure made a pig's ear out of things.

He exhaled with a hiss. He'd have to make it up to Jennifer. A grand gesture of some kind. But what? Things had gone well from when he first met her, thanks to Zeus doing a runner, chasing after a squirrel. They had made the trip to Percé for Melissa's wedding together. Things were fine then. They were fine until he discovered he was approved and the paperwork completed for him to go to Egypt. That was when things started to sour, and his genuine feelings for her were now clouded with regret and uncertainty.

Even that made no sense. With a heavy fatigue settling into his bones, Michael picked up his phone and scrolled through their messages. Jennifer was the one who started ending texts with an *x*, and he followed suit afterwards. Exhausted from his travels, his mind too weary to ponder the situation any longer, he fell asleep on top of the covers, his phone in his hand.

Jennifer's eyes, red and puffy, revealed her sleepless night. The remnants of her makeup, now a messy smear on her eyelids and cheeks, were a reminder of her neglect. Her not having to work later was a slight consolation. Cleaning her face seemed daunting, a task that would take forever. She should have removed her eye makeup before falling into bed, but she didn't, a minor act of self-neglect that now was significant.

She applied gentle eye makeup remover first, followed by a cleanser. That rid her face of the residue but did nothing to reduce the puffiness. Somewhere in her stash of cosmetics, she had a gel eye mask. She rooted through the bag, but it wasn't there. Through her dressing table drawers. Not there either. A hot shower might help.

Before entering the bathroom, she laid out clean underwear, a bra, black leggings, and a long pink V-neck T-shirt. The shade was almost identical to the gems on the cartouche. The tears pricked her eyes again with sadness and frustration. Poor choice of shirts. She tossed it aside and searched again. Another one of the same style, but in a cinnamon colour, came out of the drawer. A quick inspection showed no stains on it, so it would do. She'd put her white zip-front hoodie on if it was too chilly for just it.

Zeus whined at the bedroom door, a clear sign of his needs. He had to go outside before Jennifer did anything else. He had never had an accident in the house, and she wouldn't set a precedent now by ignoring him. Jennifer, weighted down by the depth of her responsibility, headed for the stairs. The pug was well ahead of her, rushing down the steps. The stairlift was slower than walking, but there was no danger of her falling, which had happened a few times over the years. At least when it had, she was near the landing or the bottom, so her injuries weren't severe.

By the time she reached the patio door, the dog was running in circles as if chasing its tail, which it didn't have. At least not one big enough to catch. Jennifer no sooner got the door open, and Zeus flew out the opening as fast as his short legs could carry him.

Thirty-One

Jennifer's House, Orchard Avenue, Niagara Falls, Ontario

August 9, 2018

Showered, dressed, and with fresh makeup applied, Jennifer gathered up the gift boxes containing the jewellery and shoved them in her handbag. What she had to do wasn't easy, but the sooner she did, the better it would be. Michael would be down by the falls. Zeus hadn't been to the park there since the day he got away from her. She grabbed his harness. When the tags rattled, the pug came running.

"Now, you behave today. No running off like you did the last time I took you to the park by the falls."

Zeus cocked his head as she spoke. Whether he understood her, she felt better for saying it.

Jennifer shrugged on her hoodie and stumped down the steps to the side door. With the house locked and Zeus in the passenger seat, she climbed in and fastened her seatbelt. Then, the doubt hit her. Was she doing the right thing? Should she break it off with Michael before things get any more serious? Bad things happened to people she cared about. She couldn't let that happen to him.

She took a deep breath and started the car. Driving in the city during the height of tourist season was a nightmare. People wandered across the roads without looking. Car horns blared when motorists took exception to being cut off. It would still be bad come September, but not as. By then, the kids were back in school, but there were field trips to the city and its attractions.

Clifton Hill was busy all year, if school was in session or not. And loud. Giggling girls, rowdy boys, the noise from the arcades, and loudest of all, the booming voice from the Ripley's Believe It or Not museum. Sometimes, you couldn't make out what it said; the sound distorted because of the high volume. She avoided this street whether she was in her car or walking.

There were other routes to the location where she left her car when visiting the park. They were quieter, with less traffic and people, but they took her out of her way. Yes, her Smart car was excellent on fuel, but she did not need to waste it on unnecessary miles.

Jennifer pulled into the lot only to find the traffic backed up at each toll booth. Once she paid, she drove ahead and found a spot at the far end. It put her near the Falls Incline Railway and the parkland beyond. Before opening the car, she clipped the leash onto Zeus's harness to ensure he didn't dash off before she got out of the vehicle.

There wasn't much room in the back of her Smart car, but she used it to stash her cane and cross-body purse. What if Michael didn't come down here today? What if he chose to go elsewhere? Hard as it would be, it was for the best. She had told herself so many times that it became a mantra. The sooner she did it, the sooner it would be over.

With a firm grip on Zeus's lead, she climbed out of the car, slung her purse over her shoulders, and reached for her cane. The pug leaped down and sat by her side until the door was closed and the vehicle locked.

Jennifer started towards Nikola Tesla Plaza. She couldn't deal with the Table Rock Welcome Centre crowds today. She wanted to tell Michael she couldn't accept the gifts and that he'd be better off finding someone else. Not even halfway to the statue, she was exhausted and had to find a bench to sit and rest. Her dog lay down at her feet.

She gazed at the falls, transfixed by their beauty and power. The rush of the water hurtling over the precipice wasn't all that loud from here. It was a constant background noise, like white noise. Maybe she thought of it that way because she'd lived here her entire life. To tourists, it probably was roaring.

Michael strolled through the park, his hands in his front jeans pockets. Birdsong filled the crisp air. His attention strayed from one thing to another. The ponds and their fish and frogs. He climbed the steps at the illumination tower which offered a brilliant view. From there, he saw Horseshoe Falls without streams of people blocking them as they wandered the pavements.

He paused in front of the Nikola Tesla statue. The man was a genius, and the monument commemorated his brilliance.

Michael planned to cross the parkway at the Welcome Centre, where there was no need to worry about traffic. He hadn't gone much farther when he spotted two familiar beings — one a pug lying on the grass and Jennifer sitting on a bench enjoying the sunshine. He removed his hands from his pockets and jogged over to them.

Zeus perked up at his approach. The small dog was on his feet and straining on his leash to run to him.

"Hey, I didn't expect to see you two here," he said when he reached the bench. Michael patted the dog's head. He brought them together.

"I was hoping you'd be here today."

"What's wrong? You sound upset."

Jennifer reached into her purse, pulled out the two jewellery boxes, and placed them in his hand. Afterwards, she turned away from him.

"Why are you giving these back to me?" he asked, his voice tinged with confusion and surprise.

"I'm sorry, Michael. I can't be with you," she choked back a sob, her voice trembling with sadness and regret.

With his fingers on her chin, he turned her head back so she faced him. Her beautiful green eyes were glassy with tears.

"What are you talking about?"

"Just what I said. I can't be with you. I'm sorry. Look, bad things affect people I care about. My parents, my brother were killed because of me. I'm poison. I don't deserve you. I don't deserve to be happy."

"You've got Zeus. Nothing bad has happened to him."

"It would have if you didn't stop him getting out onto the road." Jennifer stood and started back towards her car. The pug trotted alongside her, pausing periodically to look at Michael.

Michael got up, too.

"Jennifer, wait," he called after her, and jogged to catch up. "At least keep these. I bought them for you. They're yours." He pressed the boxes into her hands, his fingers lingering on hers.

"Michael, just go. Don't make it any harder for me than it already is." Jennifer stuffed the boxes back in her purse, turned and walked away. Michael stood there, his heart breaking, his world crumbling around him.

Jennifer, her heart heavy with her decision, limped back to her car. She settled Zeus in the passenger seat, tucking her purse and cane behind the driver's. As she closed the door, her seatbelt clicked into place, and a flood of tears escaped her. She had fought back her emotions for as long as possible. Michael would move on from her, she reassured herself. Just as she would have to move on from him.

The jewellery. Michael had told her to keep it, a gesture of his love and trust. She'd tuck the two boxes away in a drawer, a place where they wouldn't haunt her with reminders of what might have been. The right thing had been done. She had ended their relationship before it could turn into something more complicated, more painful. She would get over him. It would take time, but she was hopeful. And if she wasn't with him, constant worry about his safety wouldn't consume her. Each day, she believed, it would get easier, and she would find her peace.

Michael's shoulders sagged. His mouth dropped open. Did that just happen? Did Jennifer dump him? She had convinced herself since the death of her parents and brother that it was her fault. Part of the blame, perhaps. But the most significant share belonged to the other driver. The person who ran the red light. How could he get her to believe it?

Right now wasn't the time. Both he and Jennifer needed to regroup. He'd go back to his room. Search the Internet for the accident that took her family from her. Find some proof to absolve her from the blame she heaped on herself.

Should he leave Canada again? He couldn't return to Manchester because he'd given up his flat in June. Go back to Egypt on another dig? Or the Saqqara site? Or should he stay here and try to win her back?

What would Roger or Christopher do in this situation? He could send them emails, ask, hop a plane, and fly out west or to Quebec City. Or, like when he and Jennifer travelled to Percé for Melissa's wedding, go by train? The latter would stir up too many memories, so not that.

Back at the hotel, Michael logged into the hotel's free Wi-Fi and typed 'fatal accident at Stanley and 420 between 1990 and 2005.'

That brought back more results than he had planned. He tried again, adding Jennifer's surname to the search and hitting enter. That narrowed it down, but there were still several hits, but not as many.

Michael found what he was looking for in the *Niagara Falls Review.*

NIAGARA FALLS REVIEW
August 17, 1998
FAMILY DECIMATED IN TWO-VEHICLE COLLISION
Three members of a family died yesterday in a two-vehicle collision at the intersection of

Stanley Avenue and Highway 420. The dead were in a westbound Ford Taurus hit on the driver's side by a northbound Dodge Ram 1500. Three members of the family, both parents and one child, died instantly. Paramedics rushed a fourth member to the hospital in critical condition. At this time, the names are unknown. The driver of the other vehicle escaped injury.

NIAGARA FALLS REVIEW
August 18, 1998
FAMILY MEMBERS KILLED IN TWO-VEHICLE COLLISION IDENTIFIED
Police have identified the family members killed in a two-vehicle collision as 41-year-old Stephen Fox, his wife of the same age, Patricia Fox, and their 10-year-old son, Kevin.

The only family member to survive the crash was their 15-year-old daughter, Jennifer, who remains in critical condition at the Greater Niagara General Hospital.

The driver of the vehicle that collided with the Fox's car was 69-year-old Donald Raymond. Mr. Raymond refused to give a breath sample at the scene. Officers took him into police custody, where he blew 0.16, two times the legal limit.

So, the guy who hit Jennifer's family's car was drunk. Likely the reason he ran the red light. Did she ever know that? Or did her grandmother never tell her? Which side of the family was she on — mother's or father's? All Jennifer said was the woman came and raised her after she got out of the hospital. All those years of guilt. It would take a long time for her to get over it. If she ever did.

Michael opened his email program.

From: Michael Scott
<mscottarchaeology@ymail.com>
To: Christopher Scott <cscott74@gmail.com>; Roger
Scott <rogscott1@gmail.com>
Subject: Advice
Hi guys,

You both remember the girl I brought to Melissa's wedding, eh? Well, things were going really well (at least I thought so) between us. The archaeologist in charge on a dig in Egypt accepted me after Mel's nuptials. I put Jennifer on the GO train at Union Station in Toronto, took the UP Express to the airport and flew home.

Anyway, we kept in touch the entire time I was away. Jennifer even started ending her text messages with an *x*. I picked her up a couple of jewellery pieces she'd never find here, and I surprised her by returning a few days earlier than I planned.

Today, she tells me we can't be together. That she's poison. That bad things befell people she cares about. When she was 15, she got into a spot of bother with the police. Her parents had to pick her up at the police station. Her younger brother was too young to be left home alone, so they took him with them. On their way back, a drunk driver broadsided their car. Both parents and her brother died on the scene. She spent months in the hospital. She blames herself for the accident.

I don't want what we had to end like this. What should I do?

His mouse hovered over the send button. Did he hit send? Michael reread the email. He didn't want it to sound lame. Should he include the links to the two online newspaper articles he found? Unnecessary. He said what had happened. That's all his brothers needed to know. He didn't tell them the reason for her trip to the police station.

Michael clicked send, and the email vanished into the ether.

Thirty-Two

Jennifer's House, Orchard Avenue, Niagara Falls, Ontario

August 10, 2018

Jennifer was numb, bereft. Life meant nothing at the moment. It would get easier. It had to. She told herself that anyway. She did what she did to keep Michael safe from harm. Who knew what would happen to him if they stayed together? She didn't want another death on her conscience.

She was back at work today. She hoped Michael wouldn't come into the restaurant, as she couldn't handle that.

Zeus sat on the floor beside her and stared into her face. Her dog liked Michael.

"Sorry, baby, but he's gone. He won't be coming back," she said.

Showered and dressed, Jennifer left the house and drove to work. At least she could go in and out the back. If Michael came into the restaurant, she'd slip into the employees-only room and stay there until he left. Problem solved.

Jennifer's shift started at noon and continued until eight. Not a bad shift. And with her getting off before the fireworks, she'd be home with Zeus to keep him calm.

Timecard punched, she grabbed her apron off the hook and put it on. Piled her hair in a messy bun on top of her head and began her shift. There were a few customers who were regulars at this time of day. Most of them today were tourists. A man and woman approached the bar.

The woman was familiar-looking, but Jennifer couldn't place where she knew her from.

"What can I get you?" she asked.

"Jennifer? Jennifer Fox?"

The voice gave the woman's identity away.

"Emma? Emma Bradshaw?"

The woman nodded and smiled ear-to-ear.

"You two know each other?" the man asked.

"Years ago, we were best friends," Emma said. "Until the party and my parents moved me away because we couldn't be together anymore." She turned back to Jennifer. "And it's Emma Taylor now. This is my husband, Matt."

"Nice to meet you," he said, reaching over the bar to shake Jennifer's hand.

"I think I asked you already, but what can I get you?" Jennifer asked.

"I'll have a glass of white wine," said Emma.

"I'll have a small pint of Coors Light," said Matt.

Jennifer got their drinks and placed them on the bar. "Anything to eat?"

"Not at the moment."

"So, what brings you to Niagara Falls?"

"It's our fifth wedding anniversary. Matt and I met in Vancouver at the University of British Columbia and funded our education by working at The Steamworks Brewpub. We separated for a while after graduation and found each other again in Winnipeg. We got married there five years ago today."

"You've been around. Still doesn't explain why you're back here?"

"Matt has never been, and after my father accepted the transfer to Vancouver, which is how I ended up going to university there, I haven't been back. What about you? Any significant other in your life?"

"There was, but I ended it." The tears threatened to flow, and she blinked to stop them.

Business in the bar area had picked up since Emma's and Matt's arrival, so Jennifer excused herself and left to serve the other customers.

Michael's phone pinged and he picked it up. A response to the email he had sent to his brothers yesterday from Christopher.

From: Christopher Scott <cscott74@gmail.com>
To: Michael Scott <mscottarchaeology@ymail.com>;
Roger Scott <rogscott1@gmail.com>
Subject: Re: Advice
Hi Mike,
 I'm sorry you're in this situation. I'd say give Jennifer some space. Maybe that's what you need, too. Can you go back to Egypt? It might do you some good.

He might go back, get stuck into a dig, and try to get over the breakup. His room across the street from where she worked was too close. He still struggled with the situation, feeling lost and uncertain about his next steps.

His email app still showed one unread message, so he scrolled through to find it. This one was from Roger and had come in the previous day. He told him the same thing that Chris had. Give her some space. Rog didn't go as far as Chris and tell him to go back to Egypt, but that was the best idea he'd heard. Michael felt grateful for their advice, knowing they had his best interests at heart.

He scrolled through his contacts until he found the one he wanted and composed an email.

From: Michael Scott
<mscottarchaeology@ymail.com>
To: Ramadan B. Hussein

<rbhussein.archaeologist@egyptianantiquities.eg>
Subject: Return to Saqqara
Hello, Ramadan,

I'd like to return to the Saqqara site if my permits and
visas are still valid. With last month's finds, I'm sure
we'll find more buried there. However, I'm currently
going through a difficult personal situation, dealing
with a breakup, and being in Egypt, which holds many
fond memories, might provide some solace. There's
nothing to keep me in Canada now, so if you approve
my return, I can be there on the first flight from
Toronto.
Yours,
Michael

With the email sent, he could only wait for a reply. In the
meantime, he packed his belongings to prepare for checking
out. Did he text Jennifer to tell her he was leaving the city? Did
he tell her his destination? Once he knew if it would be Cairo
or elsewhere, he might.

Michael grabbed the TV remote and flicked through the
channels. Nothing appealed to him, but he had to do something
while he waited to hear from his associate, Ramadan. The time
difference meant he might not get a reply until the next day
since Egypt was seven hours ahead of where he was.

Go for a last walk to the falls, a place where Jennifer and
he used to spend a lot of time together? If so, he'd take the
route that didn't go past where Jennifer worked.

He still could not understand her reason for ending their
relationship. *Bad things happening to people I care about.* It
had been a tough couple of years for Michael, and people he
cared about suffered through terrible things, too. His father's
death, the ugly breakup with the young woman in England, and
now this situation with Jennifer added to his emotional strain.

Michael hadn't packed his laptop, so he checked for direct
flights from Pearson bound for Cairo. The Wi-Fi was open, so
he could book nothing from the hotel. Once Michael heard,

he'd take the trains to the airport and book his direct flight there. He didn't care which airline got him to his destination — as long as it was out of Canada.

With EgyptAir, he could get a direct flight to Cairo from Toronto. Direct flights to Manchester were available through almost any airline. At least now, he had some idea of the flights available. For now, he'd return to the falls via parking lots, side streets and Murray Street, a route that avoided any reminders of Jennifer.

Michael shoved his phone in one of his front pockets, his wallet in the other, and the keycard for the room in the leg pocket of his cargo pants.

It had clouded over when Michael exited the hotel. Out of habit, he glanced towards the front entrance of the Outback when he reached the street. He shook his head and chastised himself, then turned and walked in the other direction.

By the time he had reached the parkway along the river, the clouds had dispersed, and the sun bathed the surroundings in a cheerful glow. Yet, Michael's mood remained as overcast as the earlier sky. The bustling Niagara Parkway at the foot of Murray Street, with its constant flow of traffic and people, seemed to mock his internal turmoil. He crossed the westbound lanes with no problem, but the wait for the eastbound ones felt like an eternity.

Once he got across, he strode to the railing, leaned his forearms against it, and stared at the rushing water of the American Falls. From this vantage point, trees obscured Horseshoe Falls. He walked farther along the sidewalk towards the Welcome Centre. He found a vacant spot along the railing with an unobstructed view and resumed his position.

As he stood there, the wind shifted, and the mist from the cascading water enveloped him. The sound of the water crashing on the rocks below echoed his heartache. Michael, capturing the moment on his phone, realized the finality of it all. He knew he would never return here, not without Jennifer. Her absence, like the mist, had settled in his life, a permanent and unchanging fixture, a void he could never fill.

Michael checked out and called a taxi to take him to the station. The sooner he was out of Niagara Falls, the better.

Before boarding, he had to wait for the next GO train to arrive and de-board its passengers. Once he got to Union Station in Toronto, he would catch the UP Express to Pearson, whether it was Egypt or Manchester. Anticipating Ramadan's response, he hoped the reply would be waiting for him by then.

As he pulled his phone out of his pocket, it vibrated in his hand. It was an email notification. An email from the team leader on the Saqqara dig, Ramadan, sat in his inbox, holding the key to his next move.

From: Ramadan B. Hussein
<rbhussein.archaeologist@egyptianantiquities.eg>
To: MichaelScott <mscottarchaeology@ymail.com>
Subject: Re: Return to Saqqara
Michael,
Your permits, visas, and permissions are valid until December 31, 2018. This time, you will work with the Czech team at Abusir. Miroslav informed me they're on the verge of a major discovery, and your expertise could be invaluable in this endeavour.
Regards,
Ramadan

That made Michael's mind up. Egypt it was. He replied to Ramadan, advising him he would confirm his arrival time and date once he'd purchased his ticket. He had one more message to send, and that was to Jennifer, but he'd wait until just before he boarded his flight.

"Where are you staying, and for how long?" Jennifer asked Emma when she returned to see if she or her husband wanted another drink.

"We're staying at the Hilton across from the casino. I wouldn't say no to another glass of white wine."

"Coming right up. You okay, or do you want another

Coors Light, Matt?"

"If Emma's having another wine, I'll have another beer."

"Why don't you grab that table. I'll bring your drinks there."

Jennifer returned to the bar to get them their beverages. She grabbed her phone from the shelf beneath it. No messages from Michael. That was a good thing. She hadn't expected to hear anything from him since she told him she couldn't be with him. She pocketed her phone.

With a glass of wine in one hand and Matt's beer in the other, Jennifer walked back to the table they'd moved to. "I'm going to take my break now," she said to Sadie, the other girl working the area, then sat down with them. "You didn't say how long you were staying."

"We're here for a week. We both have to get back to Winnipeg. Matt's a lawyer."

"Family law. Custody, wills, probate. That kind of thing," he said. "None of the courtroom drama. Well, I shouldn't say that. Custody hearings can get quite heated."

"What about you, Emma?" Jennifer asked.

"I'm a 9-1-1 dispatcher. Not anything remotely close to what I studied in University."

"You must get some pretty interesting calls."

Jennifer's phone vibrated in her pocket. On the side of her text message icon was a red dot with a one in it. She opened the app. The text was from Michael.

You won't have to worry about running into me. I'm returning to Egypt.

Her face dropped.

"What's wrong?"

"The guy I just broke up with is taking the first flight out of Canada to Egypt."

"Why would he want to go there? Is he an Egyptian national?" Emma asked.

"No. Archaeologist."

Another message came in right after the first.

BTW, the accident wasn't your fault. The guy that hit you and killed your parents and brother was drunk.

Jennifer turned her phone to Emma so she could read the message.

"Is that true?"

"Yes. Twice the legal limit. He was speeding and ran the red light. Has no one ever told you?"

"No. My grandmother said nothing about it."

"You poor thing. Your gran probably thought she was protecting you. Instead, she let you believe it was your fault. The guilt you must feel." Emma leaned over and hugged Jennifer. "My parents had moved us across town not long after that night. Get me away from you. They thought the drinking and the party were your fault. Then, before you came out of the coma, we were already in Vancouver."

"Oh, God. I've made a terrible mistake. What am I going to do?"

Thirty-Three

Outback Steakhouse, Victoria Avenue, Niagara Falls, Ontario

August 10, 2018

What had she done? The realization hit Jennifer like a ton of bricks. Her grandmother, the one person she trusted, had kept a crucial detail from her. The other driver was drunk. This revelation turned her world upside down. She couldn't help but wonder if she had texted Michael just now, would he have replied? He was halfway around the world, or at least on his way. The mess she was in seemed to grow worse by the moment.

"Do you have a passport?" Emma asked.

"No."

"First, you go to the post office or a Service Canada outlet and get a passport application. Then you'll need passport photos taken. I know some of the drug stores in Winnipeg do them. Maybe one here does, too."

What was Emma hinting at with the mention of a passport? Could she be suggesting a journey for Jennifer to a foreign country, a country she had never set foot in before?

"What are you planning, Emma?"

"You're going to Egypt. You're going to find your man and apologize. Grovel if needs must. But you have to undo the damage you've done."

"I-I can't," Jennifer stammered, her voice a mere whisper. A heavy weight pushed on her chest, making it hard to breathe. She rested her chin in her hands, elbows on the table, trying to steady herself.

"Why not?" Emma wiggled in her chair to face her friend.

"Well, for starters, I've never flown before."

"Always a first."

"I don't know where he is."

"Would he go back to the same place he was before?"

"I don't know." Jennifer buried her face in her hands. "What about my pug, Zeus? I can't leave him behind."

"Is there anyone who can look after him?" Emma asked.

God, that girl was relentless. Jennifer should cut her losses, move on, and get over what could have been. But Emma, with her unwavering determination, wasn't about to let Jennifer off the hook without a fight.

"No. It's just Zeus and me."

"You could always board him at a kennel."

"What? No way. I've heard stories about what happens to animals at kennels. He's not staying in one."

"We'll work that out later. In order of importance, passport application and photos. Matt can be a witness. We'll find someone else because, if I remember correctly, the first time around, you need two. Then, you and I will take the completed application and photos to a passport office in Toronto unless there's one here in town. We'll get it sent off."

"But …"

"Now what?"

Jennifer knew by Emma's tone that her friend was growing impatient with her.

"But, you and Matt are here for your anniversary. If you're spending all your time with me, it won't be much of a celebration for you," Jennifer said to Emma.

"We'll still have our mornings, evenings, and nights together. You don't mind, do you, honey?" Emma asked.

Jennifer thought he looked defeated. Before the accident, when Emma decided to do something, nothing held her back. She was still like that today. Was it a good thing? Or bad? Jennifer couldn't help but wonder, her uncertainty mirroring the complexity of their relationship.

"I've got to get back to work," Jennifer said, sliding off her chair. "I'll see you both tomorrow?"

"You bet." Emma stood and hugged her friend.

Matt rolled his eyes.

"Wait, we need to exchange phone numbers and email addresses so we can keep in touch," Emma said.

The girls exchanged phones and entered their information in the contacts. When they finished, they swapped devices back to their rightful owner.

At least something in the last twenty-four hours had gone right. Maybe Emma's enthusiasm and insistence were good. It would force Jennifer out of her comfort zone, a place she'd never been until earlier this year. The train trip to Percé with Michael was way out of it. Not because she'd spent some time with a man she barely knew, but Jennifer had never ventured outside Niagara Falls, that she remembered. Her struggle with memory loss and the unfamiliarity of her comfort zone was a constant battle.

Her memory of events before the accident was sketchy. She may have gone on school trips before then to the Royal Ontario Museum or Ontario Science Centre in Toronto, but she had no recollection without concrete proof.

Back home, Jennifer let Zeus outside to burn off some energy. She watched him from the sliding doors as he did zoomies. He wiped out a few times because he ran too fast and couldn't control himself on the corners, a sight that always brought a smile to Jennifer's face.

Jennifer grabbed a salad at work after Emma and Matt left, and ate it on the fly. By the time she finished, the lettuce was soggy.

After she let the pug back in and locked the door, Jennifer searched for the photo albums. Her heart raced as she couldn't find them. Could her grandmother have hidden them in the room she used when she moved in to care for her after her release from the hospital?

She walked to the bottom of the stairs. Use the stairlift? Climb? Jennifer ascended the stairs slowly, winded after the first flight. She'd use it when she came down with the pictures.

The bedroom her grandmother used remained frozen in time, a poignant reminder of her parents' absence. Everything was just as they had left it. But where were her grandmother's belongings? The woman lived in an apartment. What did she do with her furniture? Her dishes? She didn't bring them with her. Storage? That made no sense. There was no evidence of paperwork or a key to a storage facility.

Tears pricked Jennifer's eyes now that the strangeness of nothing of her grandmother's in here had passed. All the woman had brought with her was her clothing and a framed photograph from her wedding day that used to sit on the nightstand beside the bed. Her husband had died before the move to an apartment. Where was the wedding picture now? It wasn't there. Jennifer had packed her grandmother's clothes and had taken them to the Salvation Army store on Drummond Road not long after the woman's death.

Jennifer remembered the heated arguments between her parents and grandmother when they tried to convince her to sell the house and downsize. The woman wanted to stay in the house she and her husband had made a home. In the end, she relented and moved to the seniors' complex, which strained their relationship.

Could that have been why she never mentioned the other vehicle's driver was drunk? Her grandmother was bitter over being forced out of her home by her family?

Jennifer's search for the family's hidden treasure led her to the cedar chest at the foot of her parents' bed. Among the boxes and albums, she discovered her grandmother's wedding picture, a relic of the past. The unusual placement of the photos, in the past kept on a shelf in the closet, sparked her curiosity. Had her grandmother hidden them away out of spite?

Initially, Jennifer had planned to take the pictures downstairs, but the sheer volume of them, scattered between boxes and albums, made her reconsider. Instead, she carried them across the hall to her bedroom, the one she had always known as her own. The thought of moving into the room her parents shared, and later her grandmother used until her death, unsettled her. Even her brother's room, a space frozen in time, remained untouched, save for the occasional vacuuming and dusting.

Jennifer stacked the albums on the floor next to her bed, each one a potential treasure trove of memories. Anticipating what she might find, she sat on the mattress, pulled the string off the top box, and removed the lid. She got comfortable and took out one envelope the photos along with the negatives came back from the camera store in.

She and her brother, Kevin, stood near the railing by the falls. Jennifer turned the picture over to see if a date was on the back. *July 10, 1994, Jennifer and Kevin at Niagara Falls* was in her mother's handwriting. Her brother turned six earlier that summer, and she would turn eleven in October.

The other pictures in this package were taken in the park, below the falls, and behind the falls. There was one of the four of them together near one of the ponds. One of her parents had to have asked someone to take it for them. Her mother had written on the back of every picture who was in it and the date.

Jennifer continued viewing the photos until she had gone through the entire box. Birthdays, Christmas, Easter, Halloween, first days of school. She returned the lid to the carton and started on the next one.

The pictures here were older. Jennifer's parents, Mr. and Mrs. Fox, at what might have been her father's work Christmas party. There were no children, and everyone was dressed up, the men in suits and the women in dresses. Some women wore corsages. On the back, like all the other photos, the names of every person there. This photo was different. It was an eight by ten taken by a photographer whose stamp was on the lower right corner. Her father had worked at Nabisco in the factory. Now, the plant bore a large Post sign on the upper corner of its tall building. If not for hotels and other high-rises popping up over the years, the sign would have been visible from where Jennifer worked on Victoria Avenue.

Jennifer studied the professional photograph again. There, in the corner, was the man who came into the bar every day. She was certain of it. Jennifer set that picture aside, planning to slip it into her purse for the next time she worked. She was eager to show the photo to him, to confirm her hunch that the face she recognized was a younger version of the man.

This second box was all work-related. Adult Christmas parties, children's Christmas parties, summer family picnics. Jennifer wasn't sure what she expected to find going through the old family photos.

She closed it up and grabbed the top album off the pile. It was from 1983, the year Jennifer was born. Her parents at St. Patrick's Day. It must have been a house party, although not here. Someone had to have taken it, too. Her mother wore a hideous dress that looked like a tent. She was pregnant. As the year progressed, the woman grew and the clothing didn't improve. This book ended the day after Jennifer was born. There was a photo of her in the nursery at the hospital.

A loud bang sounded from outside. Zeus dashed from where he had been and straight under her bed. The fireworks had started. If she could get to Egypt, apologize to Michael, and beg his forgiveness, she couldn't leave Zeus behind. She bought him a ThunderShirt, and it helped. The hard part was getting him into it. Once he had it on, he was fine, but it was so much of a hassle she cuddled him on her lap instead. If she went away, she would have to ensure whoever looked after him knew about his fear of fireworks and thunderstorms. Jennifer would prefer it if someone came and stayed in her house. Zeus would be more comfortable in his familiar surroundings. But who?

Jennifer coaxed the pug from under the bed and tucked him under the covers beside her. At least the fireworks only lasted five minutes. She rested her hand on his body and looked through the family albums.

If she didn't know better, she'd have sworn her parents adopted her brother. There weren't as many pictures of him as a baby as of her. When he got older, except for sports, the photos included both of them. Jennifer knew he wasn't because she had seen photographs of her mother in the same hideous maternity clothes before he was born. At least she didn't have to worry about that. Fashions had come a long way since the 1980s.

The last album she looked at was from 1998, the year of the accident. There were no photos after June that year; if there were, no one had the film developed. If she found her mother's camera, would there still be a roll of film in it? Were there still photo labs around that processed them? Nowadays, with digital cameras, there was no need for that.

By now, it was almost midnight. Time to call it a day. Get into her pyjamas, let Zeus out for his nightly ablutions and go to bed. Tomorrow was another day; maybe she'd find the camera.

Thirty-Four

Hilton Niagara Falls, Fallsview Boulevard, Niagara Falls, Ontario

August 13, 2018

Emma picked up her phone and put it back down. Did she text Jennifer? Had she overstepped her position by urging her friend to travel halfway across the world to make things right with the man she had ended it with?

Matt wasn't happy when they left the restaurant. She understood. They were supposed to be in the city celebrating their anniversary, not going off to get her friend sorted out with a passport. To top it off, Emma volunteered him to be a guarantor on the application.

The last person she expected to run into in the city was Jennifer, whom she hadn't seen since the night of the accident. Before, when they were each waiting at the police station for their parents to come and take them home, the two girls sat and held hands. Emma wasn't sure which one of them was more terrified.

At least it was quiet in their room, apart from Matt's snoring. Still, she took her phone and tiptoed into the bathroom, closing the door behind her. She tapped out a message.

When do you want to get your passport photo done and pick up the application?

Now, to wait for a response. Emma turned the volume off on her phone so the sound wouldn't wake her sleeping husband, but it made no difference. The ping sounded like a brass band; it was so loud.

Not sure I should be doing this.

Cold feet. Emma understood. She almost backed out of her wedding at the last minute, terrified of what she had gotten herself into. In the end, she was glad she went through with it. These five years with Matt were wonderful. He understood that when she gave up her career, she studied at university to get her degree and settled on being a 9-1-1 dispatcher. Her stress level was lower than ever, not that there weren't some crazy situations in her current profession. But at least now, she could leave the job at work where it belonged. Not drag it home with her.

What had Emma talked her into doing? It was like they were teens again. Jennifer followed her friend blindly. That's what the party was about. Them drinking. One of the neighbours called the police. If she had a backbone, she would stand up to Emma. But, like back then, she complied.

Jennifer snatched up her phone. She reread Michael's text. Did she respond and tell him she never knew that the other driver was drunk? First coffee. Look after Zeus. Camera. Maybe it was in the chest. She hadn't looked for anything else after finding the photos.

Once Zeus was outside, Jennifer made coffee, put his food in his dish, and poured fresh water into his bowl. A steaming mug of medium roast in one hand and her phone in the other, she sat by the patio door. That way, she'd know when he was ready to come inside. Whether he replied, she had to tell Michael she didn't know about the other driver.

I didn't know. No one ever told me. Emma from back then is in town. She confirmed your text.

After the way she had left things with him, she didn't dare sign off with an *x*. Or maybe she should? In the end, Jennifer left it at that. She didn't want him reading something into the conversation that wasn't or shouldn't be there.

Zeus was ready to come in, so she opened the door. While she was away from the table, her phone vibrated. One new text message. Had Michael responded? She opened the app. Emma.

You still live in the same place?

Why did Emma ask that? Then, she realized. Emma was coming over to her house. Dammit.

Yes.

Jennifer sent the reply. Dammit again. She wanted time to look for the missing camera to see if there was film in it. If she found it soon enough, maybe while Emma had dragged her around Niagara Falls, she could have dropped it off somewhere to be processed.

I'm coming over.

If Jennifer hoped to find the camera, she'd have to do it at light speed. Once Emma landed, there would be no time for such things.

She lifted the cedar chest lid in her parents' bedroom. The end where the pictures were was empty. Of course, it was. The boxes and albums were still in her room. Jennifer shifted the blankets at the other end into the space. She found an old camera box. Did her mother return the device here after each use? Jennifer lifted it out and removed the bright yellow lid with the image of a camera and the words Kodak Pocket Instamatic. Inside was a camera and an empty slot shaped like a film cartridge box. Three unused flash cubes were also in special moulded sections. The thing didn't look much larger than her phone.

Jennifer tugged on the wrist strap and pulled the camera out of the moulded plastic, bringing the viewfinder towards her eye. In a window to the left, there was a film cartridge and a 22. Was that the number of pictures taken or remaining? She turned the thing over. Tried to push a slide device on the bottom. Nothing happened. Slid a cover to the side on the front and revealed the lens. Okay, so that had to be open. She pushed the red button on the top. The camera clicked. Did she just take a picture? This time, the slide device moved. Okay, that advanced the film. She rechecked the number. It was now 23.

"Zeus," she called out to her pug. If there was only one picture left, he would be her model.

The dog appeared outside the door. Jennifer shifted so she was comfortable and focused on the animal. She pushed the red button and the slider on the bottom until it wouldn't move anymore. The roll must be done. Now, she had to find a place that could process it.

She pulled out her phone and Googled it. There was a place in town, but it didn't process cartridges that size. She found another: St. Catharines. This place did process 110 cartridges. That meant a bus ride, but it was not the end of the world.

The doorbell rang. It had to be Emma. No one else ever came to the front door. Jennifer struggled to her feet. She should have known better than to sit on the floor. It was terrible for her. She ached worse than usual afterwards. Because of the pain she was in, she used the stairlift to go downstairs.

Emma breezed in the door as soon as she opened it. Dressed to the nines and hair and makeup just so. Jennifer hadn't yet showered or dressed. She was still in her pyjamas and had a severe case of bedhead.

"You're not ready?" Emma asked.

"Does it look like I am?" The hairs on the back of Jennifer's neck prickled.

"Hurry. It shouldn't take long, but the sooner we go, the sooner we'll be back and can fill out your application."

"I was going through the old photos last night. They were all packed away in the cedar chest in my parents' room. Gran must have put them in there. Anyway, I woke up in the night wondering about Mum's camera. So, I went on a hunt this morning. It was in her hope chest, too. There's a film in it."

"You going to get it processed?"

"I think I should. I have to take it to St. Catharines, though. No place here does that size," Jennifer said.

"You can do that another time. Right now, shower, get dressed, wear something decent, and put on your makeup. We have a date with a passport photographer."

Jennifer sighed and turned back to the stairs. "There's coffee in the kitchen. I made it before you came." She waited for Emma to go through to the kitchen before she plopped on the stairlift and rode it upstairs.

Before she headed for the bathroom to shower, Jennifer walked into her room to get out her clothes. She chose black jeans and a rust-coloured button-up V-neck cardigan that would show a flash of midriff between the bottom of it and her pants.

Showered and wearing her long, blue velour housecoat, she padded back to the bedroom. Emma waited in there for her.

"You're wearing that?"

"Yes. What's wrong with it?"

"N-nothing."

Jennifer knew her friend long enough that her comment meant something, even though she said the opposite.

"Well, that's what I want to wear. Full stop."

She snatched her clothes off the bed, grabbed underwear and a matching bra from her dresser and clumped off to the bathroom to get dressed. No one saw her scars. No one except her and the hospital staff who cared for her after the accident.

When she returned wearing her choice of clothing, with her hair still wrapped in a towel, Emma smiled and nodded. She wasn't seeking Emma's approval of her outfit. Or anything for that matter.

Jennifer sat at her dressing table and applied her makeup. A bit of eyeliner, mascara, a natural-toned blush, and pink lip gloss. When she finished, she took her hair out of the terrycloth wrap and brushed it out. Normally, she let it dry on its own, but with Emma chomping to get going, she plugged in her hair dryer and blew her long golden hair dry.

"Okay, let's get this over," Jennifer said, resigning herself to follow Emma's lead.

Why did she let Emma walk all over her? Nothing had changed over the years. Yet, she could deal with obnoxious drunks at work and escort them out the door when necessary.

Jennifer ensured she locked the front door, and she and Emma used the side one.

"Where's your car?" she asked.

"I walked."

"I guess we take mine," Jennifer said as she pushed the unlock button on her key fob. Her little Smart car got excellent fuel mileage. A tank of gas lasted forever. As far as St. Catharines was concerned, she could drive there, but being out on the multi-lane highways made her uneasy.

"We'll go to the Shoppers on Lundy's Lane. I've seen their passport photo setup." She started the car and backed out of the driveway. Jennifer also used that pharmacy for her prescriptions but wasn't telling Emma about it. Despite the intersection of Drummond and Lundy's Lane being posted as a high accident intersection, it didn't bother her. Still, she avoided the junction of Stanley and Highway 420 like the plague — the intersection where her family was wiped out.

Five minutes after leaving the house, Jennifer pulled into the parking lot. They climbed out of the little car and walked to the entrance. Once inside, she led the way to the area near the back where the screen and stool were located for doing passport photos.

No one was there. That was normal. You had to tell the staff you were there, and someone would bring the camera and do it. The pharmacy was the closest place where there were people, so the girls walked to the prescription drop-off.

"Excuse me, but my friend needs to get a passport photo done," Emma said.

Her tone made her sound entitled, and maybe now that she was married to a lawyer, her friend thought she was.

"I'll get someone," the pharmacy clerk said.

"Service Canada on McLeod has passport applications," Emma told Jennifer. "We'll stop there on the way back to the hotel and pick one up. Back at Matt's and my room, you can fill it out, and he can complete his portion. Once that's done, you'll have to get another guarantor, and you can go back to

Service Canada. They'll check everything, see if it is okay and send it off for you."

"You seem to know an awful lot about it," Jennifer said.

"Googled it. We've had our passports since before we got married. It's the same everywhere," Emma shared.

"Don't smile. We need to see your ears. Let's do this," the store employee said, guiding Jennifer through the process. "One, two, three …"

The flash temporarily blinded her. Jennifer hoped she didn't blink. Spots danced before her eyes, so she didn't, but if she did, then it would have to be done over. She blinked a few times to get the spots to disappear, but it didn't help.

Thankfully, the pictures turned out fine. The employee stamped the backs of the two photos and put them in an envelope. Feeling relief, Jennifer paid for them, and she and Emma left the store.

Since it was easier to turn right out of the Shoppers parking lot, Jennifer turned that way then left at the traffic lights at the intersection of Dorchester. When they reached the Service Canada offices, Emma hopped out of the car and dashed inside. Jennifer heaved a sigh once she was alone. Her solitude didn't last long because her friend returned within minutes with the application.

Jennifer wasn't keen on driving to the Hilton where Emma and Matt stayed, but it was too far for her to walk. She'd have to park in the underground parking and pay through the nose for the privilege. It wouldn't be as bad if Emma would pony up the fee, but Jennifer doubted that would happen. However, she was wrong. Her friend stuffed a twenty-dollar bill in her hand to cover it before she even parked the car. Since there was no toll booth at the entrance, it had to be on the exit.

As agreed, Matt signed as guarantor, but Jennifer needed a second because it was a first-time application. Her choices were doctor, pharmacist, veterinarian, or police officer. There were others, but she would not ask a police officer. There might be no one still working in law enforcement who was there at the time of the arrest and subsequent accident. She saw the pharmacist when she collected her prescriptions. She'd try there first. Her second choice would be her family physician.

"I'm going to leave now. Let you two enjoy your anniversary trip. Have a safe trip home if I don't see you before you leave."

With hugs and kisses from Emma and Matt, Jennifer crept out of their room and towards the elevator. She wasn't very far down the hall when raised voices reached her ears.

Back home, Jennifer closed the door behind her, leaned against it, and sighed. Quiet. The way she liked it. It was great to see her childhood friend, Emma, again, but getting swept into her hold wasn't. The trick would be not seeing her for the rest of the time she and her husband were in town. It was not a simple task since Emma knew where Jennifer worked. She had to work later today. She didn't have a day off until Thursday. Jennifer planned on heading to St. Catharines that day with the film cartridge from her mother's camera. The second guarantor on her passport application must also have to wait until then.

Thirty-Five

Jennifer's House, Orchard Avenue, Niagara Falls, Ontario

August 16, 2018

Jennifer woke early Thursday morning. She wanted to go to Shoppers as soon as they opened and get the second signature on her passport application. Once completed, it was ready to mail, and, with any luck, her passport would arrive by the beginning of the following month. She could drop her application at Service Canada and have them go over it and send it, her payment, and her passport photos off for her. That way, she'd know if she had completed everything correctly.

With the coffee made and steaming mug in her hand, Jennifer let Zeus out. She took her coffee outside and sat on the deck to enjoy the sunshine before it got too hot. Her pug ran laps around the yard before he stopped to do his business. Jennifer kept a roll of bags in a sealed container by the door. She pulled one out and cleaned up his mess, then dropped the poop bag in her outside garbage can.

Zeus trotted into the house beside her and straight to his food dish. Most days, Jennifer filled it while he was outside, but this morning she'd gone out with him. After she looked after his food, she grabbed her phone and searched the bus routes and times again.

Since the bus she wanted left from the Table Rock bus stop, she could drive and park in the lot she used. Doing so, gave her a short walk to catch her bus and back to her car when she returned. The bus times worked out well for her as long as she was there by no later than two-thirty so she could purchase her return tickets. Perhaps she should try for two-fifteen. Give herself extra time in case there was a lineup.

Between online searches for transportation to get the film processed and checking and re-checking everything she required for her passport, Jennifer had accomplished little over the last few days. She had even checked to see if the metal implants in her leg would set off the airport detectors and what to do before going through one. Once she had started, she continued down the rabbit hole.

Satisfied that she had dotted every "*i*" and crossed every "*t*," she stopped the research. It was time to put it all to use, starting with her pharmacist.

After showering, applying makeup, and drying her hair, Jennifer selected her clothes for the day. She chose linen pants with an elastic waist, which would be more comfortable for travelling, and a long-sleeved ivory T-shirt. Again, Jennifer checked her purse to make sure the application was still in its envelope. It was.

Back downstairs, she locked the front and back doors and used the side door, locking it behind her. Her first stop was Shoppers Drug Mart, where she hoped her usual pharmacist was on duty. Any of them would probably be a guarantor for her, but she preferred it if the one she dealt with the most often would.

It was a short drive to the drugstore, and she was in luck.

"I need to see the pharmacist, please," she told the clerk at the prescription drop-off counter.

"And your name?"

"Jennifer Fox."

"Go sit outside the consultation area, and I'll let him know you're here."

Jennifer had just sat down, and the pharmacist called her into the room.

"I wondered if you would be my second guarantor on my passport application," she said, pulling the envelope out of her purse.

"Going on a trip, are you?"

"Yes and no. I want to, but I'm not sure if I will. Still, it doesn't hurt to have it."

"True. And I'll be more than happy to do that for you."

Jennifer pulled the application out of the envelope and handed it to him. It seemed like no time had passed, and he returned it to her.

"Anything else I can do for you today?"

"No, thank you. This was it. I appreciate you taking the time to do it."

She returned it to its envelope and tucked it back in her purse. That was easy. Would they be as friendly at Service Canada?

Jennifer could have applied for a handicap sticker for her car because of the injury to her leg, but she refused. There were people out there who were in far worse condition than she was. Let them take advantage. The only time it was an issue was at the grocery store. She had made a conscious decision not to use her injury as an excuse.

The parking area at the plaza where Service Canada had its offices was a vast expanse of asphalt, heat radiating from the surface under the midday sun. It wasn't busy, and there were spots next to the building not designated as handicapped only. Jennifer pulled into one of those, and the sound of her car's engine faded as she turned it off.

She walked straight to the reception desk. "I have my completed passport application with me, and I'd like someone to check it to make sure I've done it right."

The receptionist looked around the room. "We only have one person who does that, and she's busy now. Take a seat, and she'll be with you once she's free."

Jennifer sighed but found a place to sit by the window. She pulled her phone out of her pocket and read Michael's texts. He hadn't replied to the last one she sent. The one she wasn't sure if she even should have. If the fact the other driver had been drunk hadn't been withheld from her, she wouldn't have ended things with him. Too late now. Their relationship, once filled with promise, now seemed damaged beyond repair.

She scrolled through the thread, reading the messages. Would he go back to the same site in Egypt? Not that it was much help. He mentioned doing the tourist thing, going to Giza to see the pyramids and the Sphinx. The entire country was an archaeologist's dream come true—so much history. If she googled his name, would it come up in a search?

Why was Jennifer torturing herself like this? With the way things ended between them, thanks to her, he'd likely never want to speak to her again. It became a moot point because the passport person was now free.

"Let's have a look," the woman said, not raising her head.

"I hope I've filled it out correctly," Jennifer said as she handed over the package.

An enormous sigh.

Was she miffed because Jennifer hadn't taken it from the envelope? If something like that set her off, how did she react with other people? Jennifer assumed this woman dealt with unemployment issues, too. The woman's reaction, though minor, hinted at a deeper frustration and perhaps a weariness from dealing with bureaucratic processes.

A few grunts and more sighs before the woman looked up. "It's fine. All proper. I suppose you want it to go in our mail."

"Yes, if it's not too much trouble." Jennifer felt like she'd pushed one too many buttons.

The woman glared at her, picked up a glue stick, swiped it across the flap and sealed the envelope.

"Thank you," said Jennifer, with relief and gratitude. No further response. She felt a weight lift off her shoulders as she left the office, her task completed.

It was still before lunch, so she had time to go home, spend some time with Zeus, and have a bite to eat. However, with the buses' schedules, it was going to be late before she got home. The thought of the long journey ahead made her feel a twinge of annoyance, but she pushed it aside, focusing on the small joys that awaited her at home.

Feeling curious and concerned, Jennifer googled where Michael had gone after Melissa's wedding. She relied on her phone for most things, but today, she needed a bigger screen to absorb the information. Her cellphone was good for most things, but she preferred the larger display her laptop offered when there was a lot of text to read.

As her laptop booted, Jennifer's heart raced with anticipation. She opened a browser tab, typed 'major find in Egypt in July,' and hit enter. The number of hits she received filled her screen and continued for more pages. Leaving the initial part of her prompt the same, she added his name. The results were fewer, but the mystery still needed to be solved.

> CAIRO — 14 July 2018: Khaled al-Anani, Minister of Antiquities, announced the discovery of more than five stone coffins at Saqqara and declared it "a great archaeological discovery."
>
> Anani added the Egyptian-German mission, led by Manchester-educated archaeologist Michael Scott, uncovered a mummification workshop containing burial chambers with mummies dating back to the 26th and 27th dynasties.

That was it. So, had Michael returned to Saqqara? Jennifer, her mind racing with possibilities, opened another tab on her browser and searched for that location. That could very well be where he was. How could she find out for sure? He mentioned checking out a bazaar in Cairo. That's where he bought the cartouche and opal necklace. Saqqara was near Cairo.

What if the Canadian government denied her a passport because of the underage drinking that led to her losing her family? The authorities assured her that once she came of age, the courts expunged her record so it wouldn't affect the rest of her life. They had to have done it. Otherwise, she never would have worked at the casino.

Jennifer was getting ahead of herself again. Twenty days, plus mail time, was what she'd read about the time to process a passport. She could wait that long.

She hobbled to the kitchen, grabbed a cup of Mr. Noodles, spicy chicken flavour, from the cupboard, and turned on the kettle. This should keep her going until she returned from St. Catharines later that day. When the noodles had sat covered in the boiled water long enough, she peeled the lid off the container and ate.

Thirty-Six

Table Rock Welcome Centre, Niagara River Parkway, Niagara Falls, Ontario

August 16, 2018

Jennifer was at the bus stop by the Table Rock Welcome Centre in plenty of time to get her return tickets for her trip to and from St. Catharines. She didn't use the buses often, but sometimes taking one from her house to work would be preferable to driving. Maybe, next year, she'd invest in a monthly bus pass.

Today, she wanted the film dropped off and processed. Jennifer wasn't sure how to remove the cartridge from the camera, so the entire thing was in her purse. It wasn't a tremendous hardship; it was about the size of her cell phone, which weighed next to nothing.

When she boarded the bus, she tried to get a transfer, but because another transit company was involved, she'd have to buy her tickets at the next bus station. It would have been so much easier to just have to pay the once and have it look after all the transportation. Jennifer made a mental note to check on Google Maps to drive from her house to the photography shop.

At least the bus she boarded travelled straight to the terminal in St. Catharines. Jennifer entered the depot and bought her return tickets for this city's transit system and waited for her bus to arrive. She didn't have a long wait, and when she got to the stop closest to Frederick's Foto Source, it was a short walk to reach her destination.

She strode to the counter after she entered.

"Hi, I looked you up online and saw that you develop 110 films. There's one in this camera," Jennifer said, pulling the device out of her purse. "I wasn't sure how to remove it, and I didn't want to ruin my mother's camera." Jennifer handed it to the gentleman.

He released a catch on the back of the pocket camera and dropped the film cartridge into his hand.

"How long has it been in the camera? With age, films take on a red tone."

"1998. So you're telling me you might not be able to do anything? The film has been in the camera since before my mother died."

"Not saying I can't, but the pictures might come out redder than you expected. I don't want you to be surprised when you see them."

"Okay."

He took down Jennifer's information.

"We'll give you a call when the pictures are ready."

"Can you give me a ballpark on the cost, please?"

"About $35.00 plus tax. That includes processing the film and making prints."

"Thank you."

Jennifer turned and walked out. It was more than she expected, but it made sense. She had to know what was on that film.

As the clock struck seven, Jennifer's evening began its familiar rhythm. She let Zeus out into the backyard, then set about preparing her favourite Greek salad for supper. The dish was a riot of flavours, but the black olives and feta cheese made her taste buds dance.

While she savoured her salad, she Googled the route driving to the photography shop. If the traffic gods were on her side, she could make the trip in less than half an hour. That was better than riding buses, walking and waiting. When she returned, she'd drive to pick up the processed film and prints.

Now, she had to wait for the call to say the pictures were ready to pick up. The anticipation was exciting and nerve-wracking, as she couldn't wait to discover what was on that roll of film.

Zeus, always by her side, sat beside her chair. Jennifer broke off a tiny piece of cheese and fed it to him, a daily ritual they both enjoyed. After he gobbled it down, he looked up at her and belched. She giggled. The pug burped often. Mainly if he ate too fast. The gas came out the other end, too. At least it didn't now while she was still trying to eat.

"That's all Zeus-ie," she said. "Your food is in your dish in the kitchen.

After Jennifer had eaten her salad, she put her dishes in the dishwasher but didn't start it. Instead, she gathered her work clothes and put them in the washing machine in the basement. One day, Jennifer would move the laundry room upstairs. Maybe when she could put the past, filled with memories of her late brother Kevin, behind her where it belonged, she'd convert his room to an upstairs laundry. If not there, the other enormous closet on that level. Upstairs was where she generated the most dirty clothing. Bedding and towels, too. The few tea towels she used in the kitchen were much easier to take upstairs than a loaded clothes basket to the basement.

Thirty-Seven

Outback Steakhouse, Victoria Avenue, Niagara Falls, Ontario

August 23, 2018

Exactly a week after she dropped the film off at the shop, they called her to tell her she could pick the prints up anytime. She worked every day that week, her heart thumping with anticipation for the moment she could lay her eyes on the developed film. She was at work when the call came in but might work in a trip over the weekend. That didn't work. The store was closed on Saturdays and Sundays. Jennifer rechecked her schedule. Wednesday, she started at two o'clock in the afternoon. If Jennifer left for St. Catharines at about nine in the morning, barring complications, she could be home by noon. But she couldn't go too early because the shop didn't open until ten. So nine-thirty-ish.

Jennifer Google-mapped it again and, this time sent it to her phone. For the rest of today and all day tomorrow, she'd have to wait before discovering what was on the film she'd found in her mother's camera. Until she had the pictures in her hands and saw them, her curiosity would consume her. She wondered what the last pictures her mother had taken were, hoping they would reveal a piece of her mother's life she didn't know.

Somehow, Jennifer got through Monday. She breathed a heavy sigh of relief when the end of her shift came, the weight of the day's anticipation and anxiety lifting from her shoulders. At least the bar was busy, so there wasn't much time to think about what the photographs might contain. She knew what the last two were. She fiddled with the camera to use the entire roll.

The fireworks display had ended when Jennifer left work and walked to her car. There was always the end-of-shift cleanup, divvying up the tips and getting customers out the door and on their way. Some wanted to stay and linger over their drinks more than others. A few had tried to order another round right at closing time. She hated those people, their disregard for her time and the rules of the bar adding to her stress and anxiety.

At least Emma, her former best friend, hadn't been in since Matt had signed Jennifer's passport application as guarantor. That was one less stressor in her life at the moment. The uncertainty of not knowing where Michael was and if he'd want to speak to her was another addition to her anxiety. Topping the list was the processed film waiting for her to pick up in St. Catharines, a source of anticipation and fear.

Thirty-Eight

Jennifer's House, Orchard Avenue, Niagara Falls, Ontario

August 23, 2018

Jennifer, filled with nervous anticipation, backed out of her driveway at almost 9:45. A few minutes later, she merged into traffic on Highway 420. The directions to the camera store were on her phone in a holder on the Smart car's dashboard.

She travelled over the Garden City Skyway. Not that she could see anything, but the Welland Canal was beneath her. She would have had to exit the QEW at Glendale to stop there. She continued on to Lake Street to the plaza. Traffic was light, and she arrived at Frederick's Foto Service soon after their opening time of ten o'clock. A 7-11 with a gas bar stood at one end of the building, with the location she wanted at the opposite end.

Jennifer found a parking spot next to the store and exited the car. As she stood outside Frederick's, she couldn't help but feel a surge of emotions. Her heart was pounding, and her hands were trembling. She was about to relive a part of her life she had long forgotten.

"You have some pictures ready for me to pick up?" she

asked the gentleman behind the counter. He wasn't the same one she met on her first trip to the shop.

"Name?"

"Jennifer Fox."

He walked to the tub containing the packages of processed film sorted by last names. He riffled through the envelopes until he found hers.

"Here you go. There was a problem because of the film's age, but you can still make out the images," the gentleman said. He pointed to the handwritten note on the front of the packet and started to open it as if to show her.

"No, that's fine. The person I saw when I dropped off the film warned me the pictures might not be perfect."

The sale rang up, and Jennifer paid. She clutched the packet to her chest and rushed out of the store.

She took a deep breath and opened the outer wrapping inside her car. A smaller one was inside. Jennifer pulled out the printed images, and her heart skipped a beat at the first one. It was from Kevin's tenth birthday party. The candles on his cake were lit. He had an ear-to-ear cheesy grin on his face. It was the last birthday her brother lived to celebrate. The image was redder than expected, but it didn't matter. It was a piece of her past, a memory she thought she had lost forever.

Most of the pictures were from that party. Jennifer was in many of them, being his older sister, but her facial expressions cried boredom. Why did she have to be there? She could be hanging out with her friends. One friend in particular, Emma. Her parents were in one with the birthday boy as he blew out his candles. Someone else had taken it. Maybe she did? Although she didn't remember doing it. There were other adults there, too. Jennifer and Kevin didn't have any aunts or uncles. Both of their parents were only children. Neighbours, who came to help? Maybe the parents of her brother's friends? She couldn't help but wonder about the people who were a part of her brother's life, even if it was just for that one day.

Two pictures didn't fit in with the rest. One was of Jennifer's parents' bedroom, and the other was of Zeus. She took those to finish the roll of film.

Jennifer pulled a pen out of her purse and wrote Kevin's 10th birthday on the inside envelope. She added the same inscription to the outer envelope, too. When she got home, those pictures would go into a box for safe keeping.

Although she had little time to spare between here and home, Jennifer drove to the Welland Canal Parkway and the Visitor Centre. This place held significant memories for her. She needed to clear her head after seeing those pictures. It wasn't a long drive back to her house, so she'd be fine if traffic wasn't horrendous.

She pulled in and sat behind the wheel for a few minutes. Once she gathered herself and her emotions, Jennifer exited the car and walked towards the viewing platform. At first glance, there were no ships traversing the canal. People lined the upper level, so she only climbed to the first one. Nothing coming up from Lake Ontario, or was that down? And nothing from the other direction either. Still, standing in the fresh air relaxed her and quieted her mind.

Her parents had brought her and Kevin here as children. The viewing platform, a recent addition, didn't exist then. And you could stand on the sidewalk next to the canal. Was keeping people back for safety? Or because of the 9-11 attacks? Surprisingly, Niagara Falls didn't have a lot of extra security features at the visitor attractions right at the falls.

A ship, its hull glistening in the sunlight, entered the canal from Lake Ontario. It would take too long for it to arrive where she waited and watched. Jennifer knew how to get here. This was best done when she didn't have to work.

She returned to her car and drove back to her house on Orchard Avenue.

Zeus's entire body wiggled when she came in the side door. At least someone was happy to see her. Jennifer leaned down, and the pug rubbed his face against hers.

"Come on, Zeus-ie, I'll let you out and get your feed on. Then I have to go to work," she said, walking to the sliding doors in the dining room.

She'd love to stay home today and take more time to come to grips with what was on the roll of film. But that wouldn't pay the bills. And she didn't want to risk her boss getting angry with her and firing her. Sure, she inherited her parents' and her grandmothers' estates. She had earmarked some of that for a trip to find Michael and apologize. Her wages and tips more than covered the monthly bills and food.

While Zeus did zoomies in the backyard, Jennifer went upstairs to prepare for work. Before changing into her black jeans and Outback T-shirt, she opened one of the picture boxes, placed the package she had picked up inside, and closed the lid. That action forced her to choke back a sob. As calm and relaxed as she had been at the Welland Canal a short time before, she felt herself falling to pieces again.

Jennifer couldn't afford to call in sick despite her emotional state. She had bills to pay and a life to maintain. So, she resolved to go to work to do what they paid her for. She would serve drinks, be friendly, and escort unruly patrons out the front door. Her personal struggles would have to wait.

Thirty-Nine

Outback Steakhouse, Victoria Avenue, Niagara Falls, Ontario

August 23, 2018

Jennifer sighed as she pulled her timecard from the rack and punched the clock. This shift, starting at two o'clock, was her usual. It gave her the luxury of time to attend to her personal chores. However, it also meant missing out on being there for Zeus when the fireworks started. And in the winter, when they set them off two hours earlier, it was even worse.

The bar was quiet, with only a couple of regular customers. One of them was the man who had made the crack about Michael breaking stones while she got people stoned. She couldn't help but recall the photograph in her bag, a potential significant change in their dynamic.

"Ready for another?" she asked, nodding at his almost empty glass.

"Please. Seeing you come in has made my day. You're prettier and friendlier than most others working the bar."

His words, though flattering, were not unexpected. This guy was such a schmooze.

"Stella?"

"Yes, please."

Jennifer turned and pulled him another pint of his chosen beverage, and sat it before him. Her purse was under the bar, so she pulled out the picture and placed it in front of the customer.

"Is this you?" she asked, wondering how he would react to the revelation.

He picked up the photograph and fixed his gaze on the image as if he was about to uncover a long-lost secret, a story waiting to be told.

That was him and his wife. A Nabisco Christmas party. It had to be forty-odd years ago.

"Yes, that's me."

"I thought it was."

"And this is your father and mother. I worked with your dad. He was a good man. I knew there was something familiar about you from the first time I came in and you worked here. I can't believe it all this time. I've been sitting in this bar, and Steven Fox's daughter has been serving me. Talk about a small world."

He stopped and took a sip of his beer. "I remember the day we found out he was dead like it was yesterday. It was before the newspaper printed the names. There was an announcement over the PA system. Until then, I thought he might be sick. Steven never took a lot of time off, except for holidays, so unlike some others in the plant, he didn't take advantage."

Another sip.

"He'd be proud of the way you turned out. You were his pride and joy. Firstborns always hold that place in a parent's heart. Even your younger brother couldn't compete with you for your father's attention. He used to call you his little sunshine."

"Where's your boyfriend?"

"Somewhere in Egypt," she answered.

"So I'm in with a chance." He, a tall man with salt-and-pepper hair, arched a bushy eyebrow.

Jennifer smiled. This guy had to be at least sixty-five. That was too much of an age difference. Still, she liked him because he was a good customer and never got touchy-feely like some of the other men did. So far, he'd been a gentleman. Fingers crossed, he stayed that way.

"So why would he leave you behind halfway around the world?" he pressed, his curiosity piqued, hinting at the bond Jennifer once shared with her ex-boyfriend.

Did she want to discuss this with him?

"I broke up with him. I told him bad things affect people I care about, so he should get as far away from me as possible." The words hung heavy, a confession she couldn't take back, her voice trembling with her emotional turmoil.

"I can't believe that. What could you have done that was so bad that other people got hurt?" he asked, his eyes searching hers for answers.

Jennifer burst into tears and rushed into the women's bathroom.

Jennifer splashed cold water on her face, and leaned on the sink, taking deep breaths to stop crying. Nothing helped. The door opened. Her co-worker, Sadie, stood in the doorway, reflected in the mirror before Jennifer.

"You okay, Jen?" Sadie asked.

Jennifer shook her head.

Sadie approached and rubbed Jennifer's back. "Something is definitely wrong. Tell me about it. Maybe I can help."

"C-customer a-asked …" She broke down again.

"What did he ask?"

"Wh-what I-I d-did t-to g-get other p-people h-hurt," Jennifer said between sobs.

"I don't know your background. I've only known you since you started working here at the Outback. Do you want to talk about it? I've been told I'm a good listener."

Jennifer took some more deep breaths. Could she trust Sadie? She didn't want all and sundry to know this secret.

"I-it g-goes n-no f-further," she said.

Sadie made a cross over her heart. "What happens in the ladies' room at the Outback stays in the ladies' room at the

Outback."

Jennifer smiled, took a few more deep breaths, and told her co-worker about the accident that killed her parents and brother and left her injured. She followed on the heels of that confession telling of her break up with Michael. Not finding out the driver of the other vehicle was drunk when he broadsided the car she was in until after she'd broken things off with Michael.

"So what are you going to do now?"

"I've applied for a passport. I'm going to find Michael and apologize."

"Okay, but why do you need a passport?"

"Because he's somewhere in Egypt. He's an archaeologist."

"The guy who brought you the gorgeous necklaces."

"That's the one," Jennifer said.

A customer entered the washroom. Thankfully, the woeful tale had already been told.

"I've got to get back out there. Take your time. I'll cover for you," Sadie said and left the room.

Jennifer, her eyes red and puffy, her cheeks stained with mascara, tried to reduce the swelling. She grabbed a paper towel and ran it under cold water, hoping it would help. As she dabbed her eyes, the woman who had just entered the restroom washed up at the sink next to her.

Jennifer silently pleaded, *Don't make eye contact. Don't ask questions.* The woman departed without a second look, answering her silent prayer and leaving Jennifer to her own devices.

When she cleaned her face and reduced the puffiness around her eyes, Jennifer exited and resumed her position.

"I didn't intend to bring you to tears," her customer expressed remorse. Jennifer's heart throbbed at his words, but she couldn't muster the strength to reveal her anguish. She nodded and carried on with her duties, her pain unspoken.

"Bit of a rough day for me. That's all. Can I get you another Stella?"

"Sure. I'm walking. One more won't hurt."

Despite the tempest of emotions within her, Jennifer, with a strength forged in the crucible of her pain, pulled his pint with practiced ease. She set a fresh glass on the bar beside the one he hadn't emptied, determined to uphold her professional demeanour.

As the night stretched out before her, the memories that refused to let her be, tormented Jennifer. The camera with the undeveloped film, a relic from her past, was a constant reminder of the unresolved issues she was grappling with. She pondered, was it a mistake to unearth the past?

Forty

Jennifer's House, Orchard Avenue, Niagara Falls, Ontario

September 21, 2018

The mailbox lid dropped back into place with a metallic clatter. Jennifer had checked the box every day since the first of September for her passport or, at least, a rejection letter.

She opened the front door and stepped onto the porch. Her mailbox was to the left and under her house number plaque. Today, she received more mail than usual. Jennifer leafed through it on her way back into the house. Flyers, bills, and a thick envelope with official logos. She tore it open. In her hands was her passport. Now, the only thing stopping her from going to Egypt and finding Michael was a plane ticket. And getting the time off work. And, the most important of all, someone to look after Zeus. The thought of leaving her beloved pug behind, his big, sad eyes watching her go, was a painful one. Would Sadie do it if she asked? All Jennifer knew was she couldn't take Zeus with her.

Did she text Emma and let her know her passport arrived? No. That would invite Emma to accompany her to Egypt, a journey she felt she needed to undertake alone. What about any of Michael's family? The only one who she might contact was Lori. And she wasn't family, per se, but Chris's partner. She had hit it off well with her when they were in Percé for Melissa's wedding. They both had painful pasts. The thought of reaching out to Lori and admitting her need for help made her feel vulnerable.

Jennifer had to be at work soon. She was sure she was on with Sadie again today and would ask her about dog sitting while she was chasing around the world trying to find Michael. Once she got to Cairo, she'd find a way to Saqqara. If Michael was there, fantastic. If he wasn't, hopefully, someone on the site would know where he was. The worst that could happen was Michael wouldn't want to try again. Or if she was on a flight to Egypt and he was on one to Manchester, where he lived. She couldn't bear the thought of missing him by mere hours.

She needed to concentrate on today, starting with locking the front door. The only time Jennifer used it was to pick up the mail. Oh, and Emma when she came here last month. An entire month had passed. Incredible.

Jennifer's excitement was unmistakable as she stepped into work. "Guess what? My passport arrived today," she exclaimed.

"So you're going to Egypt to find your man. Good for you." Sadie hugged her.

"I must get the time off, book a flight, and need someone to look after my dog."

"I never knew you had a dog. What kind is he/she?"

"He's a pug, and his name is Zeus," Jennifer revealed, as she beamed with affection. She pulled out her phone, eager to share her furry friend's photo. "Here he is," she said, turning the phone towards Sadie with a proud smile.

"Aw, he's adorable. I'll look after him."

"He *is* a wonderful dog."

"I sense a but coming."

"There's one thing about Zeus that worries me," Jennifer confessed. "He's terrified of fireworks and thunderstorms."

"I live quite a way from where they set off the fireworks. With any luck, Zeus won't hear them."

That would be a blessing. One less thing Jennifer would have on her mind while she travelled.

The manager stuck his head out of his office, so she took advantage and walked in.

"I need to talk to you about taking some time off," Jennifer said.

"How much time, and when?"

"A month? And starting tomorrow?" She crossed her fingers behind her back. "Something urgent has come up, and I must leave the country."

"Family emergency?"

"Yes." Jennifer hated lying to the man, but it was an emergency, just not family, in the strictest sense of the word.

"I hate to have you away for so long, but if it's an emergency, you can have the month. Longer if you need it. Just let me know," the manager said, offering his personal cellphone number.

Jennifer felt relief wash over her. "Thank you! You don't know how much this means to me."

"Get on with your shift before I change my mind."

Jennifer floated out of the manager's office, relief and excitement washing over her. Now, she had to get a ticket. She sorted out her dog-sitting issue before she spoke to the manager, leaving her with a sense of freedom and relaxation.

"I've got the time off," she squealed to Sadie when she took her position.

"You look a lot happier since the last time I saw you," her regular customer said as he sat on a stool.

"I'm going away for a month. I will find the guy I ended it with because I now have information I didn't have before. Pint of Stella, is it?" Jennifer's voice quivered with hope as she shared her plans with the man.

"I'll miss your smiling face, and yes."

Jennifer pulled his pint and set it in front of him. As a few more people trickled in, she scanned each male face, hoping against hope that it would be Michael. If he were to show up here, she wouldn't have to embark on a journey halfway around the world to find him. But as her shift drew to a close, her heart sank. He was nowhere to be seen.

Forty-One

Jennifer's House, Orchard Avenue, Niagara Falls, Ontario

September 22, 2018

Jennifer pulled her laptop out and sat it on the coffee table. She started a search for flights to Egypt but stopped. What major city was Saqqara near? She thought she'd read Cairo when she searched before, but wanted to be sure before she booked a flight to the wrong airport. Jennifer confirmed her thought Cairo was the proper destination. She returned to her search for flights. One airline, EgyptAir, had daily flights out of Toronto. Jennifer pulled out her Mastercard to buy her ticket and stopped. Not only did she need a valid passport, but she also needed a tourist visa to enter Egypt. She hadn't counted on that, and the realization hit her like a wave of frustration.

As Jennifer delved deeper into her travel preparations, she stumbled upon a frustrating fact. Unlike with other countries, Egypt did not offer the convenience of purchasing a tourist visa at the airport if you were from Canada. Instead, she had to complete an electronic visa application through the Egyptian government website. This process required two additional passport photos. At least, she consoled herself, when she saw she could pay the visa fee by credit card.

Trying to find Michael and apologize was becoming a bigger headache than she thought. Why didn't Emma tell her she'd need a visa and a passport?

Sadie lived on Westwood Street on the opposite side of the QEW. Zeus shouldn't have to worry about fireworks there. Still, she'd ensure she packed his ThunderShirt, toys, and other doggie paraphernalia.

She found Sadie in her contacts and tapped out a message.

Hit a snag. Need to apply for a tourist visa. Was hoping to leave tomorrow, but can't until I jump through more hoops.

Now, Jennifer had to find a suitcase and a carry-on bag. That meant a trip to the store to buy something. Back to her laptop, she went and searched. She found a Samsonite store on Lundy's Lane on the far side of the QEW.

"Back in a while, Zeus-ie. Guard the house."

Jennifer grabbed her purse and phone and headed to the side door. Her keys hung on a hook nearby. She plucked them just before she exited the house and locked the door behind her.

Once in her tiny car, she fastened her seatbelt and started the engine. She then backed out of her driveway and drove off to the drug store.

Jennifer embarked on a mission to find the perfect luggage. Her first stop was Shoppers for two more passport photos. With the pictures in hand, she continued her journey up Lundy's Lane to the plaza housing the Samsonite store.

Many choices faced her, but the looming question was whether anything would fit within her budget. Some pieces were more expensive than she had expected. As she continued to browse, a store employee approached.

"Can I help you find anything?"

"I need a carry-on bag and a medium suitcase," Jennifer said. She wanted to add that it doesn't cost an arm and a leg and my first-born male child, but she kept that to herself.

"Hard shell?" The clerk knocked on one piece on display.

"Yes, I think so."

The employee showed Jennifer an array of bags, most of which she couldn't justify the cost. Even the less expensive ones were well out of her price range.

When she was about to give up hope, the clerk shared the news which could change everything. The store offered a fifty percent discount on certain items, but the sale ended at the day's close of business. If Jennifer could get a $200 bag for $100, that would bring a smile to her face.

"Which ones are they?"

"They have a red tag on them."

"Thank you."

After a thorough search, Jennifer's eyes landed on a carry-on and a matching medium-sized case. Both were on wheels and had retractable handles, ticking all the boxes on her list. With a sense of satisfaction, she prepared to take them home.

"Will the smaller one fit inside the other? I'm thinking about storage and getting them home. I drive a Smart car."

After the clerk scanned the bags, she placed the small one inside the other and zipped the outer case.

Jennifer put her card in the machine at the cash register and typed in her PIN.

The retractable handle on the small suitcase she had taken to Percé broke when she got off the GO train when she got back. If not for that, she wouldn't have had to buy another small bag. At least these new ones were brand names, so they should be more reliable.

Upon her return, Jennifer began to apply for her tourist visa. This unexpected turn meant she couldn't buy her plane ticket until the Egyptian authorities approved her visa application, a process which would take at least seven days. She needed to find Michael as soon as possible, even if it meant waiting a little longer for her trip.

As Jennifer delved deeper into the visa application process, she discovered more requirements. She needed a travel itinerary, list of accommodations, and of the places she was likely to visit, all to be submitted along with her passport and printed eVisa. It was a lot more than she had expected, and she couldn't help but feel she had rushed into this without proper preparation.

This glitch could work out in her favour. It gave her time to look into a place to stay and the places she wanted to see. Saqqara was topmost on the list. Yes, the Sphinx. Yes, the pyramids at Giza. Anything else? Likely, but at that moment, her mind went blank. If she went somewhere not on her list, would she get thrown in jail? Deported? Now, that scared her. The last place Jennifer wanted to end up was in a prison in a foreign country.

Minimum of seven days. Those words echoed through Jennifer's mind. It most likely meant working days. What if she got a flight booked for Thanksgiving weekend? That would make ten days. Might as well book a hotel at the same time.

Jennifer revisited the EgyptAir website and booked a flight leaving on October 6 and returning on November 6. Her visa was only good for thirty days, so she should stretch the time out as much as possible. If things didn't work out, she'd change the date of her return flight and come back sooner. And, if she had to, she could extend her stay, although that didn't seem probable.

Next was to find a hotel. Near the airport? Or at least one with a shuttle to get her from there to her room? One with pyramid views? On the banks of the Nile? That was too much for her to think about at the moment.

Now, she had to talk to her boss and try to move her month off to start at Thanksgiving rather than immediately. He'd given her his personal cell number. She'd send him a text.

Hate to be a pain, but can I move my month off to starting Thanksgiving weekend? I'll work until then.

While she waited for him to respond, Jennifer went to the kitchen and put the kettle on to boil. She dug in the cupboard and pulled out a container of Mr. Noodles spicy chicken. They weren't the most nourishing of foods, but to her, they were comfort food. Right now, she needed that.

Jennifer was eating when the reply from her boss came in.

All right. Just don't change your mind again.

He wasn't impressed, she could tell. Oh well. He'd have to

get over it.

Now, Jennifer realized she couldn't leave until Thanksgiving weekend because of the visa process, she thought of Zeus. She sent a text to Sadie to inform her of the plan change and to ensure Zeus would be well cared for during her absence.

Today was Jennifer's scheduled day off, so she washed the dishes she'd used that day and left them to dry on the rack when she finished her meal.

Forty-Two

Jennifer's House, Orchard Avenue, Niagara Falls, Ontario

September 28, 2018

It had been a nerve-wracking week since Jennifer had applied for her eVisa. She started checking the status the Monday after submitting her application and had checked every day since then. Today, she was too anxious to do it again for fear of the same result. Pending. But to her immense relief and joy, the status showed approved, filling her with a sense of accomplishment and satisfaction.

She didn't own a colour printer, but that didn't deter her. She downloaded the document and saved it in PDF format on her computer. Then, she transferred it to a USB stick, planning to take it to a local print shop like Staples, and print it out in colour.

That wasn't an option today since she was due at work in a couple of hours and still had to shower. It would be okay as long as she printed it before she flew out for her long-awaited vacation. Something had gone right with this trip, and she could now look forward to it with relief and excitement.

Jennifer headed upstairs to shower. Before she did, she got

her work clothes ready and laid out on the bed.

With hair in a towel turban and wrapped in a bath sheet under her long velour housecoat, Jennifer padded barefoot across the landing to her bedroom. It had been cool these past few days, so she wore a long-sleeved T-shirt under her short-sleeved uniform.

Once dressed, she sat at her dressing table and applied her makeup. She never wore a lot of products on her face, only eyeliner, mascara, a light-toned blush, and pale pink lip gloss. Of her getting ready for work routine, drying her hair took the longest.

Jennifer hobbled to the bathroom and used the blow dryer on her hair. She hoped Sadie was on her shift today so she could tell her the good news about her eVisa. She couldn't remember if she'd told her the details that marked the beginning of her journey and the end of her stay in Egypt.

Although the trip was still a way off, it now felt more real, more tangible than the mere dream it had been. The anticipation was building, tinged with nervousness. The only thing that could mar this excitement was the fear of being unable to find Michael once she arrived.

With her hair dried and brushed out, Jennifer went back to her bedroom. She pulled open the drawer where she'd placed the cartouche pendant and the opal necklace, and removed the two boxes. Tears pricked her eyes when Jennifer opened them and looked at the beautiful jewellery pieces. She hadn't worn either since she ended it with Michael. Was it time to wear them again? Wear them when she flew to Egypt or have them in her carry-on? It might be better to not show them off. She could pull them out of her luggage when she cleared Customs and put one or the other or both on then.

Today, she decided. She wore the delicate opal, symbolizing her inner strength and resilience. But instead of flaunting it, she tucked the gem inside the neck of her shirt, a silent testament to her internal debate and the complexity of her emotions. She was torn between the desire to move on and the fear of forgetting, between the need for closure and the hope for reconciliation.

Jennifer floated into the Outback. Sadie had already punched in and was pulling pints when she came around the corner.

"The Egyptian authorities approved my eVisa. I can't believe it," exclaimed Jennifer. "I have to get it printed somewhere since I don't have a colour printer. No printer of any kind."

"I'm so happy for you. I just know you'll find Michael, and things will work out," said Sadie.

"I don't leave until Thanksgiving weekend, and that's a whole week away. October 6th can't come soon enough."

"It will be here before you know it. Look who's at the bar."

Jennifer turned around. It was her regular. The one who said she was the prettiest girl in the place. She never knew his name for as long as he'd been coming in.

"Hi, pint of Stella, is it?" she asked.

"I wasn't expecting to see you. When I heard you were taking a month off, I had my drinks elsewhere. I'm unsure what brought me here today, but I'm glad I came."

"I'm still taking the month off. It got pushed back a bit. Discovered a few more hoops I had to jump through and more bureaucracy."

"I'll miss you, you know."

"Don't be silly."

"I'm not."

Jennifer placed his drink in front of him. "I'm leaving on October 6th and returning on November 6th. And I'll be back to work the following day."

"This place won't be the same without you," he said, sipping his beer.

"I bet you say that to all the girls," said Jennifer. She changed tack. "You must be retired? You're in here during the week when most people with nine-to-five jobs would be at work."

"Yes. Retired about ten years ago now. Took early

retirement to care for the missus."

Now, Jennifer wasn't sure about heading in this direction.

"So she can't be impressed with your spending so much time here."

"The poor dear had dementia. I ended up putting her in a home. When she passed, she didn't remember me." He took a cloth handkerchief from his pants pocket and blew his nose.

"I'm sorry. I wouldn't have brought it up had I known," Jennifer said in a feeble attempt at an apology. She had put her foot in it. Both feet, actually.

"It's all right. Don't worry. I come in for the company. Have a couple of Stellas and go home."

"Do you have children nearby?"

"The good lord never blessed us with kiddies."

"I've never introduced myself. I'm Jennifer. Jennifer Fox. My co-worker here is Sadie Franklin." Both girls held out their hands so he could shake them.

"I'm Bill McGregor. Pleased to meet your acquaintance, both of you." He shook hands with them both, starting with Jennifer.

"So tell me, what is this big adventure you're embarking on for a month?" Bill asked.

"I'm off to Egypt. I'm going to find the guy I ended it with and try to make it right."

"I wish you all the best in your endeavour. If I can be of any help to you, you just have to say the word." Bill took another mouthful of lager.

"Thank you."

Jennifer left him to his beer.

Oh, to be young again. Bill had aged so much in the years of his wife's illness. To say it had been hard was an understatement. It had been a blessing for both him and his wife when she took her final breath. In those last months, she had become violent, borne out of fear. She didn't know who he was or any of the staff members at the home. She picked it up and threw it if there was anything within reach. And if the 'stranger' was within arms' length, she brought her fists down in a fury. There were times the staff had to restrain her. Protection for them as well as her. Poor Grace. A tear escaped and ran down his cheek. If only he could remember the good times before her illness.

By now, Bill had finished his second Stella. "That's me off home. I'll see you next time," he said, easing his tall frame off the bar stool.

"Bye, Bill," Jennifer said.

Sadie also bade him farewell.

Bill often found solace in the company of Jennifer and Sadie, even if he didn't engage in much conversation with the bar staff. His loneliness was perceptible, but he seemed comfortable in their presence.

"He's sure taken a shine to you, Jennifer," Sadie said, teasing.

"I very much doubt that. I found out not too long ago, Bill worked with my father at the Nabisco plant."

"You noticed, right? He's not been in since I told him you were off for a month. And he turns up today, and look who's working," Sadie pointed out.

"Not that this has anything to do with it, but what if I was to bring Zeus to your house on October 5th. I've got to navigate taxis, GO trains, and UP Express and be at the airport at least three hours before my flight. Will that be okay?"

"No problem. I've told the mister we're having a houseguest for a month."

"And what did he say?"

"When I told him our guest was a dog, he laughed."

Jennifer spoke as she unloaded the dishwasher. "I'm going to miss Zeus. I'm sure he'll feel right at home at your house."

"If you haven't already had your eVisa printed by then, bring it along, and I'll print it for you."

"Thanks, but I'd rather get it done before that. I'll forget if I leave it until the last minute."

Forty-Three

October 2, 2018

Michael found himself in the esteemed company of the head of the Czech team, Miroslav Bárta, in Abusir, a site of unparalleled archaeological significance not far from Saqqara. This was an exceptional opportunity, as the Saqqara team had unearthed nothing of any magnitude since July. He appreciated Ramadan had extended this invitation and anticipated the revelations this group would bring.

Both Miroslav and Michael were immersed in the Egyptian desert. The atmosphere was electric, with a tangible excitement permeating the camp that day. The entire team was on the edge of their seats, their enthusiasm far from contained. Michael, swept up in the wave of anticipation, awaited the day's treasure.

As the sun reached its peak, a sudden shout shattered the stillness. Miroslav, the head of the Czech team, sprinted towards the source of the commotion. Michael, his heart racing with anticipation, followed suit. He couldn't bear to miss the electrifying moment of discovery.

The pit they had been excavating was about six feet deep.

The sudden appearance of an entryway into a dark chasm sparked the excitement. Illuminated by bright lights, Miroslav ducked and entered. Michael and a few others followed him. It was a tomb! But whose?

Someone had plundered this one. But was it in these times? Or ancient times? Michael had experienced both in his career as an archaeologist.

Inside, a once intact but now broken-in-two statue sat in solemn silence. Miroslav, his eyes tracing the hieroglyphs on the bottom half, made a profound revelation. "This was Kaires, a priest and royal confidante."

This artifact, a missing piece of the puzzle, provided a long-awaited answer. Yes, ancient Egyptians did place statues in their burial chambers. The significance of this find was monumental, confirming the depth of ancient Egyptian burial practices and a milestone in understanding their culture.

In Michael's opinion, this discovery surpassed the one made in July at Saqqara. The meticulously lined limestone blocks on the walls showed the ancient craftsmanship and a window into a world of artistry and dedication he admired.

Aware of how important the find was, Michael stepped back and let the team leader make the required calls.

Within hours, Antiquities Minister Khaled al-Anani, whom Michael met during the July dig's find, arrived. This began a monumental discovery that would captivate the world.

Ramadan and Miroslav organized a press conference to unveil the rare and significant archaeological find. As the event unfolded, the media was in for a once-in-a-lifetime surprise.

Miroslav spoke first. "There are multiple unique facts in this case. The tomb is in the centre of a regular pyramid field in Abusir and dates back to around 2,400 B.C. Besides the cult chapel itself, it contains several other rooms."

"Items we discovered in the burial chamber of the priest Kaires are parts of the chapel's decoration, depicting scenes from everyday life. As well, we retrieved ceramic objects included in the burial equipment."

He continued, "Another unique feature is that its chapel is

the only royal tomb from this period using basalt blocks for paving, wall panelling and the altar. This is evidence of the exceptional status of the tomb owner."

"In a nutshell, Kaires oversaw all the King's building projects and described himself as his only friend. It was his duty to be responsible for the King's routine at the Morning House, where he would wash, get dressed and have his breakfast."

"Kaires also inspected the priests and was the priest of the goddess Hathor. So, the man had many duties. However, we can say without a doubt he was close to the King. You can see his tomb from the pharaoh, Neferirkare's pyramid. So it is quite possible that this was the man Kaires claimed he was the sole friend to."

After Miroslav finished his speech, Khaled al-Anani said a few words. He assured the release over the coming days of the eagerly awaited photographs documenting the find, to provide a visual testament to this extraordinary discovery.

Forty-Four

Sadie's House, Westwood Street, Niagara Falls, Ontario

October 5, 2018

Even though it was early in the day, Jennifer opted to get Zeus delivered to Sadie's house sooner rather than later. The longer she left it, the harder it would be to say goodbye to her pet. It was kind of her co-worker to offer to look after her dog, so she would have to bring something home for her. The decor of her house would give Jennifer an idea of Sadie's likes and dislikes.

She loaded Zeus and all his paraphernalia into her Smart car and drove to her co-worker's house on Westwood. With it being on the far side of the QEW, the fireworks shouldn't bother her dog. She'd packed his ThunderShirt, which helped some. He might need it to stay in a strange house with people he didn't know.

Sadie lived almost at the end of the street. A park stood on the opposite side, closer to the highway. Zeus would like that.

When she pulled into the driveway, Sadie's little Toyota sat parked next to the house. Jennifer shut off the engine, grabbed Zeus's leash and headed to her front door. She could come back for the rest of his things after.

When Sadie opened the door, Jennifer had raised her hand to ring the bell.

"I thought I saw a little yellow car drive by," she said.

"I got all the way to the corner and had to turn around."

"So this is my wee houseguest," Sadie said, squatting to greet the pug. "We're going to get along fine." She stood and invited Jennifer and Zeus inside.

"I'll get the rest of his things."

"Why don't I give you a hand? Many hands make light work, after all," said Sadie.

With Jennifer still holding the end of the leash, the three returned to her car and retrieved the rest of the dog's things. She'd packed food, dishes, a bed, and his carrier crate in case he felt more secure sleeping in it. Then there was a bag of his favourite toys and, most importantly, his ThunderShirt.

"He doesn't travel light, does he?" Sadie said.

"No."

They left Zeus's things in the welcoming hall of Sadie's cozy house. Jennifer unclipped the leash from his harness and put it with his other belongings, a pang of sadness hitting her as she did so.

"I was going to make a coffee. You want one?" Sadie asked.

"Sure," Jennifer replied, her voice soft and filled with sadness.

Jennifer settled at the kitchen table, her hands finding solace in the coolness of the polished wood. The aroma of brewing coffee blended with Sadie's home's subtle, comforting scent. Unlike her own kitchen, which was more traditional, this one exuded a modern yet unpretentious charm.

While the coffee brewed, Sadie gave Jennifer a house tour. A keen observer, Jennifer took in the colours, fabrics, and textiles, especially in the living room. She had already planned to bring something back for Sadie — something that would blend in but stand out, a thoughtful token of her appreciation for their friendship.

"Do you still need to print your eVisa? If so, you can use the computer in here." Sadie showed Jennifer into a room set up as an office.

"I had forgotten about that. Thanks for reminding me." She sat down at the computer and logged into the website. In a few minutes, her hard copy sat in the printer's output tray.

When the two returned to the kitchen, the coffee was ready. Sadie poured two mugs, the rich, dark liquid cascaded into the ceramic with a comforting sound. She handed one to Jennifer, the warmth of the mug seeped into her hands. Sadie took the milk out of the fridge and grabbed the sugar bowl from the counter. A utensil caddy sat in the middle, so she reached in and pulled out a spoon for her guest.

Jennifer drank her coffee in silence.

"I hate to run, but I've got laundry and packing waiting for me at home," she said, taking her empty mug to the sink.

"You're all right. I believe you'll find Michael, and things will work out for you. And please, don't fret about Zeus; he's in the best of hands," Sadie reassured, her words a balm to Jennifer's worried heart.

Sadie walked Jennifer to the door and hugged her.

"You be a good boy, Zeus," Jennifer said as she walked out the front door.

She cried all the way home from Sadie's house, her heart heavy leaving Zeus behind. Not once had Jennifer ever left her pug in someone else's care save an overnight stay at the vet's. The thought of him, his big, round eyes filled with confusion and longing, waiting for her to return, tore at her heart. She knew Sadie would take excellent care of him, but it didn't make leaving Zeus any easier.

Walking into an empty house felt peculiar, but Jennifer wasted no time. She took a deep breath and started doing laundry, even her work clothes. Despite not needing them until November, she knew that washing them now would ensure they were ready for her return to work after her month-long adventure exploring Egypt.

Contemplating the weather there, Jennifer couldn't help but wonder. She was accustomed to a mix of warm, sunny days in her current location, followed by cloudy, rainy, and sometimes cold ones. But Egypt was a desert. Would the nights be chilly and the days scorching hot? This anticipation and curiosity about the new environment added a sense of adventure to her trip.

While her clothes were in the washing machine, Jennifer went upstairs to her bedroom and flung open her closet door. She pulled the cord that operated the single ceiling light — a bare bulb. Linen was a practical choice. Lightweight, easy to care for. She had found these linen trousers in Winners — pull-on, no zipper, elastic waist. They would do rather well. She liked them so much that when she tried on a pair in the store, she bought a pair in every colour they had in her size. So she had beige, black, navy, brown, olive green, and purple. Jennifer removed those hangers from the rail and laid them on the bed.

She had blouses, although she was more of a T-shirt person. She wore long ones with leggings and regular-length ones with trousers and jeans. Jennifer grabbed a selection of those, dropped them on the bed with her other clothing, and then took leggings out of her dresser. Black pairs and grey ones, too. These were her favourites because the waist came up so high; they were figure-flattering and didn't roll down when she sat.

A sweater. Where was her lightweight, ivory, thigh-length one? Jennifer went back through her closet again. She found it at the back. Did she pack a pair of jeans? Wear them?

Deciding what to take and what to wear gave her a massive headache so she took a break from selecting clothing for her trip. She returned downstairs, pulled out her laptop, and searched for what she could take in her luggage, both checked and carry-on. As Jennifer scrolled through the list, she couldn't help but feel excitement and anxiety. This was her first solo trip, and she wanted everything to be perfect.

She'd pack her toiletries and makeup in her checked bag to make going through security more manageable. That eliminated the smaller size restriction and having to put them in a plastic bag. She might still put the items inside one in her large suitcase as a precaution rather than have something spill or explode and ruin her clothing. Jennifer also packed a small emergency kit with basic first aid supplies, just in case.

During the delay, because she had to get a visa to visit Egypt, Jennifer picked up extra toiletries, makeup, a toothbrush, and toothpaste. She endured filling out forms, providing necessary documents, and paying a fee, but it was all worth it for the adventure that awaited her. She packed the new items and left her other ones at home, so when she packed her suitcase, she didn't have to get back into it.

The washing machine had stopped, so Jennifer went downstairs and moved the laundry to the dryer. She wasn't sure if there was anything in it she wanted to take.

Forty-Five

Pearson International Airport, Toronto, Ontario

October 6, 2018

Undeterred by the initial obstacles, Jennifer's determination shone through. While the taxi ride was a breeze, the rest of her journey not so much. Balancing two suitcases and her purse, she faced difficulties boarding and de-boarding the GO train. Fortunately, a compassionate stranger came to her aid, shouldering her bulky bag and ensuring its safe placement on the train. His assistance was a lifeline when the train reached Union Station, as he was there to lift it off for her.

Seated in the departure lounge, relief washed over Jennifer. Her preparation for the security checkpoint had paid off. She had informed the staff about the metal in her leg before passing through the metal detector. As expected, the hand wand detected the titanium rod, nuts, and bolts in her leg, and they gave her the green light to proceed.

When she realized her oversight, regret filled her. She had packed her cane in her checked suitcase, now making its way through the depths of the airport. The distance from the checkpoint to her current spot felt like a never-ending marathon. The smaller carry-on bag and purse were manageable, especially since the latter held her laptop. She had debated bringing it, considering she had her phone and charger. Now, she lugged a computer, its power cable, and other necessities.

Forty-Six

October 7, 2018

This was the first time on the trip that Jennifer had been frightened. The thought of her documentation not being sufficient for the Egyptian authorities and her fear of being sent back to Canada weighed heavily on her. The line moved at a snail's pace. She clutched her passport opened to the photo page with the printed copy of her eVisa, her accommodations, and a list of places to visit tucked behind it. After a long wait, she was face-to-face with a dour agent.

"What brings you to Egypt?" he asked.

"Holiday."

"And your papers?"

She handed everything across the counter to him.

He looked at her, down at her passport, back at her, then at her eVisa, and scanned the list. After what felt like an eternity, he stamped her documents and returned everything to her. Her tense shoulders relaxed. She had made it through the first hurdle of her Egyptian adventure.

Jennifer followed the crowd from her flight as they walked through the airport to the baggage hall. The carousel designated for their flight remained empty. Time stretched on as they waited, the anticipation building. Bags began to tumble down the slide and wind around. People lunged ahead and pulled their suitcases off. Hers was nowhere in sight. She tried to get closer, her impatience growing so she could reach out and grab it when it passed by her. She spotted her case and waited for it. As it was about to reach her, a tall man leaned in front of her and snatched up his own. He almost knocked her over, adding to her frustration.

Another round of waiting. This time, before Jennifer's case arrived, she leaned ahead and grabbed its handle and sighed with relief. Another hurdle overtaken. She followed behind others who had their luggage. Another Customs official inspected her paperwork again before she left the baggage hall. Beyond that, there were two ways out. One said *nothing to declare* in English and Arabic, showing she had no items to declare to the Customs. The other said *declare* again in both languages for those with items to declare. Jennifer hurried towards the 'nothing to declare' exit and into the arrivals hall.

Overwhelmed by the number of people waiting, she stopped, and someone from behind ran into her. They mumbled something unintelligible and moved around her. She was here. Jennifer was here. The realization hit her, excitement and nervousness coursing through her veins.

The intense heat enveloped Jennifer as she stepped outside the airport building, hitting her like a wall. The air was thick, smelling of sweat, sand and dryness.

She sought a quiet spot, away from the bustling crowd, to retrieve her phone and figure out the airport shuttle's schedule.

Jennifer found a spot in a corner next to a pillar. She turned her phone on and waited while it completed its power-up routine. There was a post number where the bus stopped. She didn't have to phone for it. Just wait at the designated place for its return. Not that she'd used them, but she had heard that sometimes the shuttles to and from the airport back in Toronto served more than one hotel. Was that the case here? She pondered this as she waited, observing the other travellers and the bustling activity around her.

She had booked a room at the Tahrir Plaza Suites, a reasonably priced hotel with an airport shuttle across the road from a museum. Best of all, it wasn't all that far from the market where Michael had bought her jewellery. The hotel's convenient location and amenities were key factors in her decision.

Realizing she needed Egyptian cash for the shuttle, Jennifer retreated to the terminal's air-conditioned comfort. She wandered through, checking the various shops, until she came across the currency exchange. Despite the less favourable rates, Jennifer needed cash. She approached the counter, wondering if they accepted credit or debit cards for cash advances or if it was cash for cash only.

"I need to get some Egyptian money. Can I use my credit card?" Jennifer asked.

The person behind the counter shook her head but pointed down the corridor. Jennifer walked in that direction. A short distance down was an ATM. She pulled out her Mastercard and requested one hundred Egyptian pounds (E£100). That should be enough for any cash payments she had to make.

Jennifer had yet to learn the exchange rate between Canadian dollars and Egyptian pounds. With the delay in waiting for her eVisa, she could have spent the time researching it and going to her bank to get the foreign currency before her trip. She shoved the card and cash into her wallet, secured them in her cross-body bag, and ventured out into the heat and the designated post for the shuttle.

The bus driver, a stout man with a friendly smile, loaded Jennifer's large bag into the back of the bus and lifted her small one into the passenger compartment. As the shuttle waited outside the terminal, more passengers boarded. They all looked like seasoned travellers, their chatter filling the air with various languages. To them, she must look like a rookie, her nervousness radiating from her every pore.

What had she been thinking about when she decided to try

to find her lost love, Michael, halfway around the world? There wasn't any logic in it. It was all emotion. She checked her phone again.

"Use Wi-Fi. Turn your data off," the passenger on her left said.

"Why?"

"Too expensive. Your provider will hit you with exorbitant roaming charges. The bus has Wi-Fi. Take advantage everywhere you can."

"Thank you." Jennifer entered her phone's settings, turned off her data, and selected Wi-Fi. When she found the bus's network, she chose it and connected.

The convoluted route to her hotel took forever, but the driver stopped at other hotels to let people off. She watched them when they paid, most of whom had paid with cards. That's what she would do and keep the bit of Egyptian currency she had.

Eventually, only Jennifer and the kind gentleman about her age seated on her left remained on the bus. They chatted some more and discovered they had bookings at the same hotel.

"Check-in isn't until two o'clock he said."

Jennifer looked at her watch. She was still on Canadian time, so she checked her phone. It was after nine, so it was still five hours before she could check-in.

"What do we do in the meantime?"

"Me, I like to take a walk. Our hotel is quite close to the Nile, you know."

"Where do you leave your luggage?"

"They have a secure room where they store it."

After all these years since the accident, Jennifer wasn't up to walking a great distance, not before getting her cane from her suitcase. She had about five hours. Would that be enough time to get to Saqqara and find Michael?

"I need to get to Saqqara," she said. "How do I do that?"

"I take it you mean the Necropolis?"

"I guess so. My boyfriend was on a dig there in July when they discovered the mummification chamber."

"It's about an hour away from our hotel by car."

Jennifer's heart sank. Everything about this trip was going wrong. What she hoped would be a romantic reunion had turned into a nightmare. The distance to Saqqara seemed insurmountable.

"I wanted to surprise him. Guess that won't happen now." Jennifer's voice quivered with disappointment, her shattered hopes flowing in the tears that escaped and ran down her cheek.

"Don't cry. Let me see what I can do." The gentleman's words were not just comforting; they were a lifeline. His genuine concern was obvious in his tone.

Jennifer felt a glimmer of hope and dashed away the tear, grateful for his kindness.

After a long ride, the bus arrived at their hotel. Before leaving her seat, she pulled out her credit card to pay the driver. She stood, retrieved her carry-on bag from the rack, and walked to the front. When he told her the fare, she gasped.

"Not that bad. It's only about fifteen American dollars," the other passenger said.

Jennifer could live with that. She used his machine, paid her fare, and left a tip.

Forty-Seven

Tahrir Plaza Suites, Meret Basha, Ismailia, Qasr El Nil, Cairo Governorate, Cairo, Egypt

October 7, 2018

Once she had entered the secure baggage area, Jennifer removed the cane from her oversized one and her two necklaces from her carry-on and put on both. With a glimmer of hope, she wished someone would recognize the pieces and be able to lead her to Michael.

"While you were occupied, I made a few discreet calls. I know one driver who ferries the archaeologists from the airport to the site," he revealed, his voice laced with a tantalizing hint of mystery.

"You did all this for me?" His unexpected benevolence caught her off guard, but a nagging suspicion lingered. There had to be a catch, a hidden cost. "I'm grateful." She refrained from expressing her overwhelming gratitude, wary of the unknown consequences. It got her a plus one with Michael at his sister's wedding.

"I'm Daniel Carter," he said, introducing himself with a warm smile and a firm handshake.

"Jennifer Fox," she replied as the two shook hands.

"Since we're staying in the same hotel, perhaps you'll do me the pleasure of having dinner with me one evening?"

"I'm not so sure about that. Much will depend on if I find my boyfriend."

"Fair enough. Samir Hassan is the driver I mentioned. He's on his way to Saqqara from the airport now with a passenger and has agreed to stop here and pick you up, too. He'll meet you out front." Daniel pointed out the direction.

"Thank you, again, for your help. From the beginning about the Wi-Fi to getting me to Saqqara."

"My pleasure. I hope to see you soon."

Jennifer left him to wait at the appointed pickup location. Daniel was charismatic, a quality that attracted her to him and made her wary. His persuasive nature was clear in his attempt to convince her to join him for a meal, a subtle hint at his underlying intentions.

A sleek, black Range Rover glided to a stop in the dusty drop zone in front of the hotel. From the driver's seat emerged a man of Middle Eastern descent, his tall, imposing figure commanding attention. "You. You must be the lady seeking passage to Saqqara?"

"Yes, please. You're Samir Hassan? That was the name Daniel Carter gave me."

"I am."

"Jennifer Fox," she said.

He shook her hand and tried to kiss her cheek, but Jennifer swerved out of range.

That was a little too friendly for her liking. She'd never met this man before, and his familiarity made her uneasy. She couldn't shake off the sensation that there was more to him than met the eye.

Samir eased back behind the wheel, put the vehicle in gear and set out. He engaged in a hushed conversation with the person in the front passenger seat, and their words were inaudible to Jennifer.

"So, how do you know Daniel?" Jennifer asked.

"University. And you? How do you know him?"

"I met him for the first time earlier this morning on the shuttle from the airport. He must travel a lot because he knows things I never would have dreamt of being important."

"I don't believe he's been here before, but he does much international travel."

Jennifer settled in for the ride. The traffic in the city was heavy. The farther away from Cairo they went, the thinner it became. The terrain was lush and green with trees until they were almost there.

"That building on the left. That's the Ruins of King Unas Valley Temple," Samir said.

Now, they were in the desert. That was what Jennifer had expected to see. The earlier scenery, however, was a complete surprise. Until today, she thought all of Egypt was desert. This was a new side of the country she hadn't counted on, a lush and green terrain that transformed into the barren beauty of the desert.

They came to a stop. Samir bid farewell to the front-seat passenger, an archaeologist he'd picked up at the airport, and exited the car to retrieve the man's bags from the back. Jennifer's heart raced with anticipation as she opened her door, her palms slightly sweaty.

"No. You don't get out."

"How else am I going to find my boyfriend?"

"His name."

"Michael Scott."

Another vehicle pulled up alongside Khaled's, and the driver rolled down the window. The two men spoke in their native Arabic. Jennifer didn't know what they said to each other.

"Your friend is not here."

"Where then?"

"Abusir."

"Will you take me there?"

"No. Ahmed will."

Forty-Eight

Saqqara, Badrshein, Giza Governorate, Egypt

October 7, 2018

With trepidation, Jennifer stepped out of the familiar Range Rover that had carried her this far, her hand lingering on the door handle. The sight of the unknown four-wheel-drive vehicle waiting for her was a reminder of the unfamiliar territory she was about to enter. The desert sun beat down on her, the sand beneath her feet scorching. She could hear the distant hum of insects and the soft murmur of voices within the dig site.

Ahmed exited from the driver's seat and walked around to open the front passenger door. He, too, shook her hand and kissed her cheek. "Welcome, Jennifer," the man said with a warm smile. "I hope the journey wasn't too tiring for you." He helped her inside before closing her door and returning to the vehicle. "Mr. Michael is a fortunate man to have such a lovely young woman travel as far as you have to see him."

Two Egyptian men tried to kiss her cheek in about an hour when she first met them. She dodged Samir's advances but not Ahmed's. Invading her personal space was unsettling, a stark contrast to the norms in her Western culture. The disregard for personal space was a jarring experience for her, highlighting the cultural differences she was about to navigate.

"You look concerned, my dear. Do not worry. It is a custom of ours and often happens during conversations."

That explained invading her personal space but didn't make her feel better. She felt uncomfortable; her personal space violated twice in such a short time. She tried to push the emotion aside, reminding herself she was in a different culture where such gestures were normal. But the unease lingered, a nagging reminder of the unfamiliarity of her surroundings and the situation she was in.

"I know your Michael. I drove him here when he first arrived back in June. I also took him to Cairo on two occasions. Ah, I see you're wearing the pieces he bought for you at Khan el-Khalili. They are stunning, bespoke pieces. He chose well." Ahmed's eyes twinkled with admiration and fondness as he spoke. Jennifer, flushed with nervousness, couldn't help but smile at the compliment.

"And you know Michael is at Abusir?"

"Yes. The team Michael is with is digging near the Pyramid of Neferirkare. They found the Tomb of Kaires just last week. Most exciting."

"I'm sure it was. When we get there, will I be able to go into the camp?" Jennifer asked with anticipation and nervousness. She had been planning this surprise visit for weeks, eager to see Michael in his element yet unsure how he would react to her sudden appearance. Her heart raced with excitement and anxiety, her mind filled with a thousand 'what-ifs.'

"No, I'm sorry. You'll have to remain outside the perimeter, but I will get your Michael to come to you."

"That's nice. Please don't tell Michael that I'm here. Make up something. I want to surprise him." Jennifer's voice quivered with excitement, her heart pounded in her chest as she imagined the look on Michael's face when he saw her. She had been planning this visit for weeks, orchestrating every detail to ensure the perfect surprise. The risk of spoiling it was high, but the potential reward was worth it.

"All right." Ahmed turned to Jennifer, his eyes filled with understanding and a reassuring hint of mischief. He winked, a silent promise to guard her secret, his demeanour instilling a sense of trust and comfort in Jennifer.

It was a short but bumpy drive to where Michael was working. Ahmed stopped the vehicle and climbed out.

"You stay here. I'll fetch your man. If you like, you can wait over there. I'll show you."

Jennifer exited the car and walked with the driver to the suggested location.

"He won't see you until he rounds the last corner. I'll make something up to get him to come with me," he said, turning and walking.

Forty-Nine

Abusir, Badrshein, Giza Governorate, Egypt

October 7, 2018

"Mr. Michael! Mr. Michael!" Ahmed called as he entered the site.

Michael, his mind racing with possibilities, stood and strained to locate the source of the urgent call. Ahmed was sprinting towards him. Could it be a family emergency? His heart skipped a beat at the thought. There had been no messages, no signs of distress. His phone, as always, was off.

After his trip earlier in the year, he received quite the shock when he received his cellular bill. From that time on, he only turned the device on in the morning before leaving for the day, and the same back at the camp at night. The rest of the time, he kept it turned off. When he powered it back up, there could be loads of communications from his family back home in Canada. He pulled his mobile from his inside vest pocket and turned it on. Nothing of an urgent nature, so he powered the phone off again. If not a family emergency, what?

"Mr. Michael," Ahmed said as he caught his breath. "You

need to come with me. Another find." He held Michael by both arms.

"What is it?"

"I don't know. But I've not seen anything like it in all my time working as a chauffeur for the archaeological teams."

"Okay. Just let me tell Miroslav before I leave the dig."

Ahmed nodded.

Michael took a few steps back towards the tomb they had excavated a few days prior. "Hey, Miroslav, I'm going with Ahmed for a few. He's got something he needs to show me."

There was no reply, but a hand shot up, giving him a thumbs up.

"Okay, I'm all yours," Michael said when he returned to where Ahmed stood.

"Come, come," he urged, jogging ahead. The desert wind whispered in their ears, smelling of sand and carrying the distant sound of a camel's call.

What was so vital that Ahmed was in such a state? He was wound tighter than a drum. Michael followed him but at a more sedate pace, maintaining the distance between himself and the man, thanks to his longer stride.

He had followed Ahmed to the perimeter of the dig site, a vast expanse of desert with its golden sand stretching as far as the eye could see. But there was still nothing. Ahmed's vehicle, which he used for his job, stood next to the fence.

Michael turned towards the gate. It had to be a mirage. And a beautiful one at that. He took a few more steps toward this figment of his imagination. It couldn't be. It was! Jennifer, his plus one at his sister's wedding, whom he'd fallen head over heels for, stood in the desert heat.

"Jennifer? How did you get here?" He broke into a run, his heart pounding. When he reached her, he scooped her up into the air, his joy too overwhelming to contain, and swung her around.

She shrieked, and he put her down on the desert sand again.

"I'm so sorry. I was stupid. I'm so sorry," Jennifer babbled, her voice trembling with fear and relief. "It scared me being with you after what happened to my family. I wanted nothing bad to happen to you, too."

"Hey, it's okay. You're safe now. We're safe. I understand why you did what you did." Michael embraced her tightly. He held her, filled with emotion, and whispered soothing words into her ear.

Her journey, which had transformed into a harrowing ordeal, took an unexpected turn. Jennifer found herself in the heart of the desert, enveloped in the arms of Michael, a man she had tried to distance herself from. The tragic events that befell her family led her to believe that getting too close to anyone would only invite history to repeat itself. Yet, here she was, in a moment of vulnerability and uncertainty, with the man she loved.

"You're going to burn to a crisp in this sun. Let me go tell Miroslav something has come up, and I'll be off the site for the foreseeable." He turned to Ahmed. "Will you take us into Cairo?"

Jennifer nodded in agreement, her voice too hoarse from the desert heat to speak.

"Of course."

"I'll be right back." Michael jogged off in the direction he came from a few moments earlier.

Jennifer followed him with her eyes until he disappeared around a stack of lumber, an odd sight in the barren desert. The lumber, which seemed out of place, must shore up walls and ceilings when the team worked below ground, adding to the mystery of their current situation. The last thing an archaeological team would need was a cave-in, but what could be so important that they would risk it?

After a few minutes, Michael returned, helped Jennifer into the backseat of Ahmed's vehicle, and then climbed in himself.

"Where would you like to go?" Ahmed asked.

Jennifer looked at her watch, urgency washing over her. In a short time, she'd had her phone turned on to connect to the shuttle bus's Wi-Fi, which had synced to the proper time. She realized she needed time alone to process the day's events, so she decided. "Could we go back to my hotel? I need to make myself presentable."

"Of course. Which one is it?"

"Tahrir Plaza Suites. I should be able to check in by the time we get back there."

Ahmed started the engine and turned the vehicle around. Minutes later, they travelled back along the road towards Saqqara and beyond into the lush green city. The vibrant and bustling city welcomed them back with open arms. The sound of car horns and chatter filled the air, contrasting the silence of the desert they had left behind. For Jennifer, the transition was more than a change of scenery. It was a return to safety, the familiar, and a place where she could process the day's events in peace.

Fifty

Tahrir Plaza Suites, Meret Basha, Ismailia, Qasr El Nil, Cairo Governorate, Cairo, Egypt

October 7, 2018

About an hour had passed when Ahmed pulled the vehicle to a stop in front of Jennifer's hotel.

"Goodbye, lovely lady. I hope to see you again soon," Ahmed's warm voice echoed as he shook her hand and gently kissed her cheek. "You take care now, Jennifer. Remember, if you need anything, I'm a phone call away."

While in this foreign country, she must adapt to the cultural norm of frequent handshakes and cheek kisses. These unfamiliar gestures made her heart race.

"And same to you, Mr. Michael."

Another handshake, but no kiss. Were kisses reserved for women?

"I might call you later tonight for a ride back to the camp," he said.

"But of course."

Michael escorted Jennifer into the hotel's lobby, a grand

space with marble floors and high ceilings. They walked towards the check-in desk, where a friendly hotel employee greeted them.

"I have a reservation," she said, "Jennifer Fox." She pulled the credit card she had used when she reserved her room out of her wallet and handed it across to the employee.

The front desk clerk typed her name into the computer. "Ah, yes. Your bags are already in your room."

"Thank you. I didn't expect that."

She handed Jennifer a plastic key in a paper sleeve across the counter along with her Mastercard.

"Elevators are just there."

Michael took her hand, and they walked to the lifts. They rode the next available one to the top floor.

Jennifer's single room, though small, was a haven for her. The soft scent of jasmine wafted in the air. The walls, a shade of deep red, almost like wine, seemed to radiate warmth. The soft furnishings, including a small round table and stool, were all white, inviting her to settle in and relax.

"You don't mind if I take a shower and get changed? I've been wearing these clothes since yesterday morning, Toronto time."

"Go ahead. While you do that, I'll take advantage of the hotel's Wi-Fi and check my emails."

Jennifer put her large suitcase on the bed and opened it. She found an outfit she hoped wouldn't be too hot for this weather: cream-coloured linen pull-on trousers and a matching knit top with narrow terra cotta-coloured horizontal stripes.

As Jennifer unpacked her case, she felt a surge of excitement. The online advice to adjust to the local time echoed in her mind. She was too wired to sleep but knew an early night was in order.

The last thing she did before going into the compact bathroom to shower was remove her cartouche pendant and opal necklace. She laid them on the small desk/dresser near her bed.

Jennifer stood under the rejuvenating spray of the shower.

Although she had brought some of her toiletries, shampoo, conditioner, and body wash dispensers were in the shower. She used those. If Jennifer liked them, she would continue taking advantage of them as a guest.

What Ahmed had told Michael to get him to leave a dig site and follow him didn't matter now. He had, and that was what was important. After she had ended her relationship with him, she didn't expect to see him again.

Showered, dried, and dressed, Jennifer applied her makeup. All she had to do was dry her hair and put her jewellery back on.

"Hey, you look fantastic. Not that you didn't before, but you don't have that ten-hour flight followed by a drive in and out of the desert look now," Michael said. His charming smile and warm eyes made her weak in the knees.

Jennifer walked to the small desk where she'd left her necklaces.

"Here, let me do that." He picked up the cartouche pendant.

She lifted her hair off the back of her neck, the soft strands tickling her skin, and held it out of the way to make it easier for him. Both necklaces were on in no time, and Michael had planted a soft kiss, warm and lingering, on her neck. It sent shivers, like a gentle breeze, up her back. There was still more explaining, but with luck, Michael would understand why she had done it. At that moment, she couldn't deny her growing attraction to him.

"Where do you want to go? What do you want to do?" Michael asked her.

"As long as I'm with you, that's all that matters."

"Why don't we find a place to eat. Perhaps one with a terrace and a view of the Nile. It would be a perfect start to your adventure in this ancient land," Michael suggested, his eyes sparkling with anticipation.

"Sounds wonderful."

"Grab your stuff, and we'll go."

Jennifer slipped her feet into her well-worn Birkenstock

sandals, grabbed her purse, put her room key and phone in it, then dropped the cross-body bag strap over her shoulder. She grabbed her cane last.

Michael held the door, and she stepped into the corridor.

Was she doing the right thing? The time spent with Michael in her comfort zone had been enjoyable. Even the time with him and the rest of his family at his sister's wedding in Percé had been a pleasant experience. That trip was a step out of her comfort zone, but everyone had made her feel welcome and part of the family. But now, she was halfway around the world in a country she knew little about other than the pyramids, the Sphinx, and King Tut. As she stood there, she couldn't help but question whether this adventure was worth the risk?

"We won't get any Nile views from here. We'll go to The Grill restaurant at the InterContinental Hotel. The restaurant offers a perfect view. It's on the third level and near the river, so we should get some stunning views even if we're not sitting outside. "

"How far?"

"Fifteen minutes. You okay with doing that?" Michael asked.

"Yes," she said.

Michael took her hand and led her past the museum. They crossed the bustling street at Wasim Hasan without trouble and continued in that direction. Upon reaching the end of the street, they turned left onto Nile Corniche. The hotel and restaurant were just a leisurely stroll away.

He led her here with little hassle. Today, the traffic was mild. They didn't have to endure the honks of frustrated motorists, which was always a pleasant surprise. As they walked, Michael couldn't help but steal glances at her, his heart swelling with affection. He was glad they could share this moment together, away from the chaos of their daily lives.

Fifty-One

The Grill Restaurant, Semiramis InterContinental, Cornich, El Nile, Cairo, Egypt

October 7, 2018

The restaurant hostess led them to a table on the terrace, which offered spectacular views. Watercraft, including river tour boats, plied the waterway.

"How long are you in Egypt?" Michael asked.

"I'm here until November. Figured I had to get a thirty-day eVisa, I might as well take advantage of it."

That was the best news he had heard in a long time. Would Jennifer want to spend some of it with him? He'd love to spend time with her. Michael had returned to Egypt to give her some space, as advised by his brothers. And you couldn't get much more space than that.

"When I saw you here, I couldn't believe my eyes. You were saying you were sorry and you were stupid. What was that about?" He reached across the table and held her hand.

"You probably won't believe this, but until I got your text saying the driver who broadsided our car was drunk, the night my family died, I didn't know. No one ever told me. I don't know why they didn't. Even Emma knew. But I was in a coma for some time after the accident, and by the time I came out of it, her family had moved to Vancouver. I hadn't seen her since then. And then, she and her husband walked into the restaurant one night. The same night, you sent me the text about the drunk driver. I showed it to her, and she confirmed what you had told me. But how did you find out?"

"I searched the net and found a newspaper article on the crash."

Jennifer paused and sipped water from the glass on the table.

"My grandmother never mentioned a single word. She even hid all the old family photos that used to be on the shelf in the closet in my parents' bedroom in the cedar chest. I found my mother's camera with film in it. I took it to a shop in St. Catharines to be processed. The pictures were from Kevin's birthday earlier that summer."

Michael rubbed his thumb across the back of Jennifer's hand, lost for words. How could her grandmother have kept information vital to her a secret? The same held true with moving the family pictures.

"Emma and her husband helped me get my passport so I could come and find you and apologize for being so stupid. I'm even prepared to grovel if that's what it takes. I've fallen in love with you, Michael Scott. That scares me because it's never happened before. A few teenage crushes before the accident, but nothing like this. I feared getting close to you and then something happening to you."

"There's no need to grovel. And you don't have to apologize, either. We're here together now. Let's make the most of your time in Egypt."

"But … you have to work," Jennifer said.

Michael's different approach took Jennifer aback. He seemed to take her as she was, with no need for her to seek his approval. How did she find someone like that who was so content with her?

"How did you find Ahmed?" Michael asked.

"That's a long story. It started on the shuttle bus. A passenger, a guy named Daniel Carter, told me to keep my phone off or turn off data and just use Wi-Fi. He is staying at the same hotel as me. I asked how I could get to Saqqara to find you. He called a friend of his who does the same thing as Ahmed. Can't think of his name now, but he took me to Saqqara, and then Ahmed took me over to where you were at Abusir."

"I know the guy you mean. Samir Hassan. He's an okay guy. When chauffeuring guys about, he sometimes stops in the dining tent for coffee."

"What's with all the touchy-feely stuff?"

"Takes a bit of getting used to, I agree, but Egyptians have a contrasting concept of personal space than we do."

"I'll say." Jennifer stifled a yawn, her eyelids heavy with exhaustion. The lack of sleep in the last forty-eight hours had caught up with her, her body yearning for a comfortable bed and a good night's sleep.

The hostess had left menus on the table, and their vibrant colours and exotic fonts caught Jennifer's eye. They hadn't perused them yet. Jennifer picked up the one at her place setting. The side that faced up was in Arabic, a beautiful script that she couldn't decipher. She turned it over and found the English side, the familiar words bringing her relief. "These prices are expensive," she said.

"Not really. You get used to them once you've been here awhile."

She recalled Daniel telling her that the shuttle bus fare worked out to about $15 US. Another thing she hadn't researched in the time she had before her eVisa came through.

"I feel utterly out of place, Michael," Jennifer confessed.

"Why do you say that?"

"I didn't know the exchange rate between Canadian dollars and Egyptian pounds, for starters. I used the ATM at the airport and only got one hundred pounds, thinking it would last me a few days. With that, I can't even pay for the cheapest item on the menu. And I'm likely wearing something that will get me arrested," Jennifer admitted, her voice trembling with anxiety.

"Jennifer, your clothes are fine. Egypt takes tourism seriously. They want people like you to come here. Look around. You're not dressed any differently than some other people here in the restaurant or out walking," Michael reassured her, his voice brimming with understanding and support.

That made her less uncomfortable, but she needed to be more relaxed. The tension in her shoulders and the unease in her voice were still palpable.

Michael, following Jennifer's lead, perused his menu. While their meals in the field had been satisfying, he couldn't help but yearn for something more traditional: a hearty dish of meat and potatoes. The choice was obvious: steak. But which one? The menu presented a tantalizing array of options: T-bone, Tomahawk, Tenderloin, Striploin, and Ribeye. Each cut promised a unique and mouthwatering culinary experience, heightening his anticipation for the coming meal.

"See anything you like?" he asked.

"Salmon, I think," Jennifer replied.

"Soup or starter?"

"No."

A few moments later, a waitstaff member took their orders.

"I'm going to have the grilled salmon," said Jennifer.

"Excellent. Sides and sauce?"

"Roasted mushrooms and the grilled asparagus. For sauce, I'll try your signature sauce. Can I get it on the side, too, please?"

The server nodded at Jennifer, as he jotted it down on his notepad. "Of course, Madam. The chef will prepare your order just as you like it," he assured her with a professional smile. "Yes. And you, sir?"

"I'll have the 300-gram dry-aged Ribeye, mashed potatoes, and roasted root vegetables. And I'll have the signature sauce as well."

"Anything to drink?"

"I'll have a pint of Stella if you have it."

"And you, Madam?"

"A virgin Bloody Mary."

"And what is that?"

"Bloody Mary but without the vodka."

"Ah, very well."

Jennifer took another sip of water.

"There's something I need to tell you," Michael said.

"What's that?"

"I've fallen in love with you, too. I asked my brothers what I should do after you said you couldn't see me anymore. They both told me to give you some space. So, I did. And now, here you are." Nervousness and hope filled Michael's voice as he revealed his feelings. Jennifer's reaction was surprise and joy, her eyes widened and a soft smile played on her lips.

"Your brothers are smart."

"You could have knocked me down with a feather when I saw you; that's how surprised I was. And that doesn't begin to consider how thrilled I was."

Jennifer smiled.

Her radiant smile lit up the room, and her captivating green eyes sparkled. Michael considered himself fortunate to be in the company of such a stunning woman. He could drink in her beauty forever.

Their drinks were served interrupting his rumination.

The view of Cairo and the Nile was breathtaking. Jennifer had seen nothing like it. The city, a vibrant mix of ancient and modern, with towering skyscrapers and centuries-old monuments standing side by side.

"What's that tall, thin building over there?" Jennifer asked. She had always dreamed of travelling and exploring different places; this trip to Egypt was her first big adventure.

"I'm not sure. When they bring our meals out, I'll ask."

"After we eat, can we walk by the river?"

"We can do anything you want," Michael said.

How did she get so lucky? She had a man who was willing

to do anything for her, a man who loved her. With his dark hair and warm brown eyes, Michael was the epitome of kindness and generosity.

Michael picked up his beer. "Cheers," he said.

Jennifer lifted hers, and they clinked glasses. "Cheers. To us. To Egypt."

"Most definitely."

A few minutes later, the server placed their meals on the table. The tantalizing aromas from the different dishes, the exotic spices and fresh ingredients, tickled Jennifer's nose and sent her tastebuds into overdrive. The presentation was as appealing as the scents, with vibrant colours and artistic arrangements. The sound of the busy restaurant and the sight of the bustling waitstaff added to the atmosphere.

"Before you go," Jennifer said, her eyes fixed on the towering structure, "What's that magnificent, slender building over there?" Filled with curiosity, she pointed towards the structure.

"Ah, that's Cairo Tower."

"It's beautiful. Can you go up?"

"Yes. E£70 per non-Egyptian person."

"Isn't that high?"

"You'll have to forgive my friend. She's just arrived, and this is her first time in your country."

Jennifer sighed, filled with gratitude and frustration. Michael meant well by coming to her aid, but she didn't like how it made her look. She was used to being independent and self-sufficient and didn't want to be seen as someone who always needed help. Typical dumb blonde, she thought, her self-deprecating humour masking her discomfort.

"Ah. I see. Well, that would be about $1.50 US in your money."

"That's not expensive at all." She was used to converting the exchange rate on American money at the restaurant. That happened at least once on every shift, especially in the summer when it was full-on tourist season. "Thank you." Maybe she should have asked for the US equivalent when she asked money questions. But, she didn't like being mistaken for an

American, either.

She focused on her plate and cut off a piece of salmon. It tasted delicious. Next, Jennifer tried the roasted mushrooms and, finally, the grilled asparagus. As requested, the sauce was on the side. She dipped a piece of mushroom into it and tried it. It was scrumptious. She poured some on her salmon.

"How's your food?" Michael asked.

"To die for, And that sauce," Jennifer said. "How's your steak?"

"Melt in your mouth tender. I've been dying for meat and potatoes for a long time. Sure, they feed us well on site, but it's more traditional Egyptian fare."

They continued their meal in silence for a few moments. Jennifer hadn't eaten anything this fancy before. Sometimes, she ate at the Outback. Most of her meals were salads or Mr. Noodles, toast and jam, soups, and grilled cheese sandwiches in the colder weather. Since the accident, it was only her and her grandmother. Dining at a restaurant was unheard of in the older woman's eyes, so eating out was a rare treat.

"Did you want to go to the top of Cairo Tower?" Michael asked.

"I wouldn't mind. It would be breathtaking as the sun sets and the city lights come on," Jennifer said, anticipation and romance in her voice.

"We can go tomorrow night. I'll ask Ahmed if he'll drive us."

"Won't he be working elsewhere? Like back and forth from the airport to the various dig sites?"

"I'll ask him tonight when I call him to come and take me back."

They finished their meals and drinks. Michael insisted he paid, a gesture that Jennifer found both endearing and unnecessary. She argued he shouldn't have to foot the entire bill; she would pay for herself, but, he won the argument. They hadn't been dating long and had only reunited, but since the beginning a deep bond developed along with a strong sense of mutual respect and support.

As they strolled down the street, their hands intertwined, a perceptible sense of anticipation filled the air. A towering steel wall blocked the majestic Nile, but they pressed on, their curiosity piqued. Farther along, a gap appeared, and they stepped through, reaching the railing.

They found themselves at the Nile Taxi stand, where the rhythmic lapping of the water against the riverbank provided a soothing soundtrack. The occasional birdsong added more of nature's melody to the scene. The air smelled of the river, earthy and fresh. Sailboats, their white sails billowing in the gentle breeze, glided across the water.

It was a beautiful scene. Jennifer pulled her phone out, powered it on, double-checked that she still had data turned off, and snapped pictures. Her second wind, which had perked her up before they ate, had vanished. She yawned, exhausted but content, her heart full from the day's adventures.

"Guess I should be taking you back to the hotel," Michael said.

"I have been awake for a long time."

"Early night tonight, and you'll be right as rain tomorrow."

"I hope you're right."

Michael guided her across the street, their steps in sync. As they made their way back towards the hotel, Jennifer found solace in leaning her head on his shoulder. She'd consider herself blessed if the rest of her life was filled with such simple yet profound moments.

Except for her weariness, they arrived back too soon. Michael kissed her goodnight at the hotel's entrance.

"See you tomorrow, and we'll go up Cairo Tower in the evening. Watch the sun go down."

"That sounds ever so romantic," Jennifer replied with anticipation and nervousness.

Once Jennifer was inside the hotel, Michael called Ahmed and asked the man to pick him up and take him back to Abusir.

While he waited, he replayed the time he spent with Jennifer on what could be construed as his turf. Except for her tiredness, things had gone well in his mind. Well, not one hundred percent. She gave him the stink eye at the restaurant when he told their server she had arrived earlier that day, and it was her first trip to Egypt. He admitted he could have phrased it better. The way he did it came out derogatory. That was the last thing he meant to do, and he regretted it.

Michael returned his phone to his pocket and walked towards the area where Ahmed would arrive in his vehicle. He should have called the man earlier. No, it was better this way. Had he phoned while he and Jennifer were standing by the Nile Taxi, she might have gotten the wrong impression that Michael didn't want to be with her. He might have to wait longer, but it was better this way.

While he waited for Ahmed to arrive, Michael considered options for tomorrow before going up the Cairo Tower. The possibilities excited him. Would Jennifer want to visit Khan el-Khalili? He could take her to the bespoke jewellery shop where he bought her cartouche pendant and opal necklace. There was also the museum across from her hotel. She might be interested in it. He no longer had any time to wait. Ahmed pulled in.

"Mr. Michael, did you and your lovely lady friend have a good day today?"

"Yes, we most certainly did," Michael said as he eased himself into the front passenger seat, a feat more straightforward than getting in and out of her Smart car. "She did rather well considering how long she's been awake. I don't think she slept on the plane; it was her first flight."

"Perhaps not. Will you require my services tomorrow? I have an airport pickup first thing in the morning. I'm not sure which camp I'll be going to. It could be Saqqara, or it could be Abusir."

"After you drop your passenger, is fine. I doubt Jennifer will be awake early in the morning. I was thinking of taking her to Khan el-Khalili, but I'm afraid it might be too much of a walk for her. I'm concerned about her comfort and don't want to push her too much."

"Ah, I noticed she uses a stick to walk. Not to worry, I can drive you both there."

Ahmed eased the vehicle into traffic, and soon, they were

heading out of the city toward the camp at Abusir.

Because of the heavy traffic leaving Cairo, it took about half an hour longer than usual to return to the camp.

"Thanks, Ahmed. I'll see you bright and early tomorrow," Michael said as he exited the man's four-by-four.

Lights illuminated the dining tent, so someone remained in there. After Michael had eaten at The Grill, he wasn't hungry, but with luck, Miroslav would be inside reviewing the day's progress. After they found Kaires' tomb and the statue of the man, albeit broken in half because of raiders in the past, they had discovered nothing of significance. Besides, it gave Michael a chance to talk to him. They had worked at this site without a day to themselves. At least until today, for Michael, anyway.

Miroslav stood leaning over a map with his hands on the table. He looked up and grunted when Michael came in.

"Any coffee left?" he asked.

The Czech pointed to the urn. Michael poured himself a mug. It was strong enough to peel the enamel off his teeth. He came back and perused the map in which Miroslav was so engrossed.

"I take it nothing more in the area where we found Kaires' tomb?"

"No. I'm not sure where we need to look next. The data all points to locations already covered."

"Maybe you've not gone deep enough? What if there's another tomb below this one?"

"Hmm, could be."

"I thought I should tell you more about why I'd be away from the site for the foreseeable. My Canadian girlfriend showed up yesterday to surprise me. I tell you, she was the last person I expected to see. We broke up not long before I came to Abusir. We have some catching up and a few things to set right. Once that's done, I'll be back if you still need me." The words heavy with Michael's internal conflict, torn between his desire to be with his girlfriend and his commitment to the archaeological site that had become his life.

"This woman, she means much to you?"

"Yes, she does."

"Then be with her. Make her and yourself happy."

"Thanks, Miroslav," Michael said as he walked away from the table to dump his coffee and started towards his sleeping quarters.

"Wait, one moment. Sit."

Michael sat at the table across from the Czech. Why did he want to talk with him at this time of the night?

"You realize there could be implications with your leaving. I want to see you happy, but I also want you to see both sides. Your departure could have far-reaching effects, not just on your reputation, but on your future opportunities in this field." Miroslav's voice carried a weight of concern, his words a cautionary tale for Michael.

"Okay."

"It could damage your reputation. You're not leaving under contentious circumstances, but others could question your reliability."

"I get that."

"It could become difficult for you to get positive references and recommendations for future projects. Your career advancement might suffer. And the authorities might never invite you back to work on these sites."

"You've said what you had to say. Now listen to my side. I only took two days to myself on my first dig when I came to Saqqara. I had more available to me but didn't use them, too invested in what we might find, especially after discovering the mummification workshop. All I'm asking is a few days to spend with her. Maybe using the term *foreseeable* wasn't the proper way to put it." Michael made air quotes around the word. "She's returning to Canada on November 7 when her Visa expires. I might spend more evenings offsite, but I'm certain I can work a schedule out that will be agreeable to everyone."

"Very well. You're a good man. You have great instincts. You're a valuable member of this team."

Michael stood and shook the man's hand. They had

reached a compromise, a delicate balance between personal and professional commitments, a resolution that both men could live with. That was all he could ask for.

In his bunk, Michael pulled out his laptop and started writing in his journal.

Jennifer's unexpected presence at our dig site near Abusir was a pleasant surprise. The sight of her filled me with a mix of emotions — joy, surprise, and a hint of longing. We spent a delightful day together, enjoying a delicious meal at The Grill and taking a leisurely walk by the Nile. As I walked her back to her hotel, a sense of contentment settled in, but a deep longing accompanied it for more of these moments with her.

Jennifer, in a vulnerable moment, shared her fears and concerns with me. She was worried about not being enough, about not meeting my expectations. She repeatedly apologized for what she perceived as her shortcomings. I had sought advice from my brothers. They advised me to give her space, so I did, leading me to my current state.

Tomorrow, we're embarking on an adventure to Cairo Tower to witness the sunset from the top. I'm filled with anticipation, eager to arrive early to savour the view of the desert and the pyramids before darkness sets in. Our plans before that are a mystery, but I'm confident we'll stumble upon something wonderful that will add to the beautiful memories we're creating.

He saved the document, shut down the computer, and stowed it in his backpack again. As Michael turned out the small lamp on the locker beside his bed, he couldn't help but reflect on the day's events. The unexpected encounter with Jennifer filled him with surprise and joy; their enjoyable time together left him longing for more, and the mixed emotions that followed made him feel both content and uncertain. He settled into sleep, his mind still filled with thoughts of her.

Fifty-Two

Abusir, Badrshein, Giza Governorate, Egypt

October 8, 2018

Michael woke refreshed and ready to meet the day at the entrance, where Ahmed had agreed to be. Although rudimentary, showers had been installed in the camp. They reminded him of the ones in the TV program *M*A*S*H*. Before he strolled to the dining tent, he showered and dressed.

Most flights usually got into Cairo around seven o'clock. Depending on how long it took to clear Customs and collect bags, that could take another hour. Ahmed had an airport pick-up this morning, so Michael didn't expect him to reach the camp until at least nine o'clock. He turned on his phone and sent a message to Jennifer.

Looking forward to our meeting at 10:00. It's great to have Ahmed with us for the day. Let's meet by the front door of the hotel. We can discuss our plans. x

After ensuring his data remained off, Michael left his phone turned on while he waited for a response. He tucked his phone into a vest pocket and went for breakfast. The cook had scrambled eggs, loaves of bread, cheese, yogurt, fresh fruit, olives, juice, and tea and coffee this morning.

Michael selected from everything but the olives. They weren't breakfast food in his mind. He poured himself a coffee and found a place to sit. The meals onsite were hearty. If you walked away hungry, it was your own fault. There was always water, juice, and coffee available, although breakfast was the only time of day, Michael opted for coffee. He was finishing his eggs when the reply came in.

OK. See you then at the front door of my hotel at 10:00. x

Fifty-Three

October 8, 2018

Jennifer sat her phone on the desk/dresser by her bed. The text was from him, the man she loved and who loved her back. He had signed his message with an *x*, a sign of affection. Despite her attempt to drive him away, he still loved her.

In her characteristic fashion, Jennifer embarked on her morning routine. She showered, applied her makeup, and then decided what to wear. It wouldn't be the clothes she had on yesterday. They were not dirty, but the two days in a row thing bothered her. She would wear those items again, but not today.

Jennifer pulled grey leggings out of the suitcase. That colour always looked good with pink. Next, she pulled out a pale pink, sleeveless, V-neck tunic that was longer at the back than the front. Jennifer should have taken it out sooner because of the wrinkles in it. She put it on a hanger, hung it on the shower curtain bar, and turned the shower on hot. A few minutes hanging there would steam the wrinkles out of it.

As her top hung in the bathroom, Jennifer adorned herself

with her cartouche pendant and opal necklace, her mind buzzing with anticipation. The weather concerned her. Where would Michael take her today? They couldn't do everything at once. They scheduled the tower for later, so they would be at the top at sunset. She looked forward to that. Would she need something warmer to wear later in the evening? Did the temperature drop significantly once the sun went down? Should she take a light sweater with her now? Or would they have time to return before going to the tower?

She had no more time to worry about it now. It was almost nine-thirty, and Michael had said to meet at the entrance around ten. Her top was less wrinkled than before, so she slipped it on, followed by a cursory glance in the mirror to ensure she looked presentable. Rather than take the chance of not getting back here before the tower, Jennifer took a white, lightweight, mid-thigh cardigan out of her suitcase. She tied the sleeves around her neck. The last thing she did before she left her room was pick up her keycard and phone. She used her cellphone as a camera, but if her smartwatch got out of Bluetooth range, it was difficult to pair the two devices.

A continental breakfast was served in the hotel's dining room. Jennifer, brimming with anticipation for her date with Michael, selected yogurt and honey. It was something she could eat before he came to get her. She sat at an empty table, her heart fluttering with excitement, and ate her light meal.

Jennifer stood when she saw Ahmed's sleek black vehicle pull into the grand entrance of the opulent hotel. No signs showed prices, so the breakfast had to be included in her room price. When Michael walked through the front doors, she was entering the lavish lobby adorned with sparkling crystal chandeliers, a sight that took her breath away.

"You look amazing," he said.

"Thank you. I stopped for a bite to eat. I was starving." Jennifer said.

"We can't have that." Michael put his arm around her shoulders, and they walked out the door and into the waiting four-by-four.

"Where are we going?" Jennifer asked, her curiosity piqued as she fastened her seatbelt, eager to discover the next part of their adventure.

"I thought we'd start with a trip to Khan el-Khalili."

"That's the market where you bought these pieces, right?" Jennifer fingered her necklaces.

"Yes. I think you'll like it. There's a lot more than just jewellery there."

Ahmed nodded, and they made their way.

Fifty-Four

Khan el-Khalili, El-Gamaleya, El Gamaliya, Cairo Governorate, Cairo, Egypt

October 8, 2018

Ahmed stopped the four-by-four near one of the many entrances to the market.

"You want at least two hours here?" he asked.

"At least. Thanks," Michael said.

"Why don't you let me know when you're ready to be picked up?"

"Sounds great."

Jennifer stood stock still, her mouth gaping at the sight before her. Michael held her hand, and they walked in. The sounds and smells overwhelmed her. Even at peak tourist season, there were never this many people in Niagara Falls.

Spices and incense mingled with brewed coffee and the aroma of genuine leather. They entered on a wide street, but off to the sides narrow passages overflowed with colourful displays.

Michael guided her down one cramped alley. Ahead of

them, throngs of people wove their way through the streets. The hum of customers haggling with vendors was an almost steady drone, punctuated occasionally by louder noises.

Stalls and shops lined the alley. Woven textiles, brassware gleaming in the sunlight, sparkling jewellery caught her attention, and fragrant perfume aromas wafted in the air.

They paused in front of one of the jewellery stores.

"Do you want to go in?" Michael asked.

"Is this where you bought these?" She brought her hand to the pendant and necklace.

"Yes."

"Why not?"

Michael held the door for Jennifer to enter the cramped store.

The shopkeeper remembered him right away. "You've come back. And who is this lovely lady with you?"

"This is Jennifer."

She felt the heat in her cheeks as she blushed.

"I am Amira Farouk. I see you're wearing two of our bespoke pieces."

"Yes. Michael bought them for me when he was in your country back in July." At least this woman remained professional and didn't come out and try to kiss her on the cheek.

There was so much to see in this one tiny establishment. Gold and silver necklaces, earrings, cartouche pendants in varying sizes and complexity, and bracelets. Where to look first? The array of pieces was spectacular.

While Michael remained occupied, Jennifer continued inspecting the jewellery available. She loved many of the items, but could she justify the price? She turned in another direction. Blingy dog accessories?

"Excuse me," she asked. "Are these animal collars?"

"Yes. You are interested?"

"Maybe. I have a pug back home. When I take him out, he's in a harness, so I'm unsure what size he will need."

"I would suggest going bigger. You can always punch another hole in the strap if it's too big."

244

Jennifer picked one up and held it around her neck. It would fasten. Surely, Zeus's neck wasn't that big around.

"Could I get it personalized?"

"Let me see if I have a plain leather one. We can go from there."

The woman went into the back and returned with an unadorned leather collar the same length as the one Jennifer picked out.

"What would you like on it?"

"Could I get his name in hieroglyphics?"

"Yes. And your dog's name is?"

"Zeus."

"A good, strong name. Anything else?"

"I don't know. What sort of charms could I get for it?"

Jennifer realized how Michael got swept up in the atmosphere here in the jewellery shop when he bought her the pieces she wore.

Amira bent down and picked up a tray of various charms. "We have the Ankh Symbol, which is this one here." She pointed to a cross with a loop at the top. "It's the symbol which represents life and immortality. This next one is the Eye of Horus or the All-Seeing Eye. It symbolizes protection, health, and healing in ancient Egyptian mythology. You can see it looks like an eye."

"I like these. What are these others?" Jennifer asked, pointing to them.

"This next one is the Scarab Beetle. The ancient Egyptians revered this insect as a symbol of rebirth, transformation, and protection. We have the Cartouche like you're wearing. Male or female dog?"

"Male."

"Then you wouldn't want this one. It's a Bastet Charm. In ancient Egyptian mythology, she was the goddess of home, fertility, and domesticity."

"You're right. Not that one."

"This last one is the Lotus Flower, a sign of purity, rebirth, and enlightenment in ancient Egyptian culture."

"Could I get his name in hieroglyphics here, centred across

from the buckle. Then the eye, facing towards his name. Like a left eye and a right eye. Then a scarab beetle, one on each side of the eyes, and finally lotus flowers, again on each side."

"Yes. Do you want the eye like this with the white and green?"

"Please."

"Eye of Ra. Eye of Horus," she noted. "It's the same thing; just one is the right eye, and the other is the left. If you'd like to wait, I can see if our silversmith can do this now."

"It's up to you," Michael said.

"Let's."

It took about an hour to add all the embellishments to the collar. Jennifer also purchased a silver cartouche keyring with a dark background. It had symbols, but since she didn't know if she was keeping it for herself or giving it away, she decided against having it personalized. If she gave it away, the recipient would be pleased to receive it.

Jennifer promised herself she wouldn't freak out at prices in Egyptian pounds. They would make much more sense when she looked at her Mastercard statement at home. She paid the woman, and she and Michael left the store.

While Jennifer explored the store's offerings, the rings in the glass display case drew Michael's attention. They were a sight to behold — some were reminiscent of wedding sets, with engagement rings and matching wedding bands. The gold bands glimmered under the store's warm lights, and the diamonds sparkled like stars in the night sky. Others were more traditional, boasting yellow gold or white gold bands adorned with sparkling diamonds. Yet, none of them spoke to him.

The flower with the white stone in the centre captivated Michael. It wasn't gold; it looked like sterling silver. The band, curved fit around the flower, appeared to have small pieces of the same stone mounted on it.

Michael motioned to Mrs. Farouk. He watched Jennifer, ensuring she remained preoccupied with the store's offerings. "What can you tell me about these?" Michael asked, his interest piqued as he pointed to the particular set.

The shopkeeper unlocked the case and brought out the one Michael had shown interest in. "Ah, the lotus flower and moonstone. A charming collection. The lotus flower symbolizes purity. They rise from the mud unstained and return to that murkiness each evening. The flowers open in the early morning, daybreak, symbolizing strength, resilience, and rebirth."

The delicate beauty of the bloom and its symbolism resonated with him, stirring a sense of hope and renewal within him. "I see."

"And the moonstone. It's the stone for new beginnings. It's also the stone of strength and inner growth. It soothes stress, stabilizes emotions, and protects travellers. Are you possibly thinking of proposing marriage to your young lady friend? If so, this would be the perfect set."

"Thank you for your help, Mrs. Farouk. I believe this set will be perfect for my intentions," Michael said. Excitement and nervousness filled him as he handed over his credit card to pay for the jewellery.

Michael enjoyed seeing Jennifer's reactions to what she saw outside the shop. She pointed to the ornate wooden balconies and latticework windows that overlooked where they walked. These architectural features reflected the intricate craftsmanship and the desire for privacy. They stopped farther up the lane where street performers entertained the gathered crowd. They danced and played traditional music, a vibrant display of the region's rich cultural heritage.

Michael, who had previously visited this market, led Jennifer down a quiet street. As they turned a corner, a hidden oasis was unveiled — tea houses and courtyards adorned with mosaic tiles. The sweet scent of jasmine filled the air along with the sound of water trickling from fountains. In this secret haven, stood a small eatery serving traditional food. The tantalizing aromas of the various dishes wafted towards them, heightening their anticipation

"You want to get something to eat that we can take?" he asked.

"I'm not sure what they have or if I'll like it," Jennifer said.

"How about Shawarma? It's just meat, sauces, tomatoes, lettuce and pickles wrapped in pita bread," he suggested.

"That sounds good," Jennifer agreed.

Michael ordered two Shawarma to go, and in no time, they were ready. "Let's go back to the courtyard. It's quiet, and we'll be able to eat without being jostled and end up wearing our food."

"I can't get over this place," she exclaimed before taking a bite. "Oh my God, it's delicious. Thank you for bringing me here. I love it."

At that moment, Michael realized that their shared experiences and the memories they were creating were the veritable treasures of their journey.

"I'm glad you're enjoying yourself. Maybe tomorrow, we'll do something a little less adventurous? I've never been to the museum by your hotel, but it's something I've always wanted to see."

"I've seen it in the brochures in my room. It looks interesting."

"Unless there's someplace else you'd rather go."

"As long as we're together, that's all that matters," Jennifer said. They had come a long way since they first met, and this journey solidified their growing bond.

They finished their Shawarma and returned to the hustle and bustle of the primary thoroughfare. This break from the crowds came at a welcome time. Although Jennifer wouldn't admit it, she was tiring. The sun, high in the sky, cast a warm glow over the bustling market. He didn't want her to overdo it and cause herself pain.

A short distance down the busy street, the domed rooftop and minarets of a mosque on the bazaar's borders pierced the sky.

"Seen enough for one day?"

"I'd like to pick something up for Sadie since she was good enough to look after Zeus for me."

"What were you thinking?"

"I'm not sure, but I'll know when I see it."

As they passed a stall with brassware, Jennifer's eyes lit up. Besides the gleaming brass, they had colourful glass lamps with the ankh symbol on top. The vendor, a friendly man with a toothy smile, approached and shook their hands.

Michael led her farther into the market stall. He loved how she got excited about what she saw here in Khan el-Khalili.

"Now to decide which one. Both the green and the blue would suit Sadie's decor. But I like this orange one."

"All hand-blown glass," the vendor said in Arabic.

"What did he say?" Jennifer asked.

"I'm not sure," said Michael. He turned to the vendor and asked again, using body language and gestures.

The man responded by blowing, then picked up a picture of the glass studio and showed it to them.

"Hand-blown in his studio. I get it now," Jennifer said.

That meant it would be heavy but delicate. It would be a miracle if it survived a flight to Canada with the airports at each end. Michael sensed Jennifer's worry about the lamp.

"I'd be taking it back to Canada with me," said Jennifer. "I don't want it to get broken. Can you wrap it up well?" She showed wrapping as if she were playing a game of charades.

"Naeam." He picked up the lamp with the orange globe.

"Please," Jennifer said, nodding.

The man wrapped it in tissue paper, bubble wrap, plastic film, and a cardboard box. If it didn't survive all that wrapping, it never would.

"I'll pay you the full price because of all the extra wrapping you did." Jennifer handed him her credit card.

He shook his head, then showed her an Egyptian pound note.

"Cash only."

"I saw an ATM on one of the corners in here. You stay here; I'll go get cash," Michael offered and dashed off. Luckily, the machine was at the end of the block. He returned within minutes and paid for the lamp.

"I'll get the money and repay you," Jennifer said. "I should have been the one who went to the bank machine."

"We can worry about that another time before your visa runs out and you return to Canada," Michael said, sadness tinging his voice. He didn't want to think about the end of their journey, about saying goodbye to Jennifer. But for now, they had this moment, this shared adventure, and that was enough.

Returning to Canada, a profound sense of melancholy overcame Jennifer. She realized that her thirty-day journey only provided her a fleeting glimpse into the vastness of Egypt. She had only touched the surface of two archaeological sites, caught a brief glimpse of the Nile from a restaurant, and taken a leisurely stroll after dinner. The thought of leaving this rich cultural tapestry behind was bittersweet.

Later in the day, the tower beckoned. Jennifer had learned at the restaurant that it was possible to ascend to the top, and she added it to her itinerary for her time with Michael. The prospect of standing at the pinnacle, witnessing the sunset paint the sky in hues of gold, orange, and red, filled her with anticipation and romance.

"Can we see more of this before we leave? Sitting down gave me the break I needed to keep going."

"If you're sure. What we've seen so far is pretty much everything there is. Just more vendors selling similar products."

"I'm still eager to see more," Jennifer stated, her curiosity unabated. "There's so much to explore and learn here," she added, her eyes shining with excitement.

"Okay." Michael took her hand, and the two continued down the street.

The pungent aromas of exotic spices tickled Jennifer's nose. The source of the tantalizing smell was on her right. She walked to the vibrant stall with an attractive display of spices and inhaled deeply, savouring the contrasting scents. These were fresher, more potent than the ones she bought back home. Nearby, a woman was grinding something using a traditional mortar and pestle. The rhythmic sound of her work filled the air, demonstrating the freshness of the spices.

"It smells so good," Jennifer said, inhaling the scent.

The vendor nodded.

Jennifer and Michael ventured deeper into the vibrant Khan el-Khalili. Various goods — carpets, luggage, clothing, and more spilled from stalls and storefronts. Even the bustling St. Lawrence Market in Toronto couldn't match this lively scene.

"It's well over two hours since Ahmed dropped us off. We should head back there so we don't keep him waiting."

"I thought he said to let him know when we wanted to be picked up."

"You're right. I'll give Ahmed a call now, and we'll head back to where he dropped us off." Michael punched Ahmed's number into his phone. "Ahmed. Michael. We're ready to be picked up now." There was a pause. Presumably, the other man was speaking. "Same place. Okay, see you soon." He disconnected the call and returned his phone to his inside vest pocket.

They wound their way back through the crowded streets to where Ahmed had left them earlier in the day. They arrived at about the same time.

"Where would you like to go next?" Ahmed asked as they climbed into his car.

"It's too early to go to the tower. I know we want to eat and be at the top before it gets dark, but I think it's too soon," said Jennifer.

"Yeah, maybe," Michael said.

"If you aren't too tired from all your walking in the bazaar, can I suggest a walk along the Nile?"

"We tried that yesterday, but there was a barrier between the road and the water."

"What if I drop you near the Cairo Tower. There are many places there to walk around. It's on an island in the middle of the Nile, so you'll get to see the city from a different perspective," Ahmed suggested. "Then, when you are ready to go up the tower, you're not too far away."

Jennifer and Michael considered the suggestion, imagining the unique view of the city from the island, and agreed that it was a good plan.

"I like that idea," Jennifer said.
"That's what I shall do then."

Fifty-Five

Gezira Island, Zamalek, Cairo Governorate, Cairo, Egypt

October 8, 2018

Ahmed parked his vehicle in front of the Opera subway station. "It's not a long walk to the tower from here, plus there is a lovely park just there," he said, pointing. "I think you'll like it. Enjoy your evening."

"Thank you," Jennifer said, climbing from the back seat. "Oh, Ahmed, can I leave this package in your car? I don't want to drag it around and risk leaving it behind somewhere."

Ahmed nodded. "That's fine. Off you go now and enjoy."

Holding hands, they walked into the park, a well-known spot for locals and tourists alike. It was a lush oasis amidst the bustling city. Towering palm trees, various other trees and shrubs, and meticulously maintained flowerbeds adorned the landscape. Inside the park, the city's cacophony was muted, replaced by the gentle rustling of leaves and the occasional chirping of birds. The air was crisp and clean, a contrast to the exhaust-filled streets. "If you're tired, we can find a bench and sit for a while," Michael suggested, concerned.

"I'm fine for now." Jennifer leaned over a flowering shrub to take in the delicate aroma of the blossoms. It smelled of vanilla and something citrus. She felt a sense of calm and contentment, enjoying the moment with Michael by her side.

The two strolled through the Al Horreya Garden towards the bridge they had crossed onto the island.

When they reached the roundabout, Jennifer said, "Is it safe to cross here?"

"I don't know. Guess we'll find out."

As they drew closer, Jennifer spotted a police officer directing traffic. "We should be okay. I'm certain he'll stop the cars for us."

"We can hope," said Michael.

In moments, the approaching traffic came to a halt, and they crossed the middle of the multi-lane road unharmed. The reassuring presence of the cop ensured their safety, stopping the traffic coming around the roundabout from the other direction so they could cross there. After that, they were on their own. But at least he had guided them across the busiest section, a testament to the safety measures in place.

"I'll get Ahmed to uplift us closer to the tower. I don't fancy our chances here after dark," Michael said.

"Once was enough for me."

"Some roundabouts back in the UK have traffic lights to control the flow. They could use them here."

"I saw some when we were near the market, but they weren't working. But this is the first time I've seen a police officer directing traffic anywhere," said Jennifer, curious, yet fascinated by the city's unique traffic management system.

"Me, too. To be honest, I never noticed before."

"I can't wait for dinner. I hope I don't get too dizzy in the restaurant," Jennifer said, her anticipation clear.

"It doesn't move quickly. From what I've heard, it takes almost two hours to complete a rotation."

"That's good."

The two continued until they reached the plaza where the tower was located. The tower, a hallmark of the city's rich history and architectural beauty, was a sight they had been looking forward to seeing. They stood there, taking in the view, their anticipation turning into awe.

Fifty-Six

Cairo Tower, Gezira Island, Zamalek, Cairo Governorate, Cairo, Egypt

October 8, 2018

"Do you want to eat first or go to the observation deck?" Michael asked.

"What time is it?"

He checked his watch. "Just after five."

"Let's go up first," said Jennifer. "After my Shawarma earlier, I'm not all that hungry."

Michael guided her towards the main entrance and paid for their passage.

"I could have paid for my ticket," Jennifer protested.

"It's not that much. Besides, my treat."

Though distant and small, the pyramids sparked a profound curiosity in Jennifer. Their grandeur, even from a height, verified their magnificence. The Sphinx, too, held a mysterious allure, its enigmatic smile beckoning her to unravel its secrets.

Sailboats glided along the Nile, their sails catching the last rays of sunlight. Exotic spices wafted through the air, mingling with the sounds of car horns and street vendors. The mystery of who sold what or why someone sang captivated her.

As the sun dipped lower, it turned a vibrant orange, illuminating the sky in its glow. By now, she was glad she'd brought her lightweight, long cardigan. She untied the sleeves and slipped into it.

"You cold?" Michael asked.

"Got a chill. I'm fine."

Michael's arm around her waist brought an instant warmth, enveloping her in a comforting cocoon. The heat radiating from his body gave her a profound sense of security in his embrace.

At the tower's apex, the hustle and bustle of Cairo below seemed light-years away. Yet it was below her. What would the ancient Egyptians think of the modern country? Would they embrace the change? Jennifer pondered these questions, her mind filled with awe and curiosity.

As Michael ascended Cairo Tower for the first time, a surge of anticipation and wonder filled him. He couldn't help but imagine the breathtaking sights that awaited him at such a height, perhaps things he had only glimpsed from the ground at desert dig sites. The tower, representative of modernity and progress, stood tall amidst the ancient wonders of Egypt.

When they reached the top, he let Jennifer leave the elevator ahead of him. Stepping onto the observation deck, left him awestruck. He took a few minutes to get his bearings, then guided Jennifer to a location facing south.

"Look down there. It's the pyramids on the Giza plateau. And over there is the Sphinx," he said, his voice filled with awe.

Jennifer's eyes widened, her breath caught in her throat as she took in the breathtaking sight. "Wow," she said.

He had his arm around her, the warmth of her body against his, a comforting familiarity. Her deep intake of breath, a sign of her awe and wonder.

"I can't believe all I could say about this view was wow,"

she said with disbelief.

Below them, the city sprawled in a captivating contrast of modern skyscrapers, ancient mosques, and bustling markets. The symphony of car horns and the distant Arabic chants from a nearby mosque filled the air. Plus the aroma of exotic spices wafting from the markets, added to the atmosphere. The view was a masterpiece, a canvas of life and history, a sight described as awe-inspiring.

By now, the light levels were lower, so Michael guided Jennifer to a better location to watch the sunset.

Minute by minute, the sky transformed into a kaleidoscope of fiery oranges, pinks and deep purples. The skyline cast long, dramatic shadows across the landscape. The twinkling lights of Cairo below flickered to life, painting the cityscape in a tapestry of light and shadow. The Nile shimmered in the fading light, a ribbon of silver amidst the city's vibrant hues. The romantic side of him filled him with joy, a feeling that was mirrored in Jennifer's eyes.

The woman he loved looked radiant in the changing light. Without removing his arm from around her waist, he pulled a small box from his vest pocket, opened it, and got down on one knee. When he saw the ring, he knew it was perfect for Jennifer. The lotus flower symbolized rebirth, purity, and enlightenment, and represented Jennifer's journey of moving on from the accident. The iridescent moonstone, with its sense of mystery and magic, aligned with the spiritual themes of the lotus. Mrs. Farouk at the market had explained this to him when he purchased it. He planned to share this significance with Jennifer later. At that moment, the romantic side of him filled him with overwhelming joy and love.

"Jennifer Fox, will you do me the honour of becoming my wife?"

She turned to him. Her hands flew to her mouth. Was this happening? Was she dreaming? Would she wake up at home in Niagara Falls? Her Egyptian trip had never taken place?

"I know it's not a diamond, but ..."

"Oh, Michael, I don't know what to say."

By now, a crowd had gathered around them. Some snapped pictures with their phones.

Someone yelled, "Say yes."

"Yes. Yes, I'll marry you!"

Michael removed the silver lotus flower ring from the box and placed it on her finger. Then he stood, wrapped his arms around her, and kissed her deeply. Feelings Jennifer thought she would never experience coursed through her veins.

Everyone around them applauded. They took more pictures. Before everyone left to resume what they had done before this romantic interlude, they passed along congratulatory handshakes and cheek kisses. Best of all, they had airdropped their photos onto Jennifer's phone.

She couldn't stop looking at the ring. It was gorgeous, and the stone in the middle shone blue in different lights.

"When did you get this?"

"This afternoon. You were busy looking at stuff, so I bought it then."

Tears of joy spilled down her cheeks, and she hugged him again.

"Pinch me. This can't be real. Pinch me so I know it is. Please," Jennifer begged.

Michael did as she asked and squeezed the skin on the back of her hand.

"Do you want to stay here longer or go to the restaurant?" he asked.

Fifty-Seven

The Tree Lounge, Cairo Tower, Gezira Island, Zamalek, Cairo Governorate, Cairo, Egypt

October 8, 2018

Michael and Jennifer stood outside the Al Dawar revolving restaurant, eyeing the menu posted by the entrance. Nothing on it appealed to Michael. They could go elsewhere to eat. There were other eateries close by and some in the tower.

"Did you have your heart set on eating here?" he asked.

"Not really. Wasn't there another restaurant on our way in? Something to do with trees."

"I know the one you mean."

With Jennifer in tow, Michael took the elevator, descending to the ground floor. The Tree Lounge, the restaurant they had spotted on their way in, stood tucked away in the back corner of the building. This establishment also displayed its menu outside the door, sparking a sense of curiosity in them as they paused to peruse it.

"This is more like it. I don't need a big meal after that Shawarma," Jennifer said.

"Nor do I. This place isn't as expensive as upstairs, either," Michael said.

"Probably because it's the revolving restaurant. You pay for the privilege."

"This is it," Michael declared, a wave of contentment washed over him. They had found their perfect dining spot, a place that felt just right.

A hostess escorted them to a table for two next to the windows and handed them menus. Even though Michael had looked over the menu outside the eatery, he still enjoyed taking his time and deciding. A server arrived with a jug of water and filled the goblets already on the table.

"The Tree Lounge burger sounds interesting," he said.

Jennifer turned the page. "Yes, it does."

"Two then?" he asked.

When the server returned, Michael ordered two of the house special burgers and two iced teas.

"When I call Ahmed to come for us, I'll get him to come to the side of the tower where we came in. Save us walking all that way back in the dark."

"Yes. It was bad enough in the daylight. I wouldn't want to do it at night."

Soon, their meals arrived. The burger was huge. Michael didn't think he'd be able to get it into his mouth. Jennifer must have felt the same because she cut hers in half. He'd try first and then cut it.

The burger was a masterpiece, a towering creation that seemed to defy the laws of gravity. Combining turkey, roast beef, salami, and mozzarella sticks was a delightful surprise, a symphony of flavours that danced on Michael's tongue. The crisp lettuce and juicy tomato added a refreshing touch, balancing the richness of the meat and cheese. The aroma of the sizzling meat and the sound of the crunch as Michael took his first bite added to the sensory experience.

"This is delicious," Jennifer exclaimed. "I can't believe everything that's on it."

"I know. Neither can I. Except getting here is hairy on foot; it's close to your hotel."

"And reasonably priced, too."

Their conversation occurred between bites of food, making it almost sound like a vinyl record groove where the needle was stuck.

"I've had an amazing day, Michael. I would never have ventured to the bazaar on my own. And now the tower? And getting engaged. It's just beautiful."

"It's been the same for me, too. Believe it or not, when I bought the ring this afternoon, I hadn't planned on proposing at the top of Cairo Tower. I'm unsure where I thought of doing it, but I would have before you returned home. I might see if I can get on the same flight with you. Now, I've got a reason to return to Canada," Michael confessed.

When Michael left Niagara Falls in August to come back to Egypt, Jennifer doubted she'd ever see him again. She thought she'd blown any chance of a reunion, let alone a marriage proposal. Those two things were out of the question. But here she was in Egypt with a man who loved her and who proposed to her. Who now had a reason to go to Canada. If he could get on her flight, that would be even better. But what if he couldn't? The thought sent a shiver down her spine.

They finished their enormous burgers and lingered over their iced tea. A young couple strolled by the window where they were sitting. They held hands and stopped to kiss. When they looked in the window, Jennifer averted her eyes.

Later, she'd have to text or email Sadie to check on Zeus. She hadn't done so yet and now felt a pang of guilt that was hard to ignore. But so much had happened since she found Michael, spent time with him, and was now engaged.

As if by magic, her phone pinged. She pulled it out and opened the text message. It was from Sadie and included a picture of Jennifer's pug playing with Sadie's two children. Jennifer turned her phone to show Michael the picture.

"He doesn't look like he's hard done by. I'd say Sadie and her family are spoiling him rotten," he said.

The photo added to Jennifer's guilt.

"Why don't you text Sadie our news?" Michael suggested.

Found Michael. All's well. He's asked me to marry him.

"Give me your phone. Hold your hand up, showing the ring beside your smiling face. I'll take a picture, and you can send it to Sadie."

Jennifer handed over the device.

Michael snapped at least three pictures from the different angles he held her phone. When he returned it, she inspected the photographs and selected the one she wanted to attach to her message.

Here I am, showing off my ring.

"Would you like to set a date?"

Her phone pinged again. Another message from Sadie.

Beautiful. I hope you said yes.

"Huh?" She snapped out of her reverie.

"The wedding. When would you like to get married?"

"I-I don't know. I'm still in newly engaged bliss," Jennifer said. She wasn't sure she was ready to start planning the wedding yet.

"And where?"

"Do we have to decide right now? Can't we enjoy our time here together?"

Michael reached across the table and took her hand.

"You don't have to decide right now, my love. I thought you might have a when and where in mind for when the day came? Don't most women?" His voice was gentle and understanding.

"I don't know. Do we?"

He better quit while he was ahead. Michael changed the subject away from wedding dates and locations. "I know we talked about visiting the museum tomorrow. Do you want to see if I can get us on a day tour to the pyramids and the Sphinx instead?"

"I thought you'd already done that."

"I planned to, but visited the bazaar and bought your cartouche instead," Michael said.

"Sure, why not. I want to see both."

Michael pulled out his phone, connected to the restaurant's

Wi-Fi and searched for day tours. "How about this one? Pyramids, Sphinx, and the museum. Decent price, but if you want to go into the pyramids, it's extra."

"I don't mind not going inside."

"Okay. You're picked up at your hotel at 8:30 and back at around three."

"I'll have to set an alarm on my phone so I'm up in time."

"I'm going to have to spend the night in Cairo rather than have Ahmed take me back to Abusir."

"My room isn't big enough for both of us," Jennifer said.

"I know. I was there. Not enough room to swing a cat. With any luck, the hotel will have a single room available for one night."

Michael tapped the keys on his phone with his thumbs. "There, I've booked the tour. It says on their site to bring your passport, sunscreen, sunglasses and camera."

"My passport is in my purse. Same with my eVisa."

"Dammit. My documents are back at the camp."

"So now, what?"

Michael's brow furrowed in deep concentration, his mind racing to devise a solution to untangle their predicament.

"I've got it!" he said. "I text Ahmed to come get us. Before we take you back to the hotel, I'll get him to take us to the site where I can get my things. Then, we return to Cairo, and I get out at your hotel."

"And hope they have a room."

"That, too."

That was the only problem with Michael's plan. Poor Ahmed was driving everywhere in the chaotic, bustling streets of Cairo, a city that never seemed to sleep. The day Jennifer arrived, it took an hour to get to Saqqara from her hotel, and it was farther to Abusir. Presumably, the man had a family, and if he was chauffeuring Michael and her around, he wasn't spending time with them.

"I feel compelled to pay for tonight's meal. Your generosity has been overwhelming," Jennifer said. "And I won't take no for an answer."

"Okay. It's no problem. I don't mind paying."

"No arguing."

"All right. I'll text Ahmed and have him uplift us here."

When the server returned with the bill, Jennifer calculated the tip and added it to the total.

"Thank you. It was a remarkable experience," Jennifer's voice resonated with gratitude as she tucked the customer's copy of the receipt into her purse.

"Okay, I've contacted Ahmed, and he'll collect us where I suggested," Michael said, putting his phone back into his inner vest pocket.

"Wonderful."

Michael wrapped his arm around Jennifer's shoulders and guided her into the night air. As they reached the street, he turned her around to face the majestic tower, symbolizing their shared adventure.

"It's breathtaking," Jennifer whispered. "It puts the towers back home to shame. I can't help but imagine the countless stories this one holds within its walls."

The temperature was still warm, but Jennifer shivered beside him. Was it the chill of the night or something else that caused her discomfort? He pulled her closer, hoping to provide some warmth.

People came and went from the tower. Some recognized them and nodded as they passed, while others offered congratulations.

About half an hour later, Ahmed's vehicle pulled up to where they stood. He stepped out with a warm smile on his face and opened the door for Jennifer.

"Your package is right where you left it," Ahmed reassured them, his voice steady and confident. "Safe and secure, as always. You can count on me."

"Thank you."

"Ahmed, plans have changed," Michael announced, a mischievous glint in his eye. "Tomorrow, we're embarking on a day trip that kicks off at 8:30 from Jennifer's hotel. I'll stop at the camp to retrieve some important items, then return to her hotel. I'm hoping to secure a room for the night."

"Do you want me to drop the lady at her hotel first?"

"You don't mind coming along for the ride? It means we get to spend more time together."

"No," Jennifer said.

"It's settled, Ahmed. Out to Abusir, then back into Cairo." Michael settled back in the seat and fastened the seatbelt.

Ahmed's route differed from how she had gone when she arrived. Maybe it was because they started out on the island in the Nile? At least in the city, the street lights illuminated the passages. Some buildings had floodlights focused on their façades. People might find the juxtaposed mix of old and new … no, make that ancient and modern, the more recent additions to the city vulgar.

Soon, they were outside the city and its lights. The contrast was striking — the city's artificial glow replaced by a vast, pitch-black sky adorned with stars twinkling overhead. Never had Jennifer seen so many stars. She would get out and look at the night sky when they stopped at the camp.

Traffic was light, so it took about forty-five minutes to get to Michael's work camp. She undid her seatbelt and started to exit the vehicle.

"You're not allowed on the site," Michael said.

"I know. I want to get a good look at the sky. The number of stars. It's incredible."

"Okay, but stay by the car."

Jennifer stood next to Ahmed's vehicle, her eyes fixed on the sky. At first, it was a sea of unfamiliarity. Then, a spark of recognition. Mars. To its right and closer to the horizon, Saturn. She gazed higher, her eyes tracing the familiar patterns. Cassiopeia and, below that, the Little Dipper. Those two constellations, along with the Big Dipper and Orion, were the only ones she knew well.

"I could spend all night out here looking at the stars," she said when Ahmed joined her.

"It's a beautiful night for certain."

"That's the Milky Way up there? That band of sky that's

not as dark as the rest?"

"I think so. I'm not up much on the night sky."

"I've never seen it look so breathtaking. So many stars. Back home in Canada, where I live, you never see the night sky like this. There are so many buildings and city lights that you're unable to see this clearly," Jennifer marvelled, filled with an overwhelming sense of awe.

Michael retrieved clean clothes and his paperwork for the tour the following day. He should call his mother and tell her the fantastic news. Egypt was seven hours ahead of Ottawa, so it would be mid-afternoon at home.

He pulled his phone out, pressed the contacts icon in his phone app, and scrolled to his mother's number. It rang about seven times. Michael thought about disconnecting and trying later. He had moved the phone away from his ear.

"Hello," Mrs. Scott said.

"Hi, Mom."

"Michael what are you doing calling all the way from England? Is everything all right?"

"Everything is fine. Better than, even. And I'm in Egypt. I've been on two archaeological digs here, and we've uncovered some amazing things. But that's not why I'm calling. Look, I don't have long. Remember Jennifer? The girl I brought to Melissa's wedding?"

"Yes. You met the young woman about two weeks before that."

"That's right." Michael raked his fingers through his hair.

"Just tonight, I asked her to marry me, and she said yes. I wanted to share my fantastic news with you."

"She's there, too?"

"Yes. Jennifer has a room at a hotel in Cairo. I'm staying onsite."

The conversation went quiet.

"Don't you think it's too sudden? After all, I remember your mess when you and that girl from England broke up. Are you emotionally prepared for this?"

"Yes, Mom." Michael's mother was making him feel like

a small child.

"You don't have to marry her, do you?"

That question held nothing back. "Jennifer is not pregnant. We don't have to get married."

"Oh, Michael. I'm not sure. I know you are damn the torpedoes, full steam ahead. I don't want to see you make another serious relationship mistake."

"I know you're worried. Jennifer has a good job. I have a good job."

"Where will you live?"

"Probably in Canada. I will apply to the University of Toronto for a teaching position."

"And if that doesn't work out?"

"I have to come back to Canada, Mom. I gave up my flat in Manchester." Michael paced back and forth. "Look, I've got to go. I'll talk to you soon. Love you."

"I love you, too," Mrs. Scott said.

Michael disconnected the call. That wasn't the response from his mother he had hoped for. She'll be on to the rest of the family before the end of the day. With the Scott family, news spread like wildfire. He slung his bag over his shoulder and returned to Ahmed's vehicle.

"Ready to head back to the city?" Michael said when reappeared with a duffle bag.

"Not yet," Jennifer said, walking over to him. "I'm in awe of the beautiful night sky. In the cities, you never get a view like this."

"All the times I've been out on dig sites, I've been more concerned about what was under the ground than what was well above it. I've missed out on a lot," Michael lamented.

"You most certainly have," Jennifer said.

"Well, my friends, I hate to do this, but I must guide you back into the city," Ahmed announced, his voice carrying a tone of gentle authority.

"Of course, Ahmed. I'm sorry. I got so wrapped up in the stars."

"Not to worry, lovely lady. But we'll go now."

Jennifer clambered into the vehicle while Michael stowed

his bag in the back. All too soon, they were back on the road to Cairo.

As Ahmed pulled up to the front doors of the hotel, his protective nature towards Jennifer shone through. He ensured she had her package while Michael retrieved his bag, a subtle gesture that spoke volumes. Ahmed's actions showed his commitment to Jennifer's safety. Michael knew if circumstances prevented him from accompanying Jennifer home, she would be safe if Ahmed took her to the airport.

"You want me to wait here?"

"If you don't mind. I want to make sure I have a place to stay. I'd hate to drag you back here for nothing."

"But I live in the city. It wouldn't be for nothing."

"All right. If I can't get a room, we'll go back and return early in the morning. That way I'm here when our tour starts," Michael said, shaking Ahmed's hand and hefting his bag up onto his shoulder.

He requested a single room for one night in the dimly lit lobby. They had one, but it didn't have a window, casting a shadow of disappointment on his face.

"That's fine. I don't need a window. My fiancée and I are going on a tour of the pyramids tomorrow. She's already a guest here, but, well," he said. He couldn't very well tell them the room was so small, you had to go back into the corridor to change your mind.

Fifty-Eight

Tahrir Plaza Suites, Meret Basha, Ismailia, Qasr El Nil, Cairo Governorate, Cairo, Egypt

October 9, 2018

Jennifer, brimming with anticipation, awoke and showered early for the day's excursion to the pyramids and the Sphinx. She checked and re-checked her cross-body bag, ensuring her documentation and sunscreen were in place. Wearing her necklaces from Michael and her lotus flower engagement ring, she was ready to embark on this thrilling adventure.

She dressed in brown linen trousers and an ivory tank top, and all that remained was to slip her feet into her Birkenstocks. Afterwards, she put her room key in her purse, and grabbed the cardigan she wore tied over her shoulders the day before. Jennifer doubted the latter would be required, but she'd rather have it.

After a delightful evening with Michael, he had bid her goodnight and gone to his room. It left Jennifer with a sense of mystery, not knowing which floor or room he was in. They had agreed to meet in the lobby an hour before the tour guide was to pick them up, adding a touch of suspense to their rendezvous.

Jennifer picked up her things. Michael mentioned she should have a camera with her. She had her phone, a backup battery, and a cable. Ensuring she had everything she needed, Jennifer left the room and made sure the door clicked shut when she was in the corridor.

Her room was close to the elevator, so she headed straight to it. There were four lifts, two on each side of the hallway. This morning, the lift stopped at every floor below her to collect people going down to the lobby level.

When she exited, Michael stood by a display of tourist brochures. Jennifer rushed to his side.

"Have we got time to grab a bite of breakfast and a coffee?" Jennifer asked, filled with excitement and hunger.

He checked his watch.

"Yes. Just."

They entered the dining room, where a continental breakfast was served. Jennifer selected a glass of orange juice, a blueberry muffin, a banana for the road, and a comforting cup of coffee. Michael chose apple juice, a poppy seed bagel, an apple and banana for their tour, and a steaming cup of coffee. The breakfast setup, with its inviting array of food and beverages, provided a soothing start to their day.

After making their selections, they found an empty table, sat to eat, and stowed what they'd picked up for later.

When the two exited the hotel, their tour guide, a tall man with a friendly smile, waited for them. He stood by the vehicle, a sleek, modern minibus, ready to embark on their adventure.

"Jennifer Fox? Michael Scott?" he asked. "Karim Khalil, your guide today. Please come."

They climbed into the spacious, air-conditioned vehicle, the leather seats cool against their skin. Once they fastened their seat belts, the driver eased out into the bustling traffic.

They chatted with Karim on their way to the desert. Michael had worked out in harsh conditions under the baking sun all day. Despite the heat, he preferred to wear long-sleeved shirts, long pants, and a hat that kept the sun off his face and neck. Jennifer might burn to a crisp with her fair hair and complexion.

"Do you enjoy the unique experience of riding a camel? A complimentary camel ride is part of our tour. The Wi-Fi network is available on the visor here. Connect to it if you wish," Karim offered.

"That sounds like fun," Michael said.

"The only thing not included in the tour price is if you want to go into the inner chambers of the Great Pyramid. That's an additional E£200 per person, payable to the Great Pyramid of Giza. If you're claustrophobic, it's not recommended. If you decide to, I can take you to where you'll have to pay the additional fee. Right now, your ticket price includes entry to the location. Please note that the inner chambers are not handicapped-friendly.

Did the additional fee apply to all visitors, regardless of nationality? Most places in the country charged a higher rate for non-Egyptians. However, he was content to admire them from the outside. Jennifer might be interested in exploring the interior, although, with her mobility issues, she might decide to give it a miss, too.

Fifty-Nine

The Giza Pyramid Complex, Al Haram, Giza Governorate, Egypt

October 9, 2018

They pulled into the site a little over half an hour after leaving the hotel. Karim flashed his tour guide ID at the ticket office. Michael and Jennifer had to show their passports and tour tickets.

Karim drove towards one of the many parking areas and parked the vehicle.

"Here we are. Shall we?"

He exited first and opened Jennifer's door.

"Wow," she said. "I can't believe I'm really here."

"It *is* pretty incredible," Michael agreed, taking Jennifer's hand and falling into step behind their guide.

"The Great Pyramid is the tomb of the pharaoh Khufu, the second pharaoh of the Fourth Dynasty. He succeeded his father, Sneferu." Karim told them more about the family and when people searched for it, they found his sarcophagus empty.

"That gives me the willies," Jennifer said.

"Raiders pillaged many of the ancient monuments in our country."

Karim led them around the Great Pyramid to three others on the plateau.

"Pyramid of Queen Henutsen, the second or third wife of Khufu. She could be buried in a tomb under the structure."

"Pharaohs had more than one wife?" Jennifer asked.

"Yes, they had many wives, but one was always more important to the pharaoh than the rest."

"Don't get any ideas, Michael." She laughed.

"Pyramid Of Queen Meritites I, she was the wife, and perhaps, half-sister of pharaoh Khufu. However, we've yet to determine that."

A shiver went down Michael's spine. He couldn't imagine marrying a family member. At least now, in Canada, it was more or less illegal. But there were exceptions, and it was possible depending on how many degrees of separation there were.

"And here is the pyramid of Hetepheres I. We believe her to be a minor wife of Sneferu, but without a doubt was the mother of Khufu. She was also of royal blood as her father Huni ruled at the end of the Third Dynasty."

"It's all so fascinating," Jennifer said. "I can see why you went into archaeology, Michael."

"One of the many reasons," he said.

"Now, we'll go over to the pyramid of Khafre. This is the second largest of the pyramids here in Giza. Khafre, himself, was the son of Khufu. The belief is the Great Sphinx was built for Khafre and the face is a likeness of the man from the Fourth Dynasty. This next pyramid is the smallest of the three main ones. It is the pyramid of Menkaure. Some say he was the throne successor of Bikheris, but the most convincing says he was the son of Khafre."

Karim continued, "When you see pictures of the pyramids here at Giza, you see the tombs of Khufu, his son, Khafre, and his grandson, Menkaure. Photographers don't typically include pictures of the pyramids belonging to the queens on the other side of the great one."

While Jennifer had been constantly taking pictures with her phone and making notes about which pyramids were in the frame, Michael hadn't bothered. He was confident she would share them with him.

"Now, pictures at the pyramids, and afterwards you can have your camel ride. We'll go on them over to the Sphinx."

"This is turning into the best day ever. Well, last night at Cairo Tower, today hasn't topped that yet," said Jennifer.

They had their photo taken in such a position that the three prominent pyramids were in the background. The photographer also took one using Jennifer's phone. The print of the professional shot would be ready for them when they returned from the Sphinx.

Karim led them to where three camels rested on the ground. "Before we start, just a few words. First, camels spit."

"So they're a lot like llamas," Michael said.

"Yes. Second, the beasts are slow. But we're not out to win any races. The Sphinx will still be there when we arrive. It's not going anywhere."

That drew a chuckle from Michael.

"Third, they are stubborn. And if a camel doesn't want to do something, it won't. Fourth, they are strong. Very strong. Fifth, they are adaptable. They can go for long distances without food or water. And sixth, riding a camel is fun!"

Jennifer hesitated when she got close to the camel. The animal was enormous, and its coarse hair prickled against her skin as she stood in its shadow. She had never ridden a horse before, so she had no clue how to get on or off the beast. Even when it was on its knees, the saddle was almost chest high. The camel turned its head and opened its mouth into a toothy grin, its breath warm and musky. Hopefully, that was a good sign.

Karim came to her side. "Left foot in the stirrup, swing your right leg over the animal's back. Hang onto the saddle with both hands, right here." He showed her the location.

"I don't know if I can bend my knee that much. I've had an injury in the past, and it's still not healed," Jennifer confessed, her voice tinged with uncertainty.

"I'll give you a boost to get you started," Michael said.

With his help, Jennifer found herself suspended in the air, trying to position her foot as Karim had instructed. The support she received was reassuring, and she was soon able to mount the camel.

Both men mounted their beasts with no problems. It was easy for them because they didn't have an entire hardware store in their leg and a knee that didn't have full mobility.

When her camel got to its feet, she feared falling off. "Yikes! I'm going to fall."

"You're fine. Hold on tight. You'll be okay."

The three started for the Sphinx, the golden sands stretching before them. The camels plodded along at a slow but steady pace, their hooves sinking into the soft dunes. So far, none of them had shown any stubborn tendencies. Karim was right when he said it was fun, now that she had gotten past the initial shock of the camel getting to its feet. About fifteen to twenty minutes after leaving, they reached the Sphinx, its majestic form rising from the desert.

Someone was there to get the camels to kneel, their long legs folded under them. They helped Jennifer and the others dismount, guiding their feet to the ground. The journey was over, but the memories would last a lifetime.

Jennifer massaged her bum after dismounting. "It's not the cushiest of things to sit on," she said.

Kamir and Michael laughed. The man likely rode one daily when he brought a private tour to the pyramids. Michael, maybe on his dig site. Did they use camels for the heavy work? The beast she'd ridden fluttered its long eyelashes at her. Flirting? Couldn't be.

The Sphinx was massive. They couldn't get right to it, but there was a walkway that got them close enough for excellent pictures. Jennifer took a selfie of the three of them with the Sphinx in the background. Michael used her camera to photograph her, looking like she was kissing it. She would have that one to go with the one with her finger on the point of one pyramid.

"You see why it is said the Sphinx was made in the image of Khafre, although others think it was his brother who was responsible," Kamir said.

"What happened to its nose?" Jennifer asked.

"Another point of contention, but we know it had nothing to do with a cannonball fired by one of Napoleon's soldiers. Sketches found were dated long before that time, and the nose was missing then. An Egyptian-Arab historian wrote back in the fifteenth century that the nose was destroyed in 1378 CE. Peasants made offerings to the Sphinx, hoping to control the flood cycle. The story goes that Sa'im al-Dahr was so outraged by their blatant show of devotion that he destroyed the nose and was later executed for vandalism. We still don't know if it's a fact or not."

"They didn't mess around with punishment back in the day," Michael said.

"No. Shall we go for lunch now? We'll go to Khufu's. Ride our camels back to where we picked them up. Then to the car for the trip to the restaurant."

"Yes, please. I'm getting rather peckish." Even though Jennifer had brought some fruit from the hotel, she hadn't eaten it. The surrounding vista interested her far more.

"Your fee includes your meal and non-alcoholic drinks, but if you want an alcoholic beverage, it isn't. You'll have to pay for that."

"That's fine," Jennifer and Michael said in unison, then laughed.

The ride back to the pyramids, where they started their camel ride, took longer. Jennifer's got stubborn. It dropped to its knees and refused to get up.

"Now, what do I do?" she asked.

Karim turned back, took the reins and pulled back towards him. Nothing.

"Lean forward. Maybe you leaned back and signalled your camel you wanted to get off."

Jennifer did as instructed. She practically laid on her stomach and could wrap her arms around the camel's neck if she wanted. It had the desired effect, and her camel stood up again. When it was on its feet, Karim handed her back the reins.

The rest of the return journey to the pyramids went without incident.

It took no time from when they returned the camels to them pulling into the parking lot at Khufu's.

"Do you want to sit inside or out on the patio?" Karim asked.

"I think inside. I've had enough sun for one day," Jennifer said.

"I'd rather be inside, too," said Michael.

Stepping into the restaurant's cool interior, a server who led them to a table by the window greeted them. The breathtaking view of the pyramids filled the prospect, but it was the soft murmur of conversations and the clinking of cutlery that made a cozy yet lively atmosphere. Khufu's efficient air conditioning provided immediate relief from the scorching heat, creating a comfortable environment for their dining experience.

"Can I get you anything to drink while you peruse the food menu?"

They had various drinks on the menu, including local and international options. After being in the blazing sun, Michael could murder a pint. He decided on Stella Artois, his go-to. This choice was not only a thirst quencher but also a nod to the cultural fusion that Egypt represented.

"Can I get a Stella, please?" Michael asked.

"And the lady?"

"Sparkling water."

"Make that two," Karim said.

The server nodded and went for their drinks, leaving them perusing the food menu.

"Can you still get their breakfast menu? The other selections have more than I could eat," Jennifer said, looking at the extensive menu.

"I believe so. But I'll ask when our server returns," said Karim, who was familiar with the restaurant's offerings.

At that moment, their drinks arrived.

"The lady wants to know if she can still order from the breakfast menu?" Karim said.

"Yes."

"I'd like the Balady Salad."

"And you, sir. Have you decided yet?"

Michael cast his eyes back to the menu. "I'll have the Pulled Beef Qatevef, Chicken Livers, and Sayadiyah.

Karim ordered almost the same meal, except for the Mulukhiyah with Rabbit.

Michael ate rabbit once when he lived in England and didn't know until after that's what he'd eaten. He'd seen them in the supermarket's meat section when he first arrived as a student in Manchester. He'd had one as a pet growing up, so he couldn't bring himself to eat one knowingly.

"You are wearing some lovely traditional Egyptian jewellery," Karim said.

"Thank you. The necklaces were gifts from Michael. Purchased from one shop in Khan el-Khalili."

"Nice. It is quite the bustling place, that bazaar."

"It sure is," Jennifer said.

When their meals arrived, Michael offered Jennifer samples of his food. She tried a bite of each. He had eaten many Egyptian foods, so he knew about many dishes. But not her. She opted for something she knew: cucumbers, tomatoes, onion, parsley, and salad dressing. At least she sampled his food.

When their server returned to see how they enjoyed their meals, Jennifer asked for an order of their Street-Style Fried Potatoes.

The discussion around the table turned to what they'd seen so far, what they liked, what they didn't, and the upcoming tour of the museum.

"You don't have to stick around to drive us back to the hotel. We're right across the street. We'll make our own way back," Michael said.

"If that's what you wish, sir."

Once they finished their lunch, it was time to return to the city for their tour of the Egyptian Museum. Jennifer was pleased that Michael told Karim he could leave after dropping them there. While having someone with a wealth of information with them was fantastic, it was time they had some alone time.

When they exited the minibus, Michael pressed a wad of Egyptian pound notes into Karim's hand. The man deserved a good tip after their tour.

Sixty

The Egyptian Museum, El-Tahrir Square, Ismailia, Qasr El Nil, Cairo Governorate, Cairo, Egypt

October 9, 2018

As Jennifer stepped into the museum, anticipation washed over her. She knew this was just the first of many visits. Today, they would only get a sample of what the museum offered. Michael, who had to go back to work, would accompany her on future visits. While she marvelled at the museum's grandeur, Michael handled their tickets at the booth.

With a museum map in hand, Jennifer's eyes sparkled with curiosity. She scanned the levels, each holding a treasure trove of cultural artifacts. Her gaze settled on the top level, where the staff housed King Tut's funeral mask. "Shall we start from the top and work our way down? I can't wait to see the mask up close," she suggested to Michael.

"If that's what you want, then by all means." Michael took her arm, and they headed towards the stairs. One of the museum employees saw Jennifer using her cane and stopped them before they could ascend the steps.

Little did Jennifer know, a surprise was in store for her. As she wondered why the staff member singled her out, the museum employee pressed a button. To her astonishment, a panel moved, revealing an elevator.

"This will be better, no?" he asked.

"Thank you. This is much appreciated," Jennifer replied with gratitude. She stepped into the elevator, her heart warmed by the thoughtfulness of the museum staff.

Comfortably ensconced in the device, Michael pushed the button for the top floor.

"Sure beats climbing those stairs," he said.

"I would never have thought they would have something like this hidden so cleverly. Did you know that was an elevator before it opened?"

"No. Tourism is important to the Egyptians, so they'll make places like this accessible to everyone."

When the elevator doors opened, Jennifer found herself just a few steps away from the room housing the mask. The door closed, blending with the other walls on this level. She stepped inside the adjacent gallery. The legendary funeral mask of King Tut, gleamed in solid gold behind a protective layer of plexiglass. Jennifer, eager to capture the moment, positioned her phone to avoid any glare or reflections that could mar the beauty of her photo.

Michael found himself captivated by Jennifer's reactions to the museum's ancient Egyptian artifacts. As they stood before the animal mummies, he couldn't help but wonder about the future of the statue of Kaires. Would it end up here, in this museum, known for its extensive collection of mummies and ancient relics, or in the new one that was being planned? And when it went on display, would they repair it first, or leave it in its current state, two pieces placed side by side, a testament to its rich history?

After perusing the upper level for at least an hour, Michael led Jennifer back to the hidden elevator.

They had barely begun to explore the main level when the announcement echoed through the intercom, declaring the museum's impending closure in a mere forty-five minutes. The ticking clock added a thrilling edge to their visit, clarifying that they had to make the most of their remaining time.

He escorted her around and showed her some of the more significant artifacts on this level. They saw quite a bit, although Michael would have preferred to stay longer. He could bring her here again. While he was in awe of the things on display, he kept his reactions more subdued. Jennifer; however, was like a child in a candy store. She gasped; her eyes grew as big as saucers at some things they saw.

The moment he dreaded came. The announcement that the museum was closing in five minutes.

"Let's get out of here, and we'll wander through the gardens. They're open," Michael said, the sound of his voice echoing in the grand hall of the museum.

Jennifer nodded, and they made their way to the exit.

"Are these real, or are they replicas?" Jennifer asked, pointing to one sphinx in the garden.

"Real."

"Aren't they afraid of them being stolen?"

Michael chuckled.

"What's so funny?"

"It weighs tons. There's no way anyone could walk off with it. They'd need a huge crane to lift it out of here. Something that size would draw attention that a would-be thief wouldn't want."

"I always imagined something of this historical significance would be sheltered indoors, not exposed to the elements like this," Jennifer mused, her hand reaching out. The rough surface of the rock scraped under her fingertips; the heat of the sun warming the stone.

Palm trees towered on either side of the museum's entrance as if standing guard to protect the valuable artifacts inside. Trimmed hedges bordered specific areas, accentuating the mystique of the outer area. In addition, knee-high stone walls provided seating, and people used them, taking advantage of a place to rest.

"Didn't we walk by here on my first day? I remember seeing this building when you took me to supper," Jennifer said.

"Yes, I brought you across that way. I should have mentioned the museum when we walked by."

"I think you were still in shock from seeing me at Abusir," Jennifer said.

"Could be. I admit, you had me gobsmacked," Michael said, chuckling. He couldn't help but smile at the memory of Jennifer's surprise. "Do you want to go for a meal?"

"I think I'm going to pass. I'd like to go back to my room and shower. I still smell of camel. Being out in the sun for so long has made me tired. I foresee a shower, maybe eating the fruit I took for the trip, and an early night. You're not disappointed, are you?" Jennifer asked, her voice tinged with exhaustion and a hint of worry.

"No. I'll walk you back to your hotel and then call Ahmed to see if he can pick me up and take me back to the site."

The two left the gardens before the museum, their steps slow and measured as if reluctant to leave the beauty behind. They returned to the hotel, the distance between them seeming to grow with each step.

Once across the multi-lane road between the museum and the Tahrir Plaza Suites, the rest of the walk was easy.

Michael kissed Jennifer goodbye at the entrance. "I wish I didn't have to leave," he whispered, his voice husky.

"I wish you didn't, too, but you should. I don't want to do anything that will ruin what we have," Jennifer said with desire and caution.

He kissed her again and walked to where Ahmed would pull in. Jennifer's eyes followed and watched him walk away.

Sixty-One

November 7, 2018

She couldn't believe an entire month had passed. Jennifer, who had developed a close bond with Michael, spent a great deal of time with him, although he had to go back to the dig site in Abusir. Still, they saw each other in the evenings and spent many of them strolling the streets near the hotel. Apparently, Miroslav had told Michael that staying away from the site for too long could jeopardize his career. She didn't want to cause anything like that, so she talked him into going back.

With each passing day, Jennifer's spirit of adventure grew. She ventured out more, exploring the quaint corners near her hotel. On some days, she even walked to the museum, immersing herself in the beauty of its gardens. The Egyptian Museum was a treasure trove that could consume a month of one's time. She and Michael had revisited it once, proof of their shared curiosity and love for exploration.

Now, as she sat in the departure lounge, waiting for her flight to Canada, Jennifer felt a pang of uncertainty. Michael had texted her, asking her to go ahead and he'd meet her there. But was there something more to it? Was he having second thoughts? Did he have cold feet? These questions, along with the lingering doubt about their future, swirled in her mind as she fingered her cartouche, symbolizing Michael's affection for her.

Then, a familiar face, Michael's, approached where she sat, bringing relief and a smile to her face, masking the underlying anxiety she felt about their future.

"Sorry, I'm late. Checks and balances and red tape to endure before I could leave the site. Make sure I had stolen nothing."

"Security is that tight?"

"It has to be. In the past, looters stole too many artifacts and sold them on the black market or smuggled them out of the country."

She nodded.

Soon, boarding began. Jennifer didn't rely on her cane as much in Egypt, so when it came time to pack, she put it in her checked bag.

At first, they didn't have seats together, but once everyone was onboard, the flight attendants made the arrangements so he could sit with her. At first, the man beside her didn't want to sit back in Michael's original seat, so he swapped with someone across the aisle, and that person moved back. Jennifer couldn't shake off a sense of unease, her eyes darting between the man and Michael, wondering what was going on.

The plane pushed back from the gate not long after they completed the seat shuffle. The flight crew went through the pre-flight checklist and demonstrated the safety instructions to the passengers.

Sixty-Two

Jennifer's House, Orchard Avenue, Niagara Falls, Ontario

November 7, 2018

Despite the long journey, the airport wait, the customs clearance, and the train rides, Jennifer set her heart on reuniting with Zeus. The joy of seeing her beloved pet after being away was the first thing on her mind.

During the flight, they discussed their wedding plans. While they only set some details, they had made a significant decision on the date and venue. They were excited to say their vows on December 31st at the Oakes Garden Theatre, envisioning a magical winter setting if all went well.

As the wedding was still over a month away, Jennifer clung to the hope that Michael's family would attend. The thought of their presence on such a special day filled her with a deep sense of belonging and desire.

When she reunited with Zeus, Jennifer focused her mind on a specific task. She had decided not only to present Sadie's gift, but ask her to be her maid of honour. However, one person would not be receiving an invitation — Emma. Jennifer knew all too well of the potential for Emma to take control if she found out about the wedding. In her typical fashion, when it came to Emma, Jennifer knew she would step aside and let her.

"Now, let's go get Zeus." Jennifer opened her large suitcase and removed the package containing the lamp she'd bought for Sadie. Nothing rattled when she lifted it. Still, she wouldn't rest easy until the woman opened it. The collar she had bought for Zeus lay in her handbag. She'd put it on him at Sadie's.

She shooed Michael out the side door, then, ensuring it was locked, went out behind him and closed it behind her. The last thing she did was test to ensure she secured it. Jennifer aimed her fob at the little yellow Smart car and unlocked it.

"It's miffed at me because it hasn't moved in a month," she said, climbing in behind the wheel.

Michael held Sadie's gift in his lap in the passenger seat.

Jennifer turned the key, and the engine started. No coaxing or anything else was required.

"So, where does your friend live?" Michael asked as she backed out of the driveway.

"On Westwood. It's not that far from here, but it's a subdivision that is newer than this area. They built these houses back in the 20s and 30s. Maybe even some in the 40s. Hers, I would think late 60s, early 70s."

About ten minutes later, Jennifer pulled into Sadie's driveway. She shut off the engine, undid her seatbelt and took the lamp from Michael.

They walked to the door holding hands. Jennifer's hand shook when she rang the doorbell. Why was she shaking? Nervous? Scared? Excited?

Zeus's barking got louder as he approached. Not long afterwards, the lock scraped, and Sadie opened the door.

"Oh my God, Jennifer! I didn't expect you until at least tomorrow. You must be exhausted after your flight. Come in. Come in. I want to hear everything." Sadie paused. "You must be the man Jennifer went halfway around the world for. She told me your wonderful news. Congratulations. Sorry, I can't remember your name."

"Michael Scott." He squatted in front of the pug. "Hi, Zeus. Remember me?"

The dog came forward and sniffed him. So far, her pet had rebuffed Jennifer.

"Come into the kitchen. I'll make a pot of coffee," Sadie said, ushering them to the kitchen.

"I brought you this. It's from Khan el-Khalili in Cairo. I hope it survived the flight."

Jennifer and Michael sat at the table.

Sadie opened the box and pulled out a wad of paper and plastic.

"I promise there's something in there. I asked the vendor to wrap it well because I was taking it on a plane to Canada."

"There's something in here. I can tell by the weight," Sadie said.

The wrappings fell to the floor layer by layer revealing the object.

"It's beautiful," she exclaimed. "You shouldn't have." Sadie placed the gift on the table.

"I wanted to. It's for looking after Zeus for me so I could get away. The man told me the base is hand-blown glass. And the top, the cross with the loop, is an ankh that symbolizes life and life after death. Now, I have one more favour to ask. Will you stand up with me when I get married?"

Sadie's hands flew to her face. "I don't know what to say."

"Say yes."

"Okay, okay, I will. Yes."

Jennifer stood and hugged Sadie. "Now we best get this monkey and all his goods and chattels back home."

Soon, they had all of Zeus's paraphernalia gathered and stacked by the front door. Jennifer pulled the collar she'd bought in Egypt out of her purse and fastened it around the dog's neck.

"You're sure I don't owe you anything. For food. Anything that you had to buy for my sweet boy?"

"No. You've done more than enough already," said Sadie.

"See you at work tomorrow. Do you know what shift I'm on?"

"Same as me. Two to ten."

"Perfect. See you then."

Jennifer clipped Zeus's leash to his new collar, and she and Michael carried the dog's accessories to the car.

"He doesn't travel light, does he," Michael said.

"We got off lucky when we took him to Percé. That was only a week, and most of his things fit in my suitcase. This time, it was for an entire month."

Sixty-Three

Outback Steakhouse, Victoria Avenue, Niagara Falls, Ontario

November 8, 2018

Jennifer parked her little car behind the Outback and walked in through the back door.

"The wanderer returns," her manager said.

"I have."

"You got sun, I can tell. But there's something else. You're glowing."

"Maybe it has something to do with the most thrilling news I have to share? I got engaged while I was away!" Jennifer exclaimed, her voice brimming with joy. She displayed the engagement ring on her hand, wiggling her fingers in excitement. She then punched her timecard, her heart still fluttering with the thrill of the announcement.

Bill was in his usual place, but no glass sat in front of him.

"Hi, Bill," Jennifer said as she walked by him to the tap to pour him his usual pint of Stella.

"Jennifer, you're back. It's good to see you. You're

looking well."

"Thanks. Here's your Stella." She put a cardboard coaster on the bar and set his glass on it. She knew right away who was going to receive the cartouche keyring.

Jennifer went to her purse and retrieved it.

When she returned, she handed it to Bill. "This told me it wanted to come home with me as a gift for someone special. You're that someone."

Bill's eyes widened in surprise, his voice trembling with emotion. "I-I don't know what to say. It's lovely, Jennifer, it is. I'm touched by your thoughtfulness." His gratitude was clear, and Jennifer felt a warm sense of satisfaction.

No one had ever done something so thoughtful for Bill in a long time. Not since his wife's dementia had taken over her life. Her gesture moved the man, and his emotions caught in his throat.

"There's something else. My parents are both gone, and I still feel their absence. I'd love it if you would give me away on my wedding day, Bill. I need your support." Jennifer's voice was soft, her vulnerability shining through.

"You-you're getting married?"

"Yes, I found him," Jennifer shared with joy and relief. "I apologized and tried to grovel, but he told me it wasn't necessary. So, the night we went to the top of Cairo Tower, he got down on one knee and asked me to marry him. This is my engagement ring." Jennifer held out her hand, her eyes sparkling with the memory of that special night so Bill could see it.

"It's a beautiful ring for a beautiful young lady. So when is the big day?"

"December 31st."

"New Year's Eve. A real celebration. And where?"

"Outdoors. I'm going to try to get the Oakes Garden Theatre," Jennifer said.

"That will be quite the event."

"Michael will be in later. I left him at the house. You'll get to meet him."

Bill, who had always longed for a daughter, was moved when Jennifer asked him to play a significant role in her wedding. This young woman was no ordinary one but the daughter of Stephen Fox, a former colleague taken too soon. He took a sip of his Stella. Bill felt the weight of the moment and placed the glass back on the coaster, his mind filled with anticipation for the upcoming event.

"It would be my honour to do that for you."

Overwhelmed with gratitude, Jennifer left the bar and embraced Bill. Her hug showed the depth of her feelings and the immense value she placed on his role in her wedding, a role that she considered pivotal and irreplaceable.

Bill's heart swelled with joy at the thought of walking Jennifer down the aisle. But it wasn't just the honour that filled him; it was a sense of being needed. This emotion, long forgotten, was one he cherished. The thought of being a significant part of Jennifer's special day brought back a flood of emotions and memories, making him feel alive and valued.

"I'll give you fair warning. Michael comes from a big family. They all have partners, and they all have dogs. The wedding I went to with him back in June — his youngest sister's. She has a Weiner dog, and her fiancé, now husband, has a golden retriever. His brother, Roger, has a black Labrador, and his other brother, Chris, has a Great Dane if you can imagine. I have a pug named Zeus."

"A big family and some big dogs, too."

"Now, Michael and I have to ensure we can get the venue and send out the invitations. I'm going to see if we can hold the reception here. It wouldn't be their first time closing for a private party."

"Anything you need, let me know. I'm more than happy to help."

"Thanks, Bill. You're a star."

Bill's cheeks grew hot. Jennifer had made him blush. He used to make his wife blush all the time; whether it was because of a compliment or an off-colour joke, he made her turn beet red. He finished his pint and revelled in his newfound stardom.

Michael strolled from Jennifer's house to the heart of downtown. The neighbourhood was a peaceful oasis punctuated by the occasional barking dog, children's voices, and laughter. The closer he got to the strip where the hotels were, the more the sounds of life enveloped him. While not as cacophonous as back in June and August when he stayed in the city, it was still a lively symphony.

A group of giggling teenage girls approached, their laughter echoing through the street. They didn't move into single file, forcing Michael off the sidewalk. Their parents never taught them any manners. Yet, with his calm demeanour, Michael didn't let their rudeness ruin his day. By now, he was at Stanley. Almost all the way there.

Michael had taken a stroll down Dunn Street, which ended at Fallsview. The street's name was an oxymoron because you couldn't see the falls thanks to all the high-rises. From there, he planned to turn left and walk towards the Skylon Tower. From there, he didn't have far to go. His destination was the Outback Steakhouse on Victoria Avenue.

As the clock ticked towards three-thirty in the afternoon, Michael's anticipation grew. He knew he was about to step into the familiar embrace of the Outback. He exchanged pleasantries with Bill, a regular customer, and ordered a Stella for himself.

After that, Jennifer, who had been waiting for Michael to arrive, introduced them.

"I thought I recognized you when you came in," said Bill. "You were here a few times back in the summer."

"Yes, I was." Michael shook Bill's hand, a genuine smile on his face. "Can I get you another?" he asked.

"No, thank you. I only have two, and this is my second. Your lovely fiancée looks after me quite well. I come in for the company but nurse a couple of beers so I can stay longer."

"I've asked Bill, who I discovered worked with my father, to walk me down the aisle at our wedding," Jennifer said.

Michael's mind wandered, contemplating the man who was a regular at the bar and Jennifer's parents, who were both gone. He grasped the weight of Jennifer's request and the role he would assume in her life. His own father's absence added to the gravity of the decision.

"That's nice. And I hope you accepted, Bill."

"I did."

"Good man." Did he feel that way? Did he mean what he just said? She had to have someone escort her and give her away. Which one of his brothers did he ask to stand up with him? Or rather than upset either of them, ask them both. Jennifer had Sadie. Would she ask another co-worker or someone else? She and Lori seemed to hit it off well when they met at Melissa's wedding.

Michael's mind was consumed with many tasks for their impending nuptials: acquiring a marriage license, securing a venue, hiring an officiant, and sending out invitations. And then, there was the future. Would they make this place their home? If so, he needed to find a job. Perhaps he could secure a position as an associate professor at the University of Toronto.

"I've secured the Oakes Garden Theatre for our special day," Jennifer announced with excitement. "They've advised us to consider an alternate location in case of inclement weather. I was thinking of the pavilion. It should be perfect unless we're hit with horizontal snow or sleet, right?"

"The venue will make it a unique and memorable experience, but are you sure you want to do an outdoor wedding in December?"

Jennifer ignored him and continued. "We have the venue for a two-hour time block. We just need to decide which one. I'm thinking of three to five. What do you think? They'll provide us with a list of vendors we can rent chairs from. They don't provide them."

Michael drained his glass and sat it down.

"Do you want another?"

"Only if it's required to stay longer."

Now, he sounded like Bill, who always had a witty response to everything.

Sixty-Four

Jennifer's House, Orchard Avenue, Niagara Falls, Ontario

December 31, 2018

Sadie and Lori had come to Jennifer's the previous day. Michael had a room with his brothers at one of the hotels in town, and Bill, a former co-worker of Jennifer's father, was meeting them there. Michael's sisters, mother, and Serenity were also in the city and were due to arrive at the house anytime. Jennifer had tasked them with picking up the bouquets and bringing them to the house, after which they would deliver the boutonnières to the men.

Jennifer's nerves were on edge. Had she forgotten something? They only had the venue for a mere two hours, a tight schedule that included setting up the rented chairs and tearing them down again. Thankfully, it wasn't a grand affair. The guest list included Michael's family, their respective partners, a few of her co-workers, and the Outback manager.

The girls, with their unwavering support, fussed over Jennifer's hair and makeup. Each had their particular strength.

Sadie worked on her hair, and Lori did her makeup. Jennifer had hired a limo to pick them up and drive them to the outdoor theatre.

Jennifer worried about the weather forecast. The meteorologist had predicted rain, but not before six o'clock that evening. If the rain held off, they would be snugly sheltered inside the restaurant at their reception by then. Jennifer's eyes kept darting outside. Even though they were in the pavilion, the threat of getting wet while moving to and from there if it rained was distressing.

"Will you stop? You're making me nervous," Lori said, her voice filled with amusement and concern.

"I can't help it," said Jennifer.

Sadie handed Jennifer a package wrapped in pale blue paper with a white satin bow tied around it.

"Open it."

"You didn't have to get me anything."

"I didn't."

Jennifer's eyes widened as she unwrapped the bundle. Inside was a doggie tuxedo, a surprise from Sadie.

"He can't very well be part of the wedding if he's not dressed for the part," Sadie explained, her eyes sparkling with mischief, adding to the moment's joy.

The doorbell rang.

"That must be the flowers," Jennifer said.

"I'll go. You sit." Sadie went to the front door, Zeus hot on her heels, barking. "Not flowers. Photographer."

Jennifer had forgotten about him. As part of the package, he came to the house to photograph the preparations. His footsteps echoed in the quiet house, the click of his camera a constant presence. The girls still needed to get dressed in their wedding attire. At least their shirts buttoned up the front, so they didn't have to pull them off over their heads and ruin their hair and makeup.

"I'm a bit early. Hope that's not inconvenient." He apologized as he looked around the main level of the house to determine the best location for photographs.

The girls had been using the family room off the back half

of the living room to do their hair and makeup. Their gowns were upstairs. Lori put the finishing touches on Jennifer's makeup, and they went to the bedroom where their gowns and jackets were.

Another surprise waited upstairs for Jennifer. On her gown sat a small jewellery box with a card beside it.

"Okay, now what have the two of you done."

"It wasn't us. Honest."

Jennifer was dubious, but she opened the card. It was from Michael. *Thought these would match your engagement ring, x,* it read. With shaking fingers, she picked up the small box and opened it. It was lotus flower studs with moonstone centres, identical to the ring she wore. He must have bought them at Farouk's in Khan el-Khalili the same day he bought the ring. Had Jennifer been so oblivious to what he was doing in the jewellery shop that day that she hadn't noticed? She had been busy designing the collar for Zeus and choosing the right keyring.

"Anybody home?" A female voice called from downstairs, interrupting the quiet atmosphere of the house where Jennifer, Lori, and Sadie were preparing for the special event.

"That sounds like Melissa's voice. I'll go," offered Lori, darting out of the room and down the steps, displaying the strong bond of friendship among the characters.

"I told them to use the side door and left it unlocked for them. Fingers crossed, it isn't someone else," said Jennifer.

A few minutes later, Lori reappeared with a large box.

"They're off to deliver the boutonnières to the men," she said.

Sadie slipped out of her street clothes first and into her gown. Lori, with highlights and lowlights in her light brown hair, fastened the back for her. Next, it was Lori's turn. Now, both girls were ready to help Jennifer. All the gowns were similar, but the bride's was fancier. All had fur jackets, too, for when they were outdoors. They hung on hangers downstairs.

Lori took the bouquets from the box and handed them to the others.

"Shall we?" she asked.

Michael worried that there would be a hiccup at some point today. He couldn't put a finger on it, but something niggled in the back of his mind. The girls should be here soon with the boutonnières. He and his brothers wore matching suits and had wool overcoats as well. That's where the flower would go.

Adam fidgeted on the bed. He had the TV remote and flipped through the channels, never leaving it on one station long enough to know what was on.

"Your tie is crooked. Ma will have to fix that for you when they get here," Christopher said. "She was always straightening our ties when we were kids."

"I remember yours were the crookedest of all," Michael said.

"Don't deny it, Chris. Mike's right," said Roger.

The three brothers laughed. At that moment, Chris's tie was the straightest of all. Maybe Lori had tied it for him. No, that couldn't be. She spent the night at Jennifer's with her and Sadie. It could be. He could have only loosened it enough to pull it over his head and left it tied.

Someone knocked on the door. Michael opened it to find Bill standing in the corridor.

"Come on in, meet the rest of my brothers and my nephew," he said, inviting the man in and introducing him to everyone.

A few minutes later, another rap sounded. This time, it was the women with the boutonnières.

"Michael, just look at that tie," Mrs. Scott said. "Sit down and let me fix it for you."

Roger and Christopher looked at one another and burst out laughing. Even Bill chuckled. Once Michael's mother resolved the tie situation, Michael introduced Bill.

Mrs. Scott lifted the lid off the box of boutonnières and handed one to each man and her grandson. She pulled the groom's from the box last. His was fancier than the others. She affixed them to everyone's overcoats.

"It's time we headed to the venue. Do you have a car hired?" Mrs. Scott asked.

That was it. Michael had needed to arrange a limo to transport them all to the wedding and didn't. "Dammit," he said. "I knew I'd forgotten something."

"Not to worry, bro'. We figured you'd forget, so Chris and I booked one big enough for all of us," said Roger.

"Thanks. You're a lifesaver."

"By the time we get to the lobby, it should be waiting for us out front."

They pulled the wedding together in such a short time, it was no wonder he'd forgotten. Six weeks wasn't enough time, yet Jennifer and Sadie had everything under control on the bride and bridesmaid side. That included making the arrangements for Lori to be fitted for the proper dress in Fort Mac.

Everyone filed out of the room with Michael bringing up the rear.

The girls had started down the staircase. When they reached the landing before the last turn to the main level, the photographer stopped them.

"First, the bride by herself. These stained glass windows will make an excellent backdrop."

"But the stairlift, won't it ruin the pictures?"

"You stand to the left, hand on the newel post. It's not in the frame at all now. That's right. Now look this way and smile."

Jennifer followed his instructions.

He brought the other two girls into the frame and photographed all three in landscape orientation.

"Okay, now, I think by the front door. Again, the window will add an extra dimension to the picture. A couple of shots of just the bride, followed by both of you with her."

This photo session seemed to take forever. The girls would be late getting to Oakes Garden Theatre at this rate. The photographer wanted photos in the living room by the front window. Jennifer looked out the window, so he captured more of her back. First, a couple with Zeus wearing his tuxedo with Jennifer, all three girls, and all three girls with Zeus.

"Lori, did you lock the side door after Melissa dropped off our bouquets?" Jennifer asked.

"Yes. The limo will pick us up at the street, so I thought we'd go out the front door."

"That will make an excellent photo. You three and the pug on the front steps."

"We need to put on the jackets that accompany our dresses first."

While Sadie held Jennifer's veil out of the way, Lori slipped her arms into the jacket and slid it into position. Afterwards, she and Sadie donned theirs.

Jennifer had a small clutch that she already had her phone in, along with her lip gloss. She plucked the front door key off the hook, and they walked outside, the photographer with his equipment ahead of them. They were no sooner outside, and he was snapping pictures. Jennifer had her back to him because she was locking the door.

"You with the dusty pink jacket. You first on the bottom step. You in the blue behind her on the next step, and finally the bride." He snapped more photos. "Now, just the bride. Good, and now, the bride and her dog."

The limo pulled up and cut his photo session short. He captured them as they entered the white stretch Lincoln Continental. The chauffeur helped them inside and closed the doors after them.

"I didn't think he was ever going to stop. I'm still seeing spots," Jennifer said.

"Us, too."

Sixty-Five

Oakes Garden Theatre, 5825 River Rd, Niagara Falls, Ontario

December 31, 2018

Michael and his entourage arrived at the Oakes Garden Theatre minutes before three o'clock. The chairs, arranged in the pavilion, emitted a faint scent of fresh wood. A table, covered with a white cloth that touched the ground, stood in front of the seats. A few people sat, their murmurs blending with the distant sound of birds chirping. Presumably, they were Jennifer's co-workers. From this distance, he couldn't tell.

He, his family, and Bill made their way to the sheltered location, their steps filled with anticipation, excitement, and nervousness. Roger and Christopher seated their mother and sisters, Adam, Gareth, and Serenity. Michael stood with Bill, their eyes fixed on the road, waiting for the limo with Jennifer, Sadie and Lori onboard.

"Don't worry, lad. Brides are always late for their wedding," said Bill. His voice was reassuring and held a deep sense of understanding and shared experience, a voice that carried the weight of fifty years of love and memories. "My missus was, and I was terrified she'd changed her mind. And then I saw her. We had fifty good years together before the dementia took her from me. It's a journey, lad, filled with love and memories."

"Thanks."

"I'm going to head up to the street. Be there waiting when Jennifer arrives."

Michael nodded. Even earlier in the day, New Year's Eve had Niagara Falls bustling, and conceivably traffic would hold them up. His palms were sweaty thanks to his nervous anticipation. Chris had the ring, a silver band that matched the delicate beauty of the lotus blossom. Its curved design symbolized the twists and turns of their journey, and it fit around the flower, a symbol of their love and commitment.

Bill still couldn't believe Jennifer had asked him to be part of her wedding. And not only as an invited guest but in a vital role. The doctors turned his world upside down when they revealed their diagnosis of his wife's illness. And further still when she no longer knew him. He hated to think it, but it was a blessing when she died. His beautiful wife, with no recollection of their years together. That's when he'd started going into the bar in the afternoon. It was for the company. When Jennifer started working there, it made it better. She was pretty, friendly, and always willing to chat. He pulled out a handkerchief and wiped his eyes.

At that moment, a white limousine turned the corner onto Falls Avenue and came to a stop where he stood. The driver got out and opened the doors. Bill helped the women out. They fussed over one another's gowns and Jennifer's veil. A pug in a tuxedo accompanied them.

"Thank you so much for doing this, Bill," Jennifer said, and kissed his cheek.

"Oh, don't get me any more emotional than I already am," he said.

Lori and Sadie left the bride and the 'father of the bride' behind.

"Your dog?" Bill asked.

"Yes. His name is Zeus. I've told you about him, haven't I?"

"I remember nothing other than seeing a beautiful young woman standing before me."

Just then, the strains of the wedding march reached his ears.

"It's show time."

Jennifer nodded.

Jennifer, her blonde hair cascading down her back, gripped Bill's arm in one hand and Zeus's leash in the other as they walked towards the decorated pavilion. Everyone, dressed in their finest attire, turned to watch as Lori and Sadie arrived, and after that, she, Bill, and Zeus made the last turn. The design of the building, with its grand arches, allowed them to glance in without being all the way there.

A wave of anxiety washed over Jennifer as she and Bill approached the entrance. She clung to his arm, her grip tightening with each step. He felt her tension and patted her hand. "Nervous?" he whispered, his voice a comforting murmur.

"A little," she admitted, her voice barely audible over the soft music playing in the background.

The ceremony, a non-religious one that Jennifer had carefully planned, was about to begin. She had opted for a civil ceremony that reflected her and Michael's beliefs and values. The scent of fresh flowers filled the room along with the strains of soft music at low volume. When it came time for Michael to put her wedding ring on her finger, his hands shook. She placed her right hand on his to prevent him dropping the ring, a slight gesture that spoke volumes about their relationship.

"I now pronounce you man and wife. You may kiss the bride."

The pavilion erupted in applause as they shared their first kiss as a married couple. But for Jennifer, the sound was distant, a mere echo. The man she had journeyed across the world to seek forgiveness from had granted it, and now they were bound in matrimony. This was, without a doubt, the most joyous day of her life.

Also by Melanie Robertson-King

The Consequences Collection
Tim's Magic Christmas
The Secret of Hillcrest House
A Shadow in the Past (second edition)
Shadows From Her Past
YESTERDAY TODAY ALWAYS
Cole's Notes (Revised version)
It Happened on Dufferin Terrace
It Happened in Gastown
It Happened at Percé Rock
All Aboard the Canadian with Buddy and his Four Fantastic
Furry Friends!
It Happened at Lake Louise
WHISPERS THROUGH TIME
(King Park Press)

Cole's Notes (A Short Story)
EFD1: Starship Goodwords – a cross genre anthology
(CARRICK PUBLISHING, 2012)

MELANIE ROBERTSON-KING

https://melanierobertson-king.com

Melanie Robertson-King has always been a fan of the written word. Growing up as an only child, her face was almost always buried in a book from the time she could read. Her father was one of the thousands of Home Children sent to Canada through the auspices of The Orphan Homes of Scotland, and she has been fortunate to be able to visit her father's homeland many times and even met the Princess Royal (Princess Anne) at the orphanage where he was raised.

www.ingramcontent.com/pod-product-compliance
Lightning Source LLC
Chambersburg PA
CBHW030341020726
47493CB00003B/633